# DEADLY
# DIVISION

NATHANIEL SIZEMORE

Deadly Division
By Nathaniel Sizemore

For information, contact
BDI Publishers, Atlanta, Georgia,
bdipublishers@gmail.com.

Cover Design and Layout: Tudor Maier
BDI Publishers

Atlanta, Georgia
ISBN: 978-0-9836709-7-1
SECOND EDITION

# Acknowledgments

To God, from whom all talents and blessings flow, and to my family and friends who encouraged this journey. And especially to my beautiful daughters, Elizabeth and Charlotte – dream *crazy* big!

**FACT**:

The "Johnson Amendment" is an actual provision of the U.S. tax code, which was included in 1954 by then-Senator Lyndon Johnson.

During the COVID-19 pandemic, a number of states issued controversial attendance and activity restrictions for religious institutions. The specific examples cited herein are real.

The Mediation Program for the United States District Court for the District of Columbia exists and has strict confidentiality requirements for cases that enter the Program.

*"Then you will know <u>the truth</u>, and the truth will set you free."*
John 8:32.

# Chapter 1

D r. Francis Pietrov's frail body hurried through the wide corridor of his red-brick apartment complex. He knew he had only seconds to make it to his front door before the person casting the shadow behind him would overtake him.

With his hands shaking uncontrollably, Dr. Pietrov reached into his right pants pocket, desperately searching for his keys. At the age of seventy, he was not accustomed to strenuous exercise – but now he was running for his life. His first-floor apartment was just a few feet away when the owner of the shadow emerged from the darkness, grabbed the back of his neck, and, with brutish strength, flung him to the ground. Dr. Pietrov's head slammed into the gray cement floor with such force that a flash of white light flooded his vision, followed by shapes and colors finally yielding a hazy focus on the figure looming over him. As he lifted his head, he could feel blood dripping down from his long, gray hair and into his goatee. He reached up and felt a deep, stinging cut near his right temple.

Dr. Pietrov's attacker wore a neatly pressed black suit with a crisp white shirt and polished black oxford shoes. He was athletically built with olive skin and was as fast as lighting. His dark hair was slicked back, allowing the light to bounce off of his head in the dimly lit hallway. His gaze was unpleasant, and his lips turned upward into a sinister smile.

"It's over, Pietrov," the man said calmly as he stood over his victim with his fists clenched at his side.

Dr. Pietrov realized any attempt to plead his case would be futile. This man was all business, and today, his business was to take Dr. Pietrov's life.

He shot a glance at the front door of his apartment and then quickly looked down the hall toward two other apartment doors, praying one of his neighbors would hear his cries for help.

The man followed Dr. Pietrov's gaze. "Don't make a scene. They don't have to die," he said in a deep, monotone voice.

The man made a quick downward movement, squatted, and looked Dr. Pietrov in the eye. He was so close Dr. Pietrov could smell the cheap cologne on the man's neck and could feel the warmth of his putrid breath.

"Please, please…I won't say a word. The Senator's name will never—"

Before he could finish his sentence, the man's right fist landed a punch to Dr. Pietrov's left cheek. He could feel the left side of his face going numb as he fell over onto his right shoulder, which popped and crackled as it hit the cement floor.

"Where do you want to do this?" The man seemed resolute on hurrying the process as he looked down the hall for the second time to ensure no one had heard the commotion and stumbled upon the scene.

"Inside…" Dr. Pietrov whimpered. The reality was setting in that these were his final moments. His whimper turned into tears, and he buried his head in his hands as he laid on the floor of the musty hallway.

Dr. Pietrov knew his work was controversial, but he never anticipated it would end in his murder. He let out a deep breath, trying to calm and compose himself as he accepted his fate. Dr. Pietrov hoped his work would live on, even if he did not. He knew his research would change the fabric of American life, and that's why so many powerful people were trying to bury it.

The attacker stood up and grabbed the ring of keys, which had fallen near the apartment's welcome mat. The man found the large bronze key, which slid seamlessly into the lock on the apartment's front door. He pushed the door open with one swift thrust of his forearm.

The dim fluorescent hall light floated across the dingy apartment's entryway, and cockroaches retreated into the darkness as the light cascaded in.

"Let's go!" the man barked as he tossed the keys into the apartment.

"I've done all I can," Dr. Pietrov confessed as he crawled on his hands and knees across the door's threshold. The man dismissed Dr. Pietrov's comments with a stern directive.

"Shut up and get inside."

Irritated by Dr. Pietrov's slow pace, the man grabbed him by the arm and dragged the old man into the dark. The door shut, and the last sound Dr. Pietrov heard was the sound of the man's gun cocking back, ready to dispatch him from this world.

# Chapter 2

David Stoneman stretched out his long legs on his large wooden desk. He leaned back in his chair and heard the seat springs clang as he shifted his weight. With his hands resting comfortably behind his head, he glanced out the window of his plush fifth-floor office.

A lawyer by trade, David thoroughly enjoyed the look and feel of his expensive Allen Edmonds shoes perched up on an even more expensive desk. He always combed his short black hair neatly to one side, and many described his deep green eyes as his most handsome feature. As he rocked back and forth in his desk chair, his mind began to wander.

*This is what he had worked for in law school, wasn't it? To be a thirty-year-old with a six-figure salary and a luxury lifestyle.*

He pursed his lips and nodded in approval, affirming his own thought.

David was in good spirits. He had just gotten off the phone with one of his clients, who agreed to settle a major case that David had negotiated to perfection.

David focused primarily on litigation and corporate mergers and acquisitions. He was a master at negotiating contracts and settling disputes. Unlike other settlements, however, this one was a work of art. Not only did he get a high-dollar amount for his client, but he convinced the other side to keep the settlement terms confidential. Success would be realized on all fronts, and his attorney's fees would be substantial as well.

The phone rang and interrupted David's daydreaming. It was his assistant, Rita.

Rita Valore was a smart, somewhat sarcastic woman in her late forties who understood the nature of the legal world and abided by its unwritten golden rule: *work hard, win cases, and make money for the firm.*

David hired Rita when he first started practicing law, even though she had no legal experience. He liked her candor, enthusiasm, and sass. She was blindly loyal to David for taking a chance on her.

Rita had been working with David since he moved from his solo practice in Norfolk, Virginia, to Washington, D.C. The move marked a major advancement in his career, after winning a massive case victory the year before against attorneys from Johnson, Allen, Peters & Branson, one of the most prestigious law firms in Washington. The day after the jury returned a favorable verdict for David's client, Johnson Allen, as they were called, was banging down his door trying to persuade him to join their large, high-profile legal team. They didn't lose often, but when they did, they almost always successfully recruited the attorney who beat them.

David agreed to join the firm on the condition Rita, his then paralegal/secretary/receptionist, was allowed to come with him. So, the two of them set off on a journey in search of larger paychecks and longer hours.

Working in Johnson Allen's flagship office in the heart of the nation's capital had been something David dreamed about since he was a first-year law student at Georgetown University nearly a decade earlier. The summer internships at Johnson Allen were the most competitive and coveted internships among Georgetown law students, and David was quickly eliminated from consideration each time he applied. None of that mattered now. He had finally made it to Johnson Allen and was winning cases, left and right.

Rita was calling because she wanted to walk through the final version of the client's settlement agreement. She was very conscientious about her work but tended to think out loud on her phone calls, which could be positive or negative depending on the day and the issue. Today, the conversation was positive as Rita rattled off the main sections of the settlement agreement, consistently interjecting her opinion as to whether each provision was "impressive" or simply "satisfactory."

"David, how in the world did you get the other side to keep this deal quiet?" Rita knew David was good, but not *that* good.

David laughed, "I heard through the grapevine their chairman made some inappropriate comments to one of their junior analysts at last year's Christmas party. I told him I wouldn't leak that information to his competitors if they agreed to keep the terms confidential."

"I'm not supposed to know those things, Dave...that way, when they cart you off to jail, I can honestly say I didn't know about *any* of it."

David grinned and concluded the conversation, "okay, let's get this thing signed and out of our hair."

"Sure thing, boss. I'll send a copy to the client and opposing counsel. This case is closed!"

Rita hung up the phone, and, once again, David propped his

feet up on his desk and glanced out his office window. However, before he could drift off into another daydream, his phone rang again.

"David Stoneman," he answered confidently as he rested the phone's handset between his chin and his shoulder.

"Stoneman?" the voice on the other end of the phone was deep and resonant. David quickly sat up in his chair – he recognized *that* voice.

"This is Greg Thomas. I was wondering if I could see you in my office for a minute."

"Sure thing, Mr. Thomas," David responded without hesitation.

Gregory Thomas III was the firm's managing partner and the only surviving original member of Johnson Allen. Although he was just a young associate when the named partners founded Johnson Allen in 1980, he worked his way up the partner ladder and began running the firm after Mr. Allen passed away a few years earlier.

Greg Thomas was one of the most feared and intimidating litigators in Washington. He had a reputation for taking no prisoners and having no mercy. For that, his clients were thrilled to pay four figures per hour to have him on their side of the table. Greg Thomas was the only person in the firm who could make or break your legal career with a simple phone call.

David knew this impromptu meeting was highly unusual, so he grabbed his suit jacket from the back of his desk chair and headed for the elevator and up to the famous eleventh floor for what, he hoped, would be a pat on the back.

# Chapter 3

In the District of Columbia, the Height of Buildings Act of 1910 disallows commercial buildings to exceed one-hundred thirty feet in height. Naturally, Johnson Allen pushed that limit with their downtown headquarters standing just inches short of the allowable height. The partners needed to feel like they were at the top of the legal market, both literally and figuratively. Therefore, they spared no expense when it came to maintaining the firm's exclusive image.

When the elevator doors opened on the Johnson Allen offices' eleventh floor, David Stoneman was in awe, yet again. It was stunning, much more luxurious than any of the firm's other floors. The receptionist's desk was made of imported Italian marble, and the solid wood floors shone as if they had just been polished. The firm's name hung neatly on the wall in bright golden letters that glistened underneath the intricately positioned downlights. The firm's name was also bordered by seven-foot-tall bamboo shoots sent from the firm's Shanghai office, giving the entryway an exotic, sophisticated, and balanced feel. Eucalyptus candles were burning on the corners of the receptionist's desk, meant to produce a calming aroma as people stepped off the elevators.

The eleventh floor was the profit center for Johnson Allen, a firm widely recognized as a major force in the D.C. legal market, consistently placing near the top of every law firm ranking list in the region. While Johnson Allen was primarily known for its trial practice, it also had one of the country's top mergers and acquisition practices as well. Because David had a strong background in both areas, he was a natural fit within the firm.

He worked for several partners and spent most of his nights sitting at his desk buried behind a pile of law books, papers, and old cups of coffee. David churned out more billable hours than many of his fellow associates, which meant he didn't do much else outside of the office.

He was one of the few associates who still wore a suit and tie to work every day, as he wanted to make a positive impression on the "old school" partners who disapproved of the legal community's growing dress code informality. As a result, his fellow associates shunned him for being a brown-nose, but he didn't care; he wasn't there to make friends.

Because David was married to his job, he didn't have time for a real relationship. The few women he had dated quickly moved on when they realized he would never prioritize anything over work. David didn't have time for love – he had an opportunity, and he wasn't going to waste it.

*Confidence*, David thought as he stepped off the elevator.

He shot a quick smile at the receptionist, who didn't even bother to look up from her computer, and headed down the long beige hallway, glancing at the pictures hanging on the walls between the partners' offices. Images of Rome at dusk and the San Francisco harbor in the afternoon dominated the wall space. The pictures reminded David of those motivational posters that had breathtaking landscapes underscored by inspirational phrases. However, if the motivation didn't hit you when you stepped off the elevator, you probably weren't going to last long at Johnson Allen.

David had only been to the eleventh floor half a dozen times, mostly to bring senior partners documents related to high-profile cases. Still, every time he walked onto the eleventh floor, he felt a sense of pride, a feeling that he had made it to the top just by being in the presence of some of the most brilliant legal minds in the country.

On each partner's wall hung gold-plated degrees from some of the world's most prestigious law schools. With close to twenty offices on five different continents, the firm's attorneys represented most of the elite educational institutions on the planet. David knew he was in good company and would slow his pace as he walked past the partners' offices, hoping that he would sit in one of those offices and, perhaps, even become managing partner one day.

As David approached Greg Thomas's office, he recalled his secretary's name was Stacy. She never gave him her last name, nor did she have it proudly displayed on her desk. She only gave her last name to Greg Thomas's VIP clients and other big-named partners in the firm, and David had not yet made that list.

*Perhaps today, that would change*, he thought as he walked up to her desk.

"Hi, Stacy," David said with a smile. "Mr. Thomas wanted to see me?"

"Just a minute," she murmured as she rose from her desk and disappeared behind a large wooden door. David caught his reflection in a nearby mirror. He noticed a hair out of place and began carefully placing it back into its normal position when Stacy emerged from behind the large wooden door. David's face reddened, realizing Stacy had caught him in one of his frequent grooming sessions.

"Mr. Thomas will see you now," she said in an unamused tone with one judgmental eyebrow raised.

David walked briskly around Stacy's desk with his head down and opened the large wooden door to reveal an office that was the size of David's living room. The oriental rug that covered the floor was blue with red and gold trim, and in the middle of the room was a glass table with high back, hand stitched chairs.

In the back corner of the office, a liquor cabinet with glass doors revealed top-shelf spirits, and mounted on top of the cabinet sat a humidor half-filled with full-bodied, imported cigars. David assumed the missing cigars had gone up in smoke over the years from celebrations following massive case verdicts.

As David's eyes turned to Greg Thomas, a chill flew down his spine. He was sitting behind his desk with his hands folded neatly in front of him, casting a stern look. Greg Thomas was tall and stocky, with thick salt and pepper hair and cold blue eyes. He almost always wore a three-piece suit adorned with a pocket square, which consistently matched his tie. A Harvard Law School alumnus and editor of the *Harvard Law Review*, he also completed a federal clerkship before joining Johnson Allen. David knew all about Greg Thomas's background because he continually reminded associates of his impressive resume at every opportunity.

"Sit down, Dave," Greg Thomas said in his deep, intimidating voice.

David found a chair facing his bosses' boss and sat patiently waiting for what he would say.

"Dave, how long have you been here at Johnson Allen?"

"About a year," David replied, repositioning himself in his chair.

"You've done *okay* so far, haven't you?" David bit his tongue as he tried to mask the irritation that rose up inside him from such a condescending question. David had brought millions of dollars into the firm in the last year alone. Simply stated, David had done *exceptionally well*, not just *okay*.

"I think so. Hopefully, I've exceeded expectations, sir," David diplomatically replied.

Greg Thomas sat silent for a few seconds.

"I think you've done *very* well," he finally rumbled with a chuckle as he slapped his hand on his desk. David breathed a quiet sigh of relief and waited for the big boss to bring up the next bombshell question.

"This case you're working on, the Hendson International case, you settled that one all by yourself, didn't you?" Greg Thomas asked as he leaned forward and rested his elbows on the desk.

"Yes, sir."

"Pretty impressive."

"Thank you, sir."

"But there's just one problem..." Greg Thomas noted with the wrinkles on his face drawing down into a terrifying gaze.

*Uh oh*, David thought with the spine-tingling feeling returning.

"You're too good, too early." He bellowed as his frown rose into a smile.

> Guys like you should be working with a team of partners, associates, and paralegals on these major deals. You just get them done by yourself in half the time. Shoot, son, you're not supposed to know where all the bathrooms

are in this place yet! I like my associates to be smart, insecure, billing over two-thousand hours a year, and taking orders from the folks around here we pay seven figures.

David paused, not sure if Greg Thomas was paying him a compliment, asking him a question, or reprimanding him.

"So...what's your secret?" The boss finally asked as he leaned back in his chair and folded his hands behind his head.

"Well, sir, I guess I learned how to negotiate as a little boy." By the confused look on Greg Thomas's face, David knew he had to elaborate on his statement and fast.

"You see, I never wanted to go to bed as a kid, and I would try different negotiation tactics on my parents to convince them to let me stay up and play video games." David was relieved to see Greg Thomas snicker in his oversized leather chair.

"Whatever you're doing, keep it up because your name is being mentioned at partnership meetings, and that's rare for an associate." David acted surprised to hear the news that word of his victories had reached the eleventh floor, even though Rita had already relayed that message after a coffee break with an eleventh-floor paralegal a month earlier.

"Wow, sir, I don't know what to say. I'm flattered."

"Just *tell me you'll keep it up*," Greg Thomas roared, half-kidding but half-serious.

"Yes, sir!" David enthusiastically responded with a smile.

"Well, don't let me take up any more of your time. Every minute you spend talking to me is one more minute you're not billing a client. I just wanted to give you a thumbs up on your progress."

"Thank you, sir." David nodded and stood up. Greg Thomas grabbed a file from his desk and turned his chair around, indicating the conversation was over.

Stacy appeared, almost as if on cue, and escorted David out of the large wooden door. She smiled, pointed to the elevators down the hall, and half-heartedly wished David a good day.

As David wandered back down the motivational hallway, he had an extra skip in his step. When he boarded the elevator and hit the fifth-floor button, he envisioned himself one day sitting in that big corner office congratulating other young lawyers on *their* major case victories.

Little did David know that Greg Thomas was pacing in his office and thinking about his next strategic move.

Greg Thomas had built his book of business stealing associates' clients. He would hire an ambitious associate, encourage them to bring in as many clients as possible, and then fire the associate and convince their clients to stay with him at Johnson Allen. No former associate dared to challenge Greg Thomas or even utter a word about this nefarious tactic for fear he would prevent them from securing another job elsewhere in Washington. The game was survival of the fittest, and Greg Thomas was the lion, and David was just another gazelle.

# Chapter 4

Over five hundred miles away from Washington, D.C., in Charleston, South Carolina, Pastor Tommy Felton knelt reverently at the altar in his church with sweat dripping from his tanned forehead. He had been in that prayerful position for most of the morning, praying for one of his faithful congregation member's rebellious, drug-pushing son. However, Tommy's mind kept wandering back to something else, something more sinister. He was concerned about a brief and alarming phone call he received that morning from an old friend.

Raised by his mother in a single-parent household, Tommy spent much of his childhood in the churches that lined Church Street in Charleston's historic district. Known as the "Holy City," Tommy relished in Charleston's rich religious and cultural history. To him, it was home.

He knew from a young age he wanted to pursue a career in the ministry. As a teenager, he spent his days working beach patrol at a local tourist spot and his nights memorizing scripture and helping with the local youth ministry.

After graduating from college upstate, he moved back to Charleston with a young wife and a new baby daughter. Tommy was a warm and welcoming person, and the crow's feet around his eyes evidenced his frequent smiling habit. He was a stout man who loved comfort food and never passed on dessert.

Tommy's thinning blonde hair became more vibrant in the hot summer months, and his slight Southern accent and laid-back demeanor were calming to people seeking spiritual absolution.

Decades earlier, he had accepted the position as head pastor of the New Beginnings Baptist Church on the town's outskirts. But over his thirty-year tenure as a man of the cloth, he had never heard anything like what he heard on the phone that morning.

His friend, a scientist, called and confessed something he simply could not believe. The conversation was panicked and rushed; nevertheless, the short exchange made an indelible impact on Tommy. However, staying true to his reputation for keeping confidences and bound by Clergy-Penitent confidentiality, requiring him to keep "confidential communications" as a spiritual advisor, he had no intention of speaking a word of it to a soul.

*Wait and pray*; that's all he could do.

It was just before one o'clock, as Tommy rose from his prayer position, walked into his church's spacious foyer, and stared out at scenic Charleston Harbor as he uncapped a bottle of water and took a sip. It was a hot April in South Carolina, and the sun beating down through an open window onto Tommy's head reminded him of that fact. He shut the window, left the church, hopped into his green Honda, and headed toward John's Island, where he lived with his wife, Marie, an elementary school teacher, and their dog, Sam. His daughter, Jenny, had grown up and moved to Tulsa with her husband and would visit during the holidays.

Tommy rolled down his car's windows and let the warm air massage his face as he took the backroads home. The sound of country music on the radio and the scent of pluff mud and

Spanish moss was familiar as he continued down the tree-covered, two-lane road. Tommy enjoyed his drive to and from the church as a form of therapy. But this time, his mind was burdened by his friend's telephonic confession.

*Could it really be true?* He thought as he drove under miles of moss-covered trees.

*Is it even possible?* He wondered, greatly shaken by the news.

Tommy couldn't make sense of it. All he knew was that his friend was trustworthy, and if he said it, it *had* to be true. They had known each other for many years, and his friend was a man of integrity – that's what scared him the most.

Tommy pulled his car into the long gravel driveway leading to his quaint, two-bedroom ranch house, which backed up to one of the snaking rivers along the barrier islands. As he walked in the front door, he realized his wife, Marie, was not yet home from teaching. Tommy glanced at his watch – she would likely not be home for a couple of hours.

As Tommy bumbled around his house snacking on old blueberry pie, he could not calm his mind. His thoughts continually bombarded him about what this revelation could mean for America and the rest of the world. This news could change the very course of history.

He flopped down on the dated living room couch and turned on the baseball game. However, Tommy quickly realized no amount of baseball or blueberry pie would help him. He decided it would be best for his nerves to call his friend back later that afternoon. He had questions that needed answers.

Tommy was tired. The intense mental gymnastics he had put himself through over the last few hours was exhausting. But, given his line of work, he developed a rare skill of being able to sleep even when he was distraught. It refreshed him. So, Tommy discarded his pie, flipped off the television, and decided to take a quick nap.

To remind himself to call his friend when he woke, he jotted down his friend's name and phone number on a sticky note and placed it on the refrigerator, secured with a cartoon chicken magnet. He glanced at the name one last time before he walked into the bedroom.

"Pietrov," Tommy said, "I hope you're kidding with me, buddy…"

He walked into the bedroom, and when his head hit the pillow, he was asleep in seconds.

# Chapter 5

Pastor Tommy Felton woke up with a gasp. His hands were clammy, and beads of sweat were rolling off the tip of his nose. He had been having a nightmare. A dream that was so real it took him a moment to slow his heart rate as he sat straight up in his dark bedroom. Tommy took two deep breaths trying to calm himself down. He realized his shirt was soaked in sweat as he turned and placed his feet on the cold bedroom floor. Tommy was tense and moved his head back and forth to stretch his tightened neck muscles.

His nose caught the aroma of vegetable soup on the stove, which indicated Marie was home and cooking dinner. He looked at the clock on his bedside table – it was 8:00 p.m. He had been asleep for hours, and the sun had gone down over the salt marsh. Tommy's squinted eye caught his wife's silhouette in the doorway as she walked down the hall.

"Marie?" he called out in a raspy voice.

"Yes, dear?"

"How long have you been home?"

"About an hour. I had to run some errands and stop by the store to get stuff for supper," she answered as she disappeared into the kitchen.

"Come on in, sleepyhead, it's ready."

Tommy rolled himself out of bed and stumbled into the kitchen to find dinner on the table. Steaming vegetable soup and Caesar salad caused his mouth to water as he moved toward the table to join his wife. Sam, the dog, lay quietly under the table, waiting for scraps to fall in his direction.

It didn't take long for Marie to notice Tommy was not his usual, cheerful self.

"What's wrong?" She asked as she put her cloth napkin in her lap.

"Just had a bad dream…"

"Care to share?" Marie was well-accustomed to the burdens her husband often brought home with him from the church. Today, however, he seemed more affected than usual. Tommy was silent for a few seconds but knew it was unfair to keep Marie in suspense.

"A friend of mine…a scientist in D.C. I had a dream he was dead." Tommy stared at his soup and pushed the floating vegetables around with his spoon.

Marie could sense there was more to the story.

Tommy continued, "The dream was *so* real. I saw him lying dead on the ground."

"Oh my!" Marie responded.

"Have you talked to him recently?"

"Yes…he called me very early this morning. You were still in bed." Tommy gulped down a spoonful of soup.

"Well, he's fine then, right?"

Tommy pushed his soup bowl away, sat back in his chair, crossed his arms, and looked at his wife. He shook his head.

"I don't think so, Marie...I just have a bad feeling."

"*Why* do you have a bad feeling, honey? What did he say?"

Again, Tommy shook his head, indicating he couldn't share much more. He knew what he had to do, and it couldn't wait until after dinner.

"I better call him again." Tommy rose from his chair and walked across the kitchen to the telephone. Tommy still preferred to make phone calls from his old school, rotary-dial landline, which hung at eye-level on the wall near the refrigerator, only using his cell phone in emergencies. As he picked up the phone and dialed Dr. Francis Pietrov's home phone number, he tapped his foot impatiently as he heard Dr. Pietrov's phone ring again and again. Finally, a voice answered – Tommy instantly knew something was wrong.

The voice that answered did not carry Francis Pietrov's Russian accent.

"Hello?"

"Yes, is Francis Pietrov available?"

"Are you family?"

"Yes, uh, he's my cousin." Tommy knew a little white lie was acceptable, given the circumstances. He would repent later.

"Sir, I'm with D.C. Metro Police, and I'm sorry to tell you Francis Pietrov passed away today." The manila-colored phone Tommy held in his hand fell from his ear to the floor, and the sound that it made when it crashed against the black and white checkered kitchen tile caused Sam to howl.

Tommy quickly picked up the phone by its long, coiled chord to ask a follow-up question.

"What happened?" Tommy asked as he clutched the receiver with both hands.

"Gunshot wound, but that's all I can say. I'm sorry."

Tommy was terrified by the news and was unable to speak. What he had seen in his dream had really happened.

The phone went dead, and Tommy slowly hung up the receiver.

He stood frozen with his hand on the wall. Marie sensed he was shaken and ran to his side and wrapped her arms around him.

"Are you okay?" Marie asked as she held Tommy tightly.

"No...no, I'm not. My friend is dead, and I think I know *why* he died." A feeling of fear cascaded over Tommy. He turned to Marie and grabbed her by her shoulders to get her full attention.

"Marie, he told me something this morning that he said he had only shared with one other person. He knew people were after him. He didn't tell me *who*; he just said *powerful men* were after him." Tommy was huffing and puffing as the realization set in that he and Marie may be in grave danger.

"What else did he tell you?" Marie was becoming more concerned.

"I don't want to get into the details."

Marie rolled her eyes, and Tommy could tell she was frustrated by not knowing the whole story.

"Sweetheart, you have to understand; the less you know about this, the better. And, you know I'm not allowed to share what I learn in confessions."

"This was a *confession*?" Marie acted surprised.

"It felt like one…why else would he call *me*?"

Marie nodded reluctantly and began clearing the table. Tommy's mind was racing, thinking through options of what he could do next. His first inclination was to alert the police, but they would likely laugh him off the phone.

Just then, Tommy thought he heard something on his front porch. He ran to the window facing his front yard and peeked out through the pastel yellow curtains which hung from his large bay window. His lawn was dark, and his porch lights only illuminated a few feet past his front steps.

He could have sworn he heard something. As he leaned forward and listened intently through the window, the only sounds he heard were the familiar sounds of crickets singing in the night.

"Honey?"

Tommy nearly jumped out of his skin. Marie had quietly followed her husband from the kitchen and unintentionally snuck up behind him. Just then, Sam jumped up and ran to the front door barking as loud as ever, confirming Tommy's fear.

"Stand back, Marie, I think someone's outside…"

# Chapter 6

Pastor Tommy Felton had met Dr. Francis Pietrov on a cool November morning in Charleston close to three decades before he received the news Dr. Pietrov was dead.

Tommy was standing on a small ladder polishing a bronze candle labrum in the sanctuary of the newly-created New Beginnings Baptist Church when a breeze hit his sockless ankles. He turned to find the church's front door wide open and a man who looked to be middle age with brown hair and a thick brown beard holding a bottle of vodka in his right hand and stumbling down the central aisle of the sanctuary. The man was sloshing liquor on the red carpet that adorned the center aisle, and he was moving quickly past the rows of wooden pews as he raced toward the front altar.

Tommy dropped his polishing rag and quickly stepped down from his foot ladder. The man did not appear to be threatening, but Tommy's mind ran to the location of possible weapons within arm's length if the man became violent. After scanning his surroundings, the realization set in that if this man wanted to do him harm, nothing within a ten-foot radius was going to help.

"You the preacher around here?" The man hollered with a Russian accent.

"Yessir," Tommy responded with his Southern accent.

"Nice church..." The man said as he spun around in a ballet-style motion.

"Thanks. Can I help you with something, sir?" Tommy was smiling but uneasy.

At that point, the man was in Tommy's face. He was so close he could smell the cheap vodka on the man's breath. The man stared Tommy right in the eye, which took a few seconds given how drunk he was, and with building anticipation, the man began to speak.

"Yea...you can help me with something...tell me why bad things happen to good people, preacher-boy."

Tommy wasn't sure how to respond. The man continued.

"Sometimes, I'm not sure God exists...people like you claim to speak with him regularly, but I've tried talking to him, and I don't get any answer." The man tipped backward but caught his balance and resumed his position in Tommy's personal space. After he did so, the man grew visibly more agitated.

"What a hypocrite you are!" the man yelled as he pointed at Tommy and gritted his teeth.

"Excuse me, sir?" Tommy changed his footing to a sturdier stance and braced himself for an attack.

"You...this place...giving people false hope...you should be ashamed of yourself!"

Before the man could cast another aspersion, he began to cry and collapsed into Tommy's arms. He was dead weight, and Tommy had to sink to the floor to avoid dropping him. The man wept for a couple of minutes as Tommy consoled him, and after the crying ceased, he composed himself and sat in the front pew of the large sanctuary.

"What happened, my friend?" Tommy asked in a soft, comforting tone.

"I'm all alone in this God-forsaken country; that's what happened! I should have stayed in Russia – I shouldn't have come here!" the man cried. Tommy would have to take baby steps to probe further.

"What's your name, bud?"

"Francis…Francis Pietrov." The man whimpered.

"And, how'd you end up here in America?"

The man took a deep, belabored breath and answered.

"I moved to the states after I completed my Ph.D. in Moscow. I met the love of my life in school, and after just six months, we were married and expecting a son. I knew there would be better jobs in America, so I moved here hoping to provide a better life for my family."

Tommy nodded and asked a follow-up question.

"How long have you lived in town?"

"We don't. We had a small apartment in Charlotte while I looked for work. And, last month, I was offered a job in Washington, D.C., to work on a federal grant. My wife always loved Charleston and wanted to take a family trip before we moved to D.C."

"Where is your family now, Francis?"

The man sniffled and hung his head as he continued.

"We were just outside of town. It was late, and the roads were wet. My son was asleep in the backseat, and my wife had taken off her seatbelt to put a blanket on him. That's when it happened; a truck swerved into our lane. I lost control, and…"

Dr. Pietrov could not finish his sentence before he broke down in uncontrollable tears. After a few minutes, Dr. Pietrov dried his eyes with his shirt sleeve.

"Bottom line…they died, and I walked away without a scratch." Dr. Pietrov managed with short gasps of air and tears rolling down his reddened face.

The moment was tense, but Tommy felt the need to deepen the discussion.

"So, what are you still doing in Charleston?"

"I chose to bury her and my son here underneath the palmetto trees. It's what she would have wanted. The funeral was this morning. We have no family and no close friends in the states. It was just the men digging the hole in the ground and me. Now, I have nothing…" as his crying continued.

Tommy put his arm around Dr. Pietrov again, trying to offer support to the broken man. He couldn't imagine the pain he was feeling.

"Are you still taking the job in Washington, Francis?"

"What's the point?" Dr. Pietrov responded as he wiped his nose.

Tommy dealt with people's problems on a weekly basis, but with Dr. Pietrov, he felt a keen sense he was supposed to help him during this difficult time. He took the vodka bottle out of Dr. Pietrov's hand and set it on the floor next to a stack of blue hymnals.

"We're going to get through this, Francis, and I'm going to help you. But, first, we need to sober you up."

Tommy mustered the strength to help Dr. Pietrov to his feet.

"There's a spare room in the basement which I can convert to a temporary bedroom. If you're okay with a cot and an uncomfortable pillow, you're welcome to stay here for a few days until you figure things out."

Dr. Pietrov looked at Tommy with weepy eyes.

"Why would you do that for me?"

Tommy smiled.

"Francis, you came into my church drunk as a skunk. But I think you're searching for something deeper than the contents of that bottle. So, I'm going to help you. It's what I do. Also, haven't you heard of Southern hospitality? Helpin' folks is what we do in South Carolina!" Tommy slapped Dr. Pietrov on the back.

"That's fine, pastor, but don't think for a *minute* you're going to convert me."

"Oh, don't worry, I don't work with Russians." Tommy couldn't pass up the opportunity to add a little levity and humor to the conversation.

Both men laughed as Tommy escorted Dr. Pietrov to his room.

----

A few days later, Dr. Pietrov was sober, well-groomed, and ready to start his new job at the American Institute of Biological Sciences in Washington, D.C. He looked at his reflection in the mirror and realized how far he had come in less than a week.

He had stayed in the spare room in the church's basement, and, over that week, he cultivated a friendship with Tommy. The two men spent hours each day talking about God, family, science, and dozens of other deep life topics.

Tommy helped him see the good in things and highlighted the opportunity he had to carry on with a newfound purpose. He had been given a second chance. Perhaps it was God, Tommy, or just good luck, but Dr. Pietrov was now convinced his future could be bright and that future would start by taking his new job in the nation's capital.

The pain of the loss of his wife and son was still fresh. He couldn't help but tear up when he let his thoughts return to that fateful night. In his mind, he could still hear the screeching tires and breaking glass. However, Tommy taught him to harness his despair into something positive, to use his pain to do good in the world. Most importantly, to help others who were hurting, not to mention that his Russian mother instilled in him the importance of honoring commitments and burying emotions. Dr. Pietrov had committed to taking the job in Washington, and that's what he planned to do. Perhaps if he threw himself into his work, it would take his mind off of the tragedy.

He tied a half-Windsor knot on his maroon necktie and let the tie hang neatly down the front of his crisp, starched white button down shirt. Tommy had taken him to King Street in Charleston and bought him a couple of new suits since most of his clothes had been destroyed in the accident. Dr. Pietrov offered to pay Tommy back when he received the first paycheck from his new job, but Tommy assured him that wasn't necessary. As he gathered his things, Dr. Pietrov still could not understand why Tommy had been so kind to him. He would ponder that question for years to come.

Dr. Pietrov walked up the gray concrete stairs and met Tommy in the sanctuary.

"All packed up and ready to go?" Tommy asked as he looked Dr. Pietrov up and down.

"Yes, sir, I think I'm ready."

Tommy leaned in and readjusted Dr. Pietrov's tie, which was hanging slightly to the left.

"Well, the clothes look great – you could easily pass for a D.C. big-shot!" Tommy slapped Dr. Pietrov's shoulder playfully and pointed to the front door.

"A taxi is waiting outside; I paid for the trip to the airport."

"Thanks for everything, Tommy," Dr. Pietrov said as he choked back the tears.

"I can't thank you enough…"

The men hugged, exchanged contact information, and promised to stay in touch.

"Do you have any plans when you get to D.C.?" Tommy asked as the men walked toward the door.

"Believe it or not, I have a contact who lives near Washington; a guy named Jerry Hatfield. I met him in Charlotte. He's in school at George Washington University to become a counselor, so maybe I'll look him up. It may be nice to have a friend who's a shrink to help me get my life together." Dr. Pietrov smiled.

Tommy opened the front door and waived as Dr. Pietrov ambled into the yellow cab and sped away. Tommy felt good about Francis Pietrov. He had been through a lot but was willing to move forward, which was half the battle. Even in the brief time they spent together, Tommy realized Dr. Pietrov was incredibly bright. Hopefully, one day, he would use his brilliant mind to change the world.

# Chapter 7

"He made a phone call, sir. To a preacher in South Carolina."

The fateful words echoed into the telephone receiver as the man with the suit and the slicked-back hair checked in with his commanding officer, Sergeant James Henderson, Director of the FEDERATION AGAINST RELIGIOUS COERCION AND OPPRESSION, or FARCO, for short.

Formally established in 2018 as a covert military organization meant to "deal" with religious-backed terrorism, FARCO had more than a dozen hand-picked lethal members worldwide, and their numbers were growing. In its early days, FARCO was developed to undermine Islamic extremism's message and eliminate religious and community leaders who encouraged violence against the United States.

While other organizations were addressing direct military threats, FARCO recognized that certain Islamic religious leaders were not only perpetuating the violent message but actively recruiting young people into various terrorist groups with their inflammatory religious rhetoric. FARCO sent operatives to eliminate those threats and, as they saw it, to squelch the fire at its source before the flames grew out of control.

FARCO was "off-the-books," so the U.S. government could claim plausible deniability if FARCO operatives were captured.

America could never be seen as the country suppressing any religious freedoms abroad – that would be diplomatic suicide.

Only a handful of people in the government even knew FARCO existed. And, without much oversight, in the last several years, FARCO began to branch out of the Middle East. They expanded their focus and began targeting non-Islamic religious threats in Europe and North America. However, their leading Washington insider had more ambitious plans than simply eliminating extreme religious sects.

With former Navy SEALs, Delta Force, FBI and CIA operatives, FARCO was arguably the world's most elite and lethal organization. Sergeant Henderson was their ruthless leader. His reputation for brutality in his interrogation tactics struck fear into the hearts of those who knew him. Unfortunately, the select few who knew James Henderson seemed to disappear without a trace.

Sergeant Henderson was a man who quickly rose in the ranks during Desert Storm. After the war, he spent a decade overseas as a counterintelligence operator. He was a trained killer with a genius-level IQ. Sergeant Henderson had a calculated and measured approach to completing his missions. He carefully studied his targets and knew their every move. And, when the time was right, he would strike and be gone before they knew what hit them.

Sergeant Henderson received millions of dollars for his services over the years, tax free, earning a reputation for being a formidable mercenary. He was a hulking man in excellent shape for being in his late fifties. His military-style haircut, bulging biceps, and chiseled jawline signaled to anyone who encountered him that he was not to be trifled with.

"I need to tell him," Sergeant Henderson said to the man with the slicked-back hair.

"He's not going to be happy."

Sergeant Henderson hung up the phone and leaned against the metal desk in his glass-walled office. The metal shelves next to his desk were filled with pictures of him with world leaders. Those pictures were staggered amidst plaques and gold-plated awards and medals for his military achievements and acts of valor. However, all of that was in the past. Powerful people had commissioned him to do a job, and he was not going to fail.

His gaze shifted to the main war room floor where his men were planning the strategic elimination of their targets. FARCO had state-of-the-art equipment and high-definition television monitors, which covered most of the wall space. Half a dozen FARCO operatives were at their desks facing the main monitors on the front wall. There was a bombing in Turkey, and the operatives were making small talk about possible culprits. When things like this happened, the FARCO team salivated, knowing they would likely get the call to eliminate the party responsible for the tragedy.

Sergeant Henderson opened his glass office door, which was elevated eight feet above the war room. As he walked down the metal stairs, the clanking sound of his boots on the steps caused the room to fall silent. The men looked at their commanding officer, awaiting their orders.

"Gentlemen, we got the scientist, but, unfortunately, he talked."

"Anyone got a problem knocking off a man of the cloth?"

The men looked at each other and shook their heads. A few enthusiastic arrant comments from some of the operatives implied the team was ready to finish the job.

Sergeant Henderson walked to the back of the spacious war room and looked out the tiny two-way mirrored window on the building's outer wall. He could see the U.S. Capitol Dome from FARCO's secret base in Northern Virginia. He knew he would have to make a phone call to that building shortly, and he wasn't looking forward to it. The Senator would not be happy to hear about this operational hiccup. The Senator had made it clear that this job was to be quick and clean. It had been neither.

However, Sergeant Henderson was cautiously optimistic. He had faith that his team, and his lead operative in the field, could finish the job. He pulled his secure cell phone from his pocket and re-dialed the man with the slicked-back hair to get more information.

"Where are you, presently?" Sergeant Henderson asked.

"Moving into position to pick up the pieces. Have you spoken to *Eagle*?"

"Negative. What's your time frame?"

"A few hours, at least."

"10-4, get it done. We can't have any more leaks." Sergeant Henderson hung up and began to scroll through his phone contacts. His next call would be to the Senator.

# Chapter 8

Senator Stephen Smythe secretly co-founded FARCO years before penning and sponsoring the Division Act, one of the most controversial pieces of legislation in American history. Senator Smythe was a fiercely ambitious politician who had a specific vision for America. As a devout atheist, he saw religion as one of the main threats to American culture and his political future. Senator Smythe ran his campaigns on the platform of deepening the divide between Church and State. Or, as he put it, "Liberating America from the shackles of religion."

He believed the Establishment Clause of the First Amendment to the U.S. Constitution was quite clear when it stated, "Congress *shall make no law* respecting an establishment of religion..." And, yet, over his last two terms in the Senate, he repeatedly witnessed religious grandstanding cloud the judgment of many of his impressionable Senate colleagues, while right-wing organizations criticized his own deeply-rooted, non-religious political positions. He didn't understand why progress was constantly stalled by unproductive religious chatter, and he intended to put a stop to it. Senator Smythe had tried to play the political game for years before concluding that he had to play dirty to win this fight. After that realization, FARCO was born.

He despised reciting the Pledge of Allegiance and skipped saying the phrase "*one Nation under God.*" He longed to return the pledge to the way it read before President Dwight Eisenhower included the reference to "God" in 1954. He loathed President Eisenhower for including the phrase "*In God We Trust*" on all U.S. currency two years later and declaring it America's official motto. There was no place for that subliminal religious messaging in *his* America.

More recently, during the COVID-19 pandemic shut down, Senator Smythe was strongly supportive of Governors who kept churches closed on Easter to reduce the spread of the virus. He was baffled by the fact that so many people would risk their health and the health of their families just to sit in a church on Easter Sunday. It was this type of reckless mindset that he sought to eradicate.

America had evolved, and, in his opinion, it didn't need to be chained by religious strictures and unsubstantiated promises of utopian life after death. Senator Smythe didn't buy into those lies. He was a realist and based his convictions on the tenets of hard science. As such, he felt certain that if he could successfully reduce the influence of religion in America, the country would be free to realize its true potential. The Division Act was the first step in that process, and FARCO's expanded scope would be a key asset in pursuing his objectives.

Today, however, he was nervous. Information had recently come to light that could undermine his entire political position. He anxiously bit his fingernails as he looked out his window at the rolling hills of Virginia across the Potomac River.

He didn't know if Sergeant Henderson and the FARCO team could get the job done. His doubts caused him to consider taking matters into his own hands.

"Sir?" the voice of his aide, Tim, disrupted his thought.

"Are we going to finish writing the speech for tomorrow's breakfast?"

"Yea, let's get on with it," the Senator said unenthusiastically as he moved away from the window.

Senator Smythe paced back and forth on his brown office carpet. Tim was seated in a cherry-colored leather chair in the corner of the room next to a two-hundred-year-old bookshelf and a white marble fireplace that sat under a large gold-trimmed mirror. The Senator stopped his pacing and sat down on the right side of his red and yellow silk couch, propping his shoes up on the coffee table.

Tim could tell he was unsettled. Senator Smythe tended to fidget aimlessly when something was bothering him. Nevertheless, Tim ignored his bosses's idiosyncrasies and continued.

"Okay, so we left off talking about the Division Act, and we discussed how religious tax breaks give churches an unfair advantage over other organizations, blah, blah, blah—"

Senator Smythe interrupted, "Yes, and look up some facts and figures about how much government revenue is lost each year in religious tax shelters, and how the Supreme Court has addressed this issue in the past, etcetera."

Tim was reviewing his notes and thumbing through his research files as the Senator was talking. Senator Smythe did not like to repeat himself and glared at his aide for not acknowledging his comment. Tim looked up from his papers and realized the Senator was waiting for a response.

"Uh, yes, sir…I already included a quote from Justice Douglas' dissenting opinion in *Walz v. Tax Commission of the City of*

*New York*, which addresses public financial support afforded to religious organizations. In that case, Justice Douglas said that the tax-exempt status of religious organizations is evidence they are receiving a financial benefit simply because of their faith."

"Good, good! Yea, I like that! Senator Smythe put his hand to his chin, rubbed the unshaven stubble along his jawline, and continued.

"If we fund them, we should be able to regulate them. Thus, the justification for the restrictions we put in place."

"Sir, I'm not sure we should mention *the restrictions*…there are several lawsuits pending which address the constitutionality of those restrictions, and it may not be prudent to mention them at this breakfast."

Senator Smythe ignored Tim's comment and continued, "Also, make sure to include that these churches don't pay property tax. Shoot, *anyone* can just start a new religion these days and get out of paying taxes! It's one of the biggest loopholes in our country, Ryan."

"It's actually *Tim*, sir. And, just as a reminder, a recent Gallup poll showed the majority of Americans identify with the Christian faith. So, your position does affect followers of the Christian faith more than other religions, FYI."

Again, the Senator glared at Tim, got up from his couch, and walked toward the young man.

"Listen, kid, you're new here, and I don't care what your name is, and I don't care to hear your opinions. I'm a sitting U.S. Senator, and you're a little pissant trying to ride my coattails into law school, or whatever it is you're trying to do after this."

Tim sat frozen in his chair. Senator Smythe continued.

"All I care about is what you can do for *me*. So, do yourself a favor and keep your ignorant opinions to yourself, got it?" Senator Smythe said, looming over Tim as he cowered in his seat.

"Yes, sir. I'm sorry, sir." Tim quickly rose from his chair and left the Senator's office in a hurry, clearly distressed.

Ever since the Division Act was passed less than a year earlier, it garnered intense scrutiny from Republicans and Democrats alike. Senator Smythe knew it would not have passed without a Democratic Congress and Democratic President. The Act was already embroiled in dozens of federal lawsuits challenging the constitutionality of most of its provisions. Like many lawsuits before, they would inevitably trickle through the court system for the next year and end up at the U.S. Supreme Court.

The most hotly contested section of the Division Act was the provision that restricted mass prayer gatherings in religious services. While Senator Smythe simply abhorred the tradition, he needed a legitimate reason to restrict this practice nationwide, once and for all.

Luckily for him, the COVID-19 pandemic offered the perfect excuse he needed. He used the social distancing policy justification from the pandemic to show that mass prayer gatherings, or "corporate prayer," as it was more formally called, promoted the spread of infectious diseases. And, churchgoers piling up on one another to pray at the altar and lay hands on each other presented a soft target to drive home his point. He had a mountain of evidence to show this practice was responsible for spreading deadly viral diseases. For that reason, corporate prayer was one of the Division Act's restricted practices. Senator Smythe knew that provision was likely unconstitutional, but, for now, it was law.

He also knew that the court of public opinion would be decisive as the Division Act made its way through the federal court system. So, every speech the Senator gave over the next six months would have to strongly support and defend his legislation. Senator Smythe knew the price of *his* version of political freedom would come at a cost and may even cost the lives of innocent Americans. But he didn't care – the end would justify the means.

The Senator grabbed his suit jacket off of the back of his door. The blue pinstripes on his suit pleasantly accented the silk handkerchief which hung out of his left-breast coat pocket. His red tie was the proverbial "power tie" meant to intimidate his opponents and exude confidence to his constituents. This was a tactic he learned as he climbed the political ladder in Massachusetts on his way to the Senate. He glanced in the mirror and ran a comb through his thinning, dyed-brown hair, and pulled his pants up over his growing gut. Senator Smythe popped a mint in his mouth, straightened his tie, and left his office to do some glad-handing down the hall.

# Chapter 9

Pastor Tommy Felton ran into his bedroom, dove under the bed, and grabbed his red, wooden Louisville Slugger baseball bat, which rested against a dusty plastic container full of spare linens near the base of the bed's headboard. As he rose from the hardwood floor, he saw Marie scurry toward the front door and heard the loud click of the door's gray deadbolt as she turned it to the lock position.

"Get behind me, Marie, and get Sam." The dog was barking relentlessly.

"I'm scared, Tommy. What do you think it is?" Marie asked in a whisper as she huddled behind her husband.

"I don't know, but I have to check it out."

"No, Tommy, we're safe inside the house. Just stay here," Marie pleaded.

"Take the dog and get in the bedroom." He waived Marie back, and she retreated into the master bedroom holding Sam.

Once Tommy heard the bedroom door shut, he slowly unlocked the front door, turned the doorknob, and pulled the door toward him. The night was calm, and the moon shone brightly in the sky. Though the front porch lights were on, they didn't illuminate much of the side yard.

He flicked the switch to turn on the sidelights. One sidelight was burnt out, but the remaining bulbs offered decent visibility. Tommy heard something rustling in one of the large, green bushes to the right of the porch. He clasped his fingers tightly around the handle of the bat and drew it back to a swinging position above his right shoulder. Tommy's tenure as the first baseman for his church's softball team equipped him with the skill of swinging a bat and hitting the mark. Tonight, his mark would likely be another person. As he sidestepped down his front porch stairs, he saw the bushes shake again as he drew closer.

"Who's there?" he yelled apprehensively as he gripped the bat more tightly.

No answer. He looked down his dark gravel driveway. It was pitch black. His closest neighbor was a quarter of a mile away through thick palmetto trees. His home's seclusion was a plus when he and Marie first moved in, but tonight it seemed like a curse. He continued to inch toward the shaking bushes.

"You have five seconds to come out of there, or I'm gonna hit you with this bat. You got it?" No answer.

"I've already called the police." Again, no answer.

Tommy suddenly realized that amidst all of the chaos, he had actually forgotten to call the police. It was too late now, and he hoped Marie made the call from the bedroom and the police were already on their way. Unfortunately, he didn't hear any sirens nor see any lights, so he suspected he would have to deal with this issue himself.

"Five, four, three, two, one. Come out now!"

Nothing. He lost control and found himself running toward the large bushes. Pure adrenaline was pumping through his veins, and he knew he would either have to kill or be killed. He felt the leaves and branches tear at his short-sleeved polo shirt and cut into his skin as he swung the bat repeatedly.

At that moment, he saw a deer dart out from behind the bush and into the darkness of his backyard. Tommy fell to his knees and dropped the bat in relief.

*It was just a deer. Thank God.*

After his heart rate slowed down considerably, he felt a warm trickle down his left arm. He was cut and bleeding. He used his hand to catch some of the blood and wiped his hand in the tall green grass.

"Marie?" Tommy hollered.

"Tommy, are you okay?" Marie asked, as she ran into the yard with Sam.

"Yes, honey, it was just a deer."

"Oh Tommy, your arm…I'll get some bandages." Marie darted back into the house and quickly re-emerged with an old washrag and some gauze.

"Did you call the police?" Tommy asked as Marie wiped the blood from the cuts on his arm.

"No, you didn't tell me to," Marie responded as she wrapped the gauze around his left forearm.

Tommy grinned and saw an opportunity to offer some sarcastic constructive feedback.

"Marie, in the future…when you see me in the front yard with a bat ready to hit someone in the bushes…please do me a favor and call the police."

Marie stopped her wrapping and looked at him, unamused. After nearly forty years of marriage, she was used to his sarcasm. She grinned, shook her head, and went back to wrapping his bleeding arm. His cuts were deep, and the first layer of gauze was already stained red.

After a few silent seconds, Marie decided to respond in kind.

"Sure thing, honey; I just thought you could handle *Bambi* all by yourself." She smiled and called for Sam, who was barking at an animal in the distance.

After several minutes, Tommy and Marie were sitting in the kitchen enjoying a glass of sweet tea and laughing about the evening's excitement and the scary deer that gave them such a fright. As the lights in the quaint Felton house turned off that night, the man with the slicked-back hair was standing in the darkness, waiting. He would give them a couple of hours; then, he would get started. It would have to look like an accident.

# Chapter 10

Tommy smelled the gasoline in his sleep and thought he was dreaming. But when he felt the liquid hit his feet, he knew it was real. His eyes opened, and he realized his mouth had been covered with duct tape. Confusion set in. Tommy grabbed for his bat, which he had laid on the nightstand next to his alarm clock, but it was missing. He then reached for the light switch on the antique lamp next to the bed, and when the light came on, he could not believe his eyes. A 9-millimeter handgun was inches from his face. The gunman removed the tape from Tommy's mouth.

"Who—"

"Who am I?" the man with the slicked-back hair finished Tommy's question and then answered it.

"I'm the last person you're ever going to see, pastor," the man threatened as he loomed over Tommy.

Tommy turned in the bed to find Marie was missing.

"Where's my wife? What have you done with her?!" Tommy grew panicked and angry.

"She's close…but she's in trouble if you don't cooperate."

"Okay, what do you want?" Tommy frantically asked.

"What did Francis Pietrov tell you this morning?"

"Francis, who?" The butt of the gun struck Tommy right below his left eye and knocked his head to the side. He looked back at his assailant.

"I won't ask again. You'd better start talking," the man said, pushing the gun up against Tommy's forehead.

Tommy realized he couldn't play dumb with this man. He obviously already knew Dr. Pietrov had contacted him. So Tommy decided it was best to tell the truth and hope for mercy.

"He told me everything..." Tommy reluctantly confessed.

"And, because you're here, I guess he was telling the truth." The man smirked and hit the pastor again.

"Does anyone else know? Your wife?"

"No! I swear, she doesn't know anything. Please, just let her go!"

"Okay...I believe you," the man said as he leaned back and brought his gun down to his side.

Tommy breathed a sigh of relief. It looked as if he had de-escalated the situation. The man leaned forward again and whispered in Tommy's ear.

"Say your prayers, pastor. It's time to see if that God of yours really does exist." The man wound up and swung the gun with full force at Tommy's head. For a split second, Tommy heard a crack on the left side of his face, and then the world went black.

----

As Tommy regained consciousness, the sweltering heat was unbearable. Through a foggy red haze, he saw his bedroom engulfed in flames. The fire had reached his pajama pants, and he used his right hand to forcefully pat out the small flames on the back of his right leg. Then he heard it. Marie was screaming his name.

"Tommy!! Tommy, help me!!" she cried.

He used all his strength to stand up and make it to his bedroom door. His head was throbbing from the blow to his face, and dizziness momentarily caused him to wobble on his feet. However, he had to ignore the pain. He had to get to Marie. The white bedroom door was closed and burning but, with a leap of faith, Tommy covered his head with his arms and put all of his body weight into the middle of the door. His momentum and the flimsiness of the wood pushed him through, and he landed face down in the front hallway.

He heard more screams from Marie. Her voice was screeching. The screams sounded like they were coming from the kitchen. His quaint home was falling down around him, and it seemed like it took an eternity for him to stumble through the flame-ridden hallway toward the kitchen.

Tommy tripped over something in the hall and fell to his knees. It was warm and fluffy. It was Sam, and he was dead. Anger welled up inside Tommy, but he began to panic when he realized Marie's screams had stopped. All he heard was the sound of crackling wood and drywall around him. He could feel the smoke and the heat burning his eyes as he squinted to find his way to the kitchen. It became harder to breathe with every step, and he began to cough and gasp for air. Thick black smoke was all around him. When Tommy reached the kitchen, he saw his wife tied to a chair. Her head was down, and the room was full of smoke.

He ran to her and, with supernatural strength, he picked up the chair holding his wife and sprinted toward the front door. Surprisingly, the door was open, and Tommy flung himself forward and out onto the porch as he panted for fresh air. In doing so, he dropped his wife, still bound in the chair, down the porch steps and into the front yard. The force of the fall broke the chair in half, and Marie's lifeless body rolled a few feet further into the front yard.

Tommy swiftly crawled to her side with tears gushing down his burnt face. She was almost unrecognizable. He knew there was nothing he could do. She was gone. Tommy heard the sound of sirens coming up his gravel driveway, but all he could do was hold his beloved Marie in his arms and weep.

Within a matter of seconds, firefighters were racing around the house with their long hoses trying to salvage what was left of Tommy's home. They rushed to Tommy's side to make sure he was not seriously injured, and an EMS squad did everything they could to try to resuscitate Marie, but it was no use. She was declared dead at the scene.

Tommy stood up and was overwhelmed by grief, which contrasted discordantly with the image before him. The sun was coming up, and the majestic orange and red colors painted in the sky seemed to mirror the flames' colors that had now enveloped the home, which held so many family memories.

The paramedics put a white sheet over Marie's body, lifted her onto a stretcher and into an ambulance.

A local police car arrived on the scene, and two officers got out. Tommy recognized one of the deputies as a member of his congregation.

"What happened *herre*, *Tahmmy*?" The officer asked with a thick, backwoods, Southern drawl as he put a hand on Tommy's charred shoulder.

"A man did this…he held me at gunpoint and tied up Marie and set the house on fire. A man did this. A man did this!" The emotions began to overwhelm Tommy, and he felt like he was going to blackout.

The deputy looked at his partner and whispered to him to call for backup.

"It's okay, *Tahm*, we're gonna find 'em. What did the man look *lahke*?"

"I don't know, uh, he had dark hair which was brushed back, and he was wearing a black suit, but no tie. Early thirties, maybe."

The officer dutifully took notes on a small notepad he pulled from his uniform pocket.

"Did he say *anythang* to *ya*?"

Tommy's mind became quite clear at that moment, and he realized he shouldn't say another word. He knew if the man with the slicked-back hair found out he was still alive, he would come after him again and anyone he talked with about this ordeal. Tommy's demeanor immediately changed.

"I will not answer any other questions without an attorney present."

The officer, his friend, looked up from his notepad, confused.

"*Tahmmy*, you're not a person of interest *herre*, buddy; I just need some—" Tommy interrupted his friend.

"I said, I'm not answering any more questions," Tommy resolutely responded.

The officer closed his notebook and walked back to his squad car. He spent a minute talking with his partner before returning.

"*Tahmmy*, unfortunately, since you're being uncooperative, we're gonna need *ya* to come down to the station for additional *questionin'*. You're more than welcome to have your attorney meet *ya* down *therre*."

"Fine. But I'm not under arrest, right?"

"No, *Tahm*, you're not under arrest. We just need to figure out what happened *herre*. So, you can drive yourself, but we need *ya* to follow us to the station, okay?"

Tommy nodded. By now, the house was a pile of smoldering rubble. The firefighters had put out most of the large flames, but black smoke was still pouring out of the debris into the crisp, blue morning sky. Tommy looked at the ambulance carrying his wife.

"Where will they take Marie?" He asked the officer.

"They'll take her to the Charleston County Coroner's Office. I'll make sure *ya* get the address after we finish our *lil'* chat. Do you have any clean clothes, buddy?"

Tommy looked down and realized he was still in his pajama pants and t-shirt, which had been burnt and reeked of smoke. Luckily, he kept spare gym clothes and tennis shoes in his car. Given his home's seclusion, Tommy always left his car unlocked with his wallet, keys, and cell phone in the center console, a habit he formed after years of misplacing those items around the house.

He walked to his green Honda, opened the trunk, and stood behind the car while he changed. The grass was damp as he sat down and slid on his old gray tennis shoes.

"Okay, let's get on with this," Tommy said to the officer as he shut the trunk, walked around to his car's driver side, and got behind the wheel. Tommy could tell the officer was taken aback by his uncharacteristic curt responses, but he knew the less conversation, the better.

"*Ya* know where the station is, in case we get separated?" His friend asked as he opened the door to the cruiser.

"Yea…you know I've been there many times to talk with folks."

The officer smiled and nodded as he got into the cruiser and turned on the engine. The blue and red lights were blinding as Tommy followed the police down his gravel driveway and onto Betsy Kerrison Parkway, heading toward downtown Charleston.

As Tommy obediently followed his friend's squad car, he had one hand on the steering wheel and scrolled through his cell phone with the other hand in search of his attorney's phone number. As he looked for the number, reality set in.

*I can't tell my lawyer or the police why the man was at my house. That could put more people in danger.* His mind was racing.

*What about Jenny? How am I going to tell her what happened?*

He knew his daughter would immediately come to his aid if he called her and explained the situation. But that would put her at risk, too.

*No, there has to be another way*, he thought as the street light in front of him turned yellow. The police cruiser continued through the intersection as Tommy stopped at the red light to think for a minute.

*If the man realizes I'm still alive, he could come after me to finish the job. If I talk to anyone, they could be his next target. I have to get out of town!*

Once the police were safely out of sight, Tommy made a right turn onto a side road and headed for the highway. He had a couple hundred dollars in cash in his wallet, which would allow him to get by until he figured things out.

*But, where should I go?* He thought as his heart began to race. Tommy knew his police escort would soon realize he had diverted, and the entire police department would be looking for him within the hour. Paranoia set in – Tommy glanced in the rear-view mirror, expecting to see flashing red and blue lights. Instead, he saw nothing, just an empty road.

Then the idea hit him; *I should go to Washington, D.C.! That's where Francis lived. Maybe I can find someone who worked with him who can help me.*

Tommy set the coordinates in his phone for the nation's capital. He didn't know what he was looking for but knew that he was as good as dead if he stayed in South Carolina.

# Chapter 11

The partnership meeting at Johnson Allen started at 10 a.m. on the second Tuesday of each month. April's meeting was no exception. The partners and senior partners filed in one-by-one. As was the firm's policy, the meeting had to be held in the eleventh-floor conference room with video equipment set up for the partners in Johnson Allen's satellite offices to join virtually. The partnership couldn't risk having the meeting in the first-floor conference space for fear that lowly associates could eavesdrop.

The room was well-appointed, with floor-to-ceiling windows on the outside wall. Views of the top of the White House and the Washington Monument could be seen from every chair. The barista stand on the wall near the room's entrance carried high-end espresso and dessert options that would appease even the most discerning palate. The conference room table was white marble and on the far wall hung an eighty-inch television upon which sat a high-tech, interactive camera and audio device. With the hundreds of thousands of dollars that went into the décor and operability of the partners' conference room, it seemed they could practically rule the world from that table.

The firm's partners came in all shapes, sizes, and colors, yet they all had one thing in common – they were brilliant legal scholars. The men often wore bespoke suits of various shades and patterns, all from the finest men's clothing stores in Washington.

The women donned pantsuits, or dark skirts with silk blouses, occasionally adorned with a vibrant scarf to round out their professional look.

Traditionally, the partners made small chat before each partnership meeting. They would compliment each other but mostly brag about *their* new clients or high-profile case victories. The partners at Johnson Allen knew they were the best of the best and took every opportunity to remind each other of that fact. It was an elite group of bulldogs and sages. Still, they won cases, and that was all that mattered.

Greg Thomas walked into the partners' conference room, finishing a bagel and carrying a cup of hot coffee as he took his position at the head of the long marble conference table. He turned on the interactive television and ensured that partners from the firm's satellite offices were virtually present and accounted for.

"Let's get started, shall we?" He said as the meeting got underway. Greg Thomas's assistant, Stacy, took a seat in one of the chairs in the back of the room and opened up her laptop to type notes for the meeting minutes. She was instructed to use discernment when taking her notes because Greg Thomas did not want anything controversial included. She got the point and kept the meeting minutes thin.

"The first line of business is Associate David Stoneman." Greg Thomas looked up to see blank faces. He could sense David's name was unknown to most of the room.

"David is a newer associate who sits on the fifth floor and has become a real hotshot over the last year," Greg Thomas summarized as he took a large gulp of his steaming coffee.

Whispers and nods cascaded over the group causing a ripple effect of acknowledgment and head nods.

"Not a fan!" Came a voice from the middle of the table. Laughs and chuckles followed.

"Seriously, people, we need to resolve this issue now and get on to more important firm business!" Greg Thomas roared as he placed his cup on an ivory coaster and flipped through his meeting documents.

He continued, "Unfortunately, it has come to my attention Mr. Stoneman has been significantly inflating his billable hours, and I have been receiving complaints from some of his clients," Greg Thomas lied.

"How many hours has he overbilled?" One partner asked.

Greg Thomas looked at his notebook, pretending to calculate the fake numbers.

"He's billed nearly seven hundred hours to date, but I have information that two hundred of those hours were fraudulently recorded."

Greg Thomas continued, "Frankly, he's completely replaceable. So, I suggest we terminate Mr. Stoneman immediately to avoid a PR issue or a formal complaint against the firm. I'll speak to his clients and let them know he's no longer with Johnson Allen. Hopefully, they'll stay on with *me* as their replacement counsel…"

Several partners in the room shot glances at each other, realizing what Greg Thomas was doing. However, no one spoke up for fear their tenure at the firm would end abruptly.

Another partner, who was not wise to Greg Thomas's nefarious strategy, suggested the partnership give David a chance to explain himself before they fired him. He interjected that the overbillings could be inadvertent and easily explained.

Greg Thomas quickly replied with a canned comment, "Johnson Allen only wants to retain associates who represent the highest standards of legal ethics. If Stoneman insists on bilking clients, he needs to go *now* before we sink too much money into him and before he tarnishes the reputation of this firm."

A nod of approval from the questioning partner gave rise to a momentary silence in the room.

"Any other thoughts before we vote on this?" Greg Thomas asked as he briefly scanned the room for additional unwelcomed comments. Every other partner in the room knew Greg Thomas was resolute in his decision and didn't dare ask another question.

"Show of hands…all those in favor of terminating David Stoneman's employment at Johnson Allen raise your hand." The partners' hands went up one by one – even the partners in the satellite offices raised their hands. Whether it was out of sheer ambivalence or fear of Greg Thomas's retaliation if they voted against him, every partner voted to fire David.

"Good, let me know if you have a lead on someone to replace him. Send all resumes to me for review."

"Okay, moving on to the important stuff…"

----

An hour later, when the partnership meeting had adjourned, Greg Thomas walked down the eleventh-floor hallway toward his corner office. Before he walked through the large wooden door, he instructed Stacy to call David and ask him to meet in the first-floor conference space. Stacy smiled, knowing exactly what that meant for David.

"That's why I don't bother to learn their names," she said jokingly as she dialed David's extension.

Greg Thomas smirked and disappeared behind the large wooden door. He needed a drink before this meeting. He had to come up with a good excuse for firing a guy whose success he was just applauding.

He knew he couldn't allege David had overbilled clients because that simply wasn't true, and Greg Thomas suspected David would secure sworn statements from all of his clients supporting that fact. The real reason was *money* – the firm would earn a boatload off of David's clients, and Greg Thomas's commission checks would be an additional six figures per year. He poured a glass of bourbon and sat at his desk. He wrote the words "corporate restructuring" on his notepad and gulped down his drink.

# Chapter 12

D avid Stoneman was filled with excitement as he rode the elevator down to the first floor. Perhaps he was being made a partner earlier than he expected, or maybe he was being honored in front of the entire partnership committee for his recent successes. Either way, the news had to be good.

He received a call from Greg Thomas's secretary inviting him to the first-floor conference space to meet with Greg Thomas for the second time that week. That was almost unheard of for a young associate. When the ding of the elevator signaled David had arrived on the first floor, he stood up straight and buttoned the top button of his coat jacket. As he stepped off the elevator, the "click-clack" of his shoes resonated throughout the foyer as he strolled up to the front desk receptionist and inquired in which conference room he was expected.

"Number one," the receptionist responded.

*Of course, it had to be the large conference room*, David thought with elation and building anticipation.

When Greg Thomas did something, he did it *big*. Conference room one was reserved for VIP clients, complete with champagne, oversized leather chairs, and plantation shutters on the windows. The chandelier hanging in the center of the room was worth tens of thousands of dollars and exuded an image of wealth and sophistication for all clients to admire. After all, the clients probably didn't realize they were paying for that extravagance.

David pushed open the heavy door to the large conference room. When the door swung open, he was surprised to find the room nearly empty. The only chairs occupied were the two closest to the door.

Greg Thomas and Clive Sneedle, the human resources director, were sitting casually and finishing their lunch, which had been ordered in from a local steakhouse.

"Come on in, Dave," Greg Thomas beckoned as he removed his bib and took another bite of his half-eaten ribeye steak.

David was confused.

*What could this mean? Why is Clive Sneedle here? Have I done something wrong?*

"Have a seat, David," Mr. Sneedle said in his squeaky robotic voice. David sat down at the head of the table and looked at Greg Thomas, who was still focused on the remaining portions of his lunch.

Then, Mr. Sneedle uttered the infamous words, "David, we have to let you go." A feeling of disbelief overwhelmed him.

Greg Thomas chimed in as he licked the steak sauce off of his fingers.

"Dave, after the partnership meeting today, we reviewed the quarterly revenue numbers, and they were just not as strong as we had hoped. Consequently, we have to do some *corporate restructuring* to thin out some of our associates and support staff."

"I'm sorry, what!?" That was all David could manage to say.

Greg Thomas continued, "Dave, you're the new guy, and we have to cut the last folks in the door, that's how it works…sorry."

David couldn't hold in his emotions any longer.

"That's it?!" David said as he raised his voice and leaned forward in his chair.

"After all that crap you told me, you're firing me?!"

"Uh, yes, that's correct…please don't make a scene, David," Mr. Sneedle pleaded.

"This is ridiculous! I made a lot of money for this firm, and you were just congratulating me in your office on the Hendson International settlement."

"Well, Dave, after reviewing the quarterly numbers, it simply wasn't enough," Greg Thomas stated firmly as he took a bite of creamed spinach.

David's blood began to boil.

"Well, I'm taking Hendson International with me when I go… they're *my* client, and I'm taking them," David threatened.

Greg Thomas wiped his mouth with a white cloth napkin, sat casually back in his chair, and scowled at David.

"You're not taking *any* clients with you, Dave," Greg Thomas replied as he pursed his lips and stared daggers at David across the table.

David had just poked the bear.

"If you even *think* about taking business away from this firm, I will unleash every litigator in this place to bleed you dry in court for the next three years until you file for bankruptcy."

David suspected Greg Thomas's bite would be just as bad as his bark, maybe even worse.

"However, if you go quietly, you'll be given two months' severance." Greg Thomas leaned in, putting his elbows on the table, and looked David right in the eye.

He continued, "And, you know what? You're going to take it because you don't have any other choice, Dave."

David knew that was the truth.

Clive Sneedle squirmed in his chair. He was uncomfortable in these situations and never knew what Greg Thomas was going to say next. He chimed into the conversation to prevent further threats.

"I'll email the paperwork to your personal email address, David. As of this meeting, you no longer have access to the firm's email account or any client files. We'll send a notification, on firm letterhead, to your clients telling them you are no longer with the firm. You can contact them directly if you choose to do so." Mr. Sneedle seemed mechanical and rehearsed in his statements.

Without another word, Greg Thomas and Clive Sneedle got up from their seats, left their lunch plates on the table, and walked out the conference room door. The meeting was over.

The elevator ride back to the fifth floor was a long one for David. When the elevator stopped, and David stepped off, Rita met him in the hallway.

"Oh David, I'm so sorry, I just heard the news." Rita gave him a big hug.

"Wow, good news travels fast," David said as he looked over Rita's shoulder to find the entire floor staring at him, waiting to see how he would react – he had no intention of giving them a show.

He simply walked into his plush office and stared out the window at the sky. The clouds had rolled in, and the once-blue sky carried a dark gray haze. David picked up an empty banker's box and started packing up his personal items.

*What do I do now?* He wondered as he took an inventory of his belongings. David glanced up and saw his Georgetown Law degree proudly displayed on the wall above his computer screen. He reached up and lifted it from its resting place and carefully laid it in the box.

Rita stood in the doorway, unsure how to help her boss. As David began taking his other pictures down, he broke the silence.

"So, are they keeping *you?*"

"No. They axed me, too. Sneedle's twitchy little sidekick met with me while Sneedle met with you. Two months of severance ain't bad, right?"

David didn't respond. He was already thinking about the dozens of other blue-chip law firms in town that would be interested in hiring him. He knew a lot of folks and was confident he would land another job within a few weeks.

Over the next hour, many of David's colleagues stopped by his office to bid him good luck in his future endeavors. They acted sad to see him go, but most of them were secretly excited that their chances to make partner had just increased. He packed up the last bit of his personal items and turned his key card in to the front desk receptionist. David told Rita he would call her in a couple days to discuss what they would do next. The truth was, he had no clue, but Rita looked to him for guidance in such things, and he had to pretend everything was going to be okay.

# Chapter 13

Pastor Tommy Felton had been on the road for three straight hours. His hands were still shaking, and he couldn't imagine feeling worse. Tommy had watched the love of his life die, and now, he was a fugitive on the run. He had painful burns on his arms and face from the fire and would undoubtedly carry physical and emotional scars for the rest of his life. He still had to call his daughter, Jenny, in Oklahoma and tell her what had happened.

*How am I even going to begin the conversation?* He wondered as he located his cell phone on the car's passenger seat. As he searched for his daughter's cell number, he paused for a moment.

*If they tracked Francis Pietrov's phone call to me, they might still be monitoring my calls.*

He decided to take a different approach. Even though she lived in Tulsa, Jenny worked for a large marketing firm headquartered in New York City. Tommy pulled over into a rest area, looked up the company's main phone line, and dialed.

A receptionist answered, and Tommy asked to be connected to Jenny's direct office line in Tulsa. After a few rings, Jenny picked up.

"Jenny…it's dad. I can't talk long, but I have something very important to tell you. Are you sitting down?"

"Yea, dad, what's going on?" Tommy could hear the concern in his daughter's voice.

"Jenny, your mother's been killed in a fire. I'm so sorry to have to tell you this way, sweetheart." Jenny began crying on the other end of the phone, and it gutted Tommy that he couldn't be there to comfort her. Nevertheless, Tommy's emotion was overcome by a sense of urgency to warn his baby girl.

"Jenny, Jenny…listen to me…you need to know something. . .it wasn't an accident. Your mother was murdered."

"What!? Dad, what are you—" Tommy interrupted, "I think the killer may be after me too. They're likely tracking my phone calls, so I'm going to lay low for a few weeks. Do not try to reach me, and do not go to Charleston – it's not safe. I can't tell you anymore. Do you understand?"

"Dad, no, wait, *who* is tracking your calls? *Who* killed mom? Dad, this doesn't make any sense!" Jenny broke down in hysterical crying. In the background noise, Tommy could hear the muffled voices of Jenny's concerned co-workers.

"I know, sweetheart. I promise I'll explain everything when I return. But trust me, this is the only way to keep you safe until I get more information. You're all I have left; please listen to me!"

Tommy could tell his daughter was inconsolable on the other end of the phone, but through her tears, she managed a question.

"Where's mom's body?"

"They'll probably keep your mother at the county coroner's office until I get back. And, listen…they may contact you and say I'm a suspect in her death. But it's not true, and I promise I'll explain everything later."

"A suspect?! Dad, what are you talking about?!" Jenny pleaded with her father for answers.

Tommy gave Jenny one final instruction.

"Jenny, if the police call you, tell them we spoke, and tell them you *don't* know where I am…I have to go, but I love you, and I'll call you as soon as I can."

"No, dad, wait…" Tommy reluctantly hung up on his daughter. He wanted to keep the call brief, just in case it was being tracked.

Tommy looked down at his phone. If anyone was tracking his call log, the outgoing number would show a New York area code and would, hopefully, divert attention away from his daughter in Tulsa. He was protecting Jenny but felt horrible about what he had just done – he turned his little girl's world upside down in less than a minute. Tommy put his burnt face in his charred hands and wept. His salty tears felt like daggers to his open wounds, but he was so overcome with grief, he couldn't stop.

After a couple of moments, he settled back into his drive and began thinking about the last twenty-four hours. This had been the worst day of his life. His life had fundamentally changed, and what's worse, he wasn't sure what to do next. However, he was sure about *one thing* – he was not going to live in fear. When it was his time to go, whether by a bullet, old age, or bad luck, he would accept his fate graciously and pass on to be reunited with his beloved Marie.

Still, Tommy didn't know what to expect when he arrived in Washington.

*Am I heading into the storm instead of away from it?* He couldn't be sure, but his mind wandered to the ominous possibilities.

All he knew was that Dr. Pietrov must have been telling him

the truth, and there were forces at work trying to keep that truth hidden. Tommy realized he might be the only other person alive who knew this momentous secret, and he wasn't going to let it die with him if he could help it. Tommy pushed his foot down on the accelerator, and his Honda increased speed as it flew down the highway. He had to finish what Dr. Pietrov started and was determined to find more answers once he reached his destination.

*Wait a second!* he thought.

*I know who can help me – that counselor Francis was always talking about. His buddy in D.C. What was that guy's name?*

Tommy only spoke to Francis Pietrov a couple times a year, at most. But every time they talked, Dr. Pietrov would go on and on about his best friend in Washington, but Tommy could not remember his name. They had become friends when Francis first moved to D.C. decades earlier. Suddenly, it hit Tommy.

"*Hatfield!* Yes, *Jerry Hatfield!*" Tommy audibly shouted in his car. He didn't know if Jerry would have any answers, but that seemed like a good place to start.

# Chapter 14

David Stoneman loaded the box of his personal belongings into his black BMW. He took one last look at the eleven-story office building he had been so proud to call his own. All of that was finished now. He had been fired, and Greg Thomas had stolen his clients. David learned his lesson and would not make the same mistakes again. At his next firm, he would be more guarded and even more cutthroat. It wouldn't take long before David was a full-blown attorney stereotype.

Rita Valore had already left. She promised to spend the evening scouring the classifieds in search of their next job. That's one thing David loved about Rita – she was fiercely loyal. David appreciated that about her.

A bar seemed to be the most appropriate next stop for him, given the circumstances, but David needed more than a stiff drink. He needed direction from someone who could set him on the right path and reassure him everything would be okay.

He shut the trunk of his car and drove aimlessly around the city for about an hour to clear his head and search for the perfect spot to drown his sorrows. David saw a familiar pub on an inviting side street a couple of blocks from the Foggy Bottom-GWU metro station. He had been to this particular bar in the past for a casual pint, but today was different. David simply wanted to drink until he was numb. He found a parking spot on the street, parked his car, and walked down the sidewalk toward the pub.

Because he was near George Washington University, he passed dozens of jovial students chatting with friends as they headed to and from classes with their backpacks ornamented on their backs. David envied them. They were not yet aware of the world's cold and competitive nature, but they would soon learn.

As he strode down the sidewalk, he passed the Fellowship Presbyterian Church on his right. He had seen the church before on previous visits to this pub, but he never darkened the door. The church was small but adorned with ionic architecture, which gave the building a storied and historic look and feel. Work afforded David little free time, and he was not going to spend his spare moments in church. Moreover, he was not religious *at all*. He went to church on Christmas and Easter, but that was it.

As David walked past the church's front steps, he peeked down the alley to the left of the building to find a homeless man rummaging through the trash cans. He stopped and watched the man for a moment as the unfortunate soul opened old Styrofoam take-out containers and poured scraps of leftover food into his mouth.

An unfamiliar feeling hit David – gratitude. He realized that even though this was arguably the worst day of his life, he still had it better than the man eating out of the garbage.

His thought was interrupted by the triumphant sound of a pipe organ, which bellowed harmoniously from the Fellowship Presbyterian Church. For some reason, David felt drawn to the music. It was pleasant, and the musical notes put him at ease. As David walked backward a few paces, he heard voices coming from inside the church doors. Out of sheer curiosity, he decided to stop in for a couple of minutes and simply enjoy the music.

After all, the pub would be open for several more hours, and he would have plenty of time to get drunk later.

It was lightly raining now, and David quickened his pace up the church's front steps to avoid getting soaked. As he entered the foyer, he was met by a small elderly lady with silver hair and broad wire-rimmed glasses. She asked if he was there for the special service. David quickly shook his head and told her he just wanted to listen to the music for a while. Despite his objections, the elderly lady insisted on introducing him to a few church members, and, before David could stop her, she disappeared down a side hallway.

As David was waiting for her return, he glanced around the foyer. A painting of Jesus caught his eye. It hung above the welcome center table to the right of the front door. It depicted a man with a scruffy beard, flowing brown hair with a halo above his head, which neatly accented his white robe.

"Captivating, isn't he?" David heard a soothing voice behind him.

He spun around to find an older gentleman in a cardigan sweater and flowing curly white hair.

"Uh, yes, he is," David politely responded.

"My name is Jerry Hatfield, and I'm a counselor on staff here. Welcome to Fellowship Presbyterian." Jerry extended his hand.

"David Stoneman," David mechanically responded with a firm return handshake.

"I think there's been a mistake…I don't need a counselor; I just wanted to listen to the organ for a minute. So, thanks for your time but I—" Jerry smiled and interrupted.

"I understand, and I also *don't believe you*," he said with a heartfelt smile. David was taken aback by the man's warmth and curt response.

"Excuse me?"

"Unfortunately for you, but fortunately for me, I have an acute power of perception, Dave, especially when it comes to human emotional states. Here, let me prove it to you." Jerry looked David up and down and continued.

"You're wearing an expensive suit and tie, which means you're a professional *something*. You're too old and too well dressed to work on Capitol Hill, and I don't recognize your face as a legislator. And, judging by the bags under your eyes, I suspect you are either a consultant or attorney who is a workaholic and who had one heck of a day."

"That's pretty good, I—" Jerry interrupted David again.

"Oh, I'm just getting started! You were on your way to the bar down the street when your conscience told you to clear your head before you downed a few beers…am I close?"

David smiled and nodded, "Attorney, and, yes, I had a rough day."

"Well, son, you've come to the right place. Let's get you some coffee, and we can talk the whole thing out."

David knew he had done the right thing by going into the church and not the bar. And, even though he was hesitant to admit it, this was exactly what he needed.

"Also, we have a special service tonight at six; I hope you can stay for that."

"Thanks, but I have plans," David lied.

"No, you don't. But that's okay – I won't push it." Jerry grinned.

The two men disappeared down the side hallway and into a small Sunday school room to begin their conversation about the day's events.

----

As the six o'clock special service started at the Fellowship Presbyterian Church, David reluctantly found himself seated in a pew in the back of the sanctuary. He planned to stay for just a short while and was only willing to do so because Jerry Hatfield wouldn't take no for an answer. He had spilled his emotional guts to Jerry, who was very encouraging and easy to talk to. David was surprised to learn Jerry was a volunteer counselor at the church and had recently retired from a successful private counseling practice. So, his interest in helping David seemed sincere.

Jerry walked up the center aisle and sat down next to David.

"Tonight, a young woman I work with, Sarah Mercer, is going to be sharing her *unbelievable* story."

"What kind of story?" David inquired as he repositioned himself in the hard wooden pew.

"Sarah is a single mom who just lost one of her sons. Very sad. I think she's handling it pretty well, all things considered." Jerry's comment was intended to encourage David to put his personal crisis into perspective.

The organ slowly began to play *Amazing Grace* as an attractive woman with shoulder-length blonde hair and brown eyes, who looked to be around thirty years old, stepped onto the stage with a microphone. She was of average height and modestly dressed, wearing an off-brand blouse and blue jeans. She gripped the mic tightly with both hands, and, even from the back pew, David could see her shoulders tense as she began to speak.

"Thank you so much for coming out tonight." She said in a soft, sweet voice.

"For those of you who knew my son, you know he was a kind and thoughtful kid." She paused for a moment. Suddenly, her demeanor changed, and she became visibly upset and emotional as she continued.

"But what most of you may not know is…the *government* did this…that Division Act…that's what killed him! All these rules – they killed my son!" Sarah Mercer broke down and cried on the stage in front of the entire congregation. Jerry quickly left his seat and ran to the stage to help his patient. Others interceded as well and tried to comfort her.

David was uncertain of what to do. *Was this normal behavior at this church?* he wondered as he scanned the other attendees, trying to gauge their responses.

The pastor took the microphone from Sarah as Jerry led her out the sanctuary's side door. He thanked Sarah for her willingness to share and began to preach an alternative sermon to salvage the service, but David wasn't listening. He was too distracted by what had just happened.

*The Division Act?* He thought.

David knew what it was but hadn't thought much about it. He remembered the Division Act was a bill recently passed in Congress, but he hadn't paid attention to the details. David was puzzled by Sarah's comments, and he tended to overanalyze things.

*How could the Division Act be responsible for the death of this woman's son?* David pondered. After trying to make sense of the looming question, he concluded Sarah might just be crazy and on the verge of a mental breakdown. She had just lost a child, and Jerry mentioned she was seeing him professionally.

After nearly twenty minutes, the sermon concluded, and the small crowd disbursed. As people filtered up the aisle and out into the church's foyer, David scanned the sanctuary. His gaze stopped on a man who looked out of place. The man had just walked in the back doors and found a seat on the opposite side of the sanctuary. He looked like he had been in some sort of accident. The man was wearing gym clothes and had a bloody bandage wrapped around his left forearm and what appeared to be fresh burns on the side of his neck and face.

David grew uneasy by the man's presence and decided to get some air outside. It was still drizzling, but David didn't care; he just needed to get out of there for a minute.

As he loitered on the sidewalk, he heard the church door open; it was the man with the burns and the bandages. David was startled, and a little nervous as the man approached him.

"Excuse me?" The man said, with what sounded like a Southern accent.

"Look, I don't have any money," came David's kneejerk reply.

"Do I really look *that* bad?" The man smiled and laughed.

David was embarrassed by his judgmental comment and tried to recover.

"I'm *so* sorry; what can I do for you, sir?"

"I was wondering if you're on staff here at the church," the man said as he pointed back toward the building.

"No, actually, this is my first time attending. There's a gentleman inside who can probably help you; his name is Jerry."

"Jerry Hatfield?!" The man seemed thrilled to hear that name.

"Yea, he should still be inside."

"Okay, great. Thank you for your help!" the man said enthusiastically as he rushed back into the church.

David looked down the street and saw the neon bar lights beckoning him, but he no longer wanted a drink. For some reason, he was curious to learn more about Sarah Mercer's story. By now, David's clothes were wet, and he could feel the rain dripping down the side of his face. At that moment, David uncharacteristically acted upon an impulse.

Before he could second-guess his actions, David found himself walking back into the church and down the central aisle toward Sarah Mercer, who had returned to the sanctuary. He passed the man with the burns, who was talking to Jerry Hatfield in one of the pews midway down the center aisle. When David reached Sarah, he couldn't believe what came out of his mouth.

"Ma'am, I'm so sorry for your loss, but I have to ask, how in the world did the Division Act kill your son?"

# Chapter 15

Sarah Mercer was stunned.

*Who was this stranger asking about her son's death? Who does he think he is?*

Jerry Hatfield overheard David's abrupt question and, sensing Sarah's offense, quickly excused himself from his conversation and ran to David's defense.

"Sarah, this is David Stoneman. I'm sure he didn't mean to be that direct." Jerry shot a reproving look at David, indicating he shouldn't ask any more bombshell questions.

"Well, I don't think it's any of *your* business, Mr. Stoneman…" Sarah barked as she looked David up and down, sizing him up. The scene then escalated.

"Do you work for the government?!" Sarah angrily asked as she took a step forward and clenched her fists. David knew he needed to weigh his next words carefully.

"No, ma'am. I'm just a lawyer who wants to learn more about your son, that's all. Forgive me if I overstepped any boundaries." David put his hands up, demonstrating his surrender.

Jerry frowned at David and put his arm around Sarah.

"I'll give you five minutes," Sarah reluctantly responded as she nodded at Jerry, indicating she would be okay telling her story.

As the remaining members of the congregation filed out of the Fellowship Presbyterian Church, David and Sarah sat on the carpeted steps leading up to the sanctuary stage. Jerry resumed his conversation with the man with the burns, and they disappeared into the foyer as Sarah began to tell David her sad story.

> I had twin boys, Samuel and Mark. Two years ago, we were evicted from our apartment, and I lost my job less than a week after that. In the middle of that chaos, I noticed Mark was lethargic, complaining of stomach cramps, frequently breaking out in cold sweats, and he would convulse for no reason. He kept reassuring me he was okay, and I thought it might just be related to stress, but the symptoms got worse. I insisted we go to the emergency room, even though we didn't have health insurance. I was desperate to get him seen right away. The emergency room doctor, a lady named Pam Winters, took pity on us and ran some tests free of charge. A few days later, we got the results. Dr. Winters said Mark had a rare gastrointestinal cancer, and the mortality rate was very high. We were devastated. That's when I found Fellowship Presbyterian and Jerry Hatfield. Jerry helped us get through some difficult days.

Even though emotional stories didn't easily move David, he felt sorry for Sarah. She took a deep breath and continued.

"The church's congregation learned about our situation, and they showered us with food, money, and prayers as a result. One person even let us stay at their vacant apartment near the hospital while Mark was undergoing cancer treatment. They were truly a blessing."

Sarah wiped her eyes with a tissue as the difficult memories flooded back.

"Jerry worked with the pastor to set up *weekly* prayer meetings where, after the Wednesday night church service, people would come down to the altar and pray for healing for Mark. Not just short, wishful prayers, but *deep, emotional* prayers where they would speak out healing scriptures and lay hands on him. Sometimes there were dozens of people huddled at the altar for close to an hour. It was amazing to watch."

David interrupted, "Where was the boy's father?"

"Dead," she responded curtly.

"My husband ran with the wrong crowd and was killed when I was pregnant with the boys. It was tough. We weren't even able to have an open casket funeral for him."

David realized he had potentially raised another sensitive topic and quickly tried to move on.

"I'm sorry to hear that. Please continue."

"The prayers of the church's congregation *actually worked*. Mark gradually got better. It was the prayer; I just know it! Dr. Winters said it was the treatment, but *I know* it was the prayers."

David was highly skeptical but didn't want to sound condescending.

"*How* do you know it was the prayers?" He questioned. Sarah leaned in and grew more excited.

"Because the medical treatments were given twice a week – once on Tuesday and once on Thursday."

"Okay...so what does that mean?" David was trying to put the pieces together.

"We would hold the prayer meetings on Wednesday nights and, like clockwork, every Thursday morning, the test results before the Thursday treatment were significantly better than any of the other days of the week."

"Did the medical treatments change over time?" David inquired as he repositioned himself on the steps.

"No...and we even skipped a week of treatment altogether but kept the group prayer meeting, and Mark's condition *still* improved. I just know it was the prayers, Mr. Stoneman!"

"Forgive me for sounding incredulous, but didn't you go to church on Sundays too? What was so special about Wednesdays' service?"

Sarah nodded, appreciating his skepticism, "Yes, we were at church every Sunday, but the group prayer meetings for Mark were only on Wednesday night after the service. For some reason, Mark's body responded when *the group* huddled around him to pray on Wednesday nights. I'm telling you, that's what did it!" Sarah said confidently.

"Okay...Ms. Mercer, again, forgive me for being indelicate, but didn't your son eventually pass away? Help me understand what I'm missing here." David was puzzled but trying not to pour salt into Sarah's emotional wounds.

"Yes, my *other* son, *Samuel,* passed away. Mark and Samuel were twins. I was describing *Mark's* recovery. He got sick first and recovered from the illness. Samuel got the same condition later and died."

"But how does Samuel's death connect to the Division Act?"

"I'm not great at explaining these types of things, but I'll do my best." Sarah paused for a moment and looked up while trying to think through how she could easily explain the connection.

"One of the Division Act sections prevents churches from holding prayer meetings…or something like that. So, after the Act was passed, we couldn't hold the Wednesday night prayer meetings for Samuel as we did for Mark. The medical treatments were the same for both boys. The *only* difference was the prayer meetings!"

David was nodding but did not believe Sarah's story. He knew the Division Act was a popular news story for the last few months, and a number of lawsuits had been filed challenging its constitutionality. Still, David was so preoccupied with his work he had failed to pay attention to the specifics. Regardless, to David, Sarah's version of her story was a way for her to vent her anger and frustration, perhaps even her own guilt for her son's death – in other words, her story was likely nothing more than a psychological defense mechanism. However, it wasn't David's place to tell her that. Still curious, David asked another question.

"But how do you know whether or not—"

Preoccupied with her previous statement, Sarah cut David off to explain further.

> After *Mark* was healed of his cancer, Samuel began to display similar symptoms. So, I took Samuel to see Dr. Winters. She told me Samuel had the same rare gastrointestinal cancer as Mark. Dr. Winters thought the cancerous cells possibly began to form when the boys were in the womb together, and the tumors must have been growing without obvious symptoms for years.

Once again, we went through the *same* treatments, and once again, I took Samuel to Wednesday prayer meetings, like we did with Mark.

At this point, David could tell Sarah was becoming more emotional.

"We were able to hold just a few Wednesday prayer meetings, and Samuel's condition was improving, just like Mark. But then the Division Act was passed, and our prayer meetings became illegal, so we had to stop…" Sarah put her hand on her forehead and teared up.

She blew her nose with a tissue and concluded the story, "The medical treatments didn't work, and Samuel's condition deteriorated. He died a couple of months ago."

David wasn't buying it. He was, however, angry with himself for not paying more attention when the Division Act was passed – he usually followed new federal legislation more closely. This one had fallen between the cracks for him.

Regardless, while his heart went out to Sarah for her loss, David didn't believe her account of the events. The story, however, was a tear-jerker and would, no doubt, make a fascinating court case. That's when the thought hit David; *this is the type of case that would be covered by national news! This is the type of case that could put me back in the spotlight!*

David felt energized, but he had to be careful how he approached the topic with Sarah. He also needed to better understand the Division Act's nuances but wouldn't bother grilling Sarah about it.

"I'm *so* sorry, Ms. Mercer."

"Please, call me Sarah." She wiped her red nose and grabbed another tissue from her pocket.

David smiled and decided to ask his question but hoped his true intentions would not be blatantly obvious.

"Sarah...I have some free time on my hands these days. Let me do some research into the Division Act, okay? Maybe there's *something* I can do to help you and Mark during this difficult time." Sarah looked surprised but nodded in approval.

They then both stood up. David gave Sarah a firm handshake and took down her contact information. He briefly said goodbye to Jerry Hatfield and quickly left the church. On his way home, he stopped at a cafe for a large cup of black coffee. It was going to be a long night.

# Chapter 16

David Stoneman could not let this injustice stand. It didn't matter that he didn't really believe Sarah's theory – what happened to the Mercer family was tragic, and he would lead the charge to right the wrong. David may have still been angry at Johnson Allen. Nonetheless, his focus now transitioned to recognizing a potential opportunity related to the civil injustice experienced by Sarah Mercer and her twin boys. As he drove the dark streets of Georgetown, he called Rita Valore.

"Hello"? Rita answered in a gruff voice.

David glanced at his car's dashboard. It was 10:00 p.m.

"Rita, I'm sorry to call so late, but I have to talk to you," David said excitedly as he waited at a red light.

"David, I was asleep, and you sound like you've had too much caffeine. What do you need?"

"Come by my apartment tomorrow morning at 8:30; we're going to do some pro bono work."

"Okay…" Rita responded halfheartedly.

"How are we going to fund that, Dave? Our gravy train just stopped, remember?"

"Come on, Rita. Have a little faith! You know how much they paid me at the firm. The severance I'm getting will bankroll us for at least a couple of months. You don't have to put in any of your own money; just help me for a couple of weeks then, I promise, I'll start calling my white-shoe firm contacts. Sound good?"

"Whatever. See ya in a few hours," Rita said as she hung up.

As David drove down M Street, he observed college students stumbling out of the bars and restaurants. They looked happy and full of life. David thought back to his days in college and law school. The world seemed so simple – study and go out with friends. That was all he used to do. Now things had become more complicated. It also didn't help that he was getting pressure from his mother to settle down, get married, and start a family. However, all of that would have to wait; he had a new goal: justice for the Mercer family and fame and fortune for himself.

David had been in Washington long enough to be numb to the constant barrage of political posturing for which the city was known. However, all the diplomacy in the world could not cover up the fact that a boy was dead because of a piece of ridiculous and unconstitutional legislation.

*Wait a second!* he thought as he snapped back to reality.

*Why am I buying into this stuff? This is absurd. There's not a shred of evidence to prove Samuel Mercer died because of the Division Act.*

Nevertheless, David knew he had to help in *some* way, but he wasn't going to be able to step into the limelight without a clever case strategy. He suspected the lawsuits challenging the Division Act's constitutionality would be tied up in the federal court system for years. The process would be slow, boring, and overhyped by special interest groups. The news coverage would likely dwindle as the tedious legal battles ensued month after month, and the public grew disinterested. He knew he had to strike now while the iron was hot.

*Yet Sarah's case seemed different*, he thought. *But in what way?*

David continued to drive Georgetown's cobblestoned streets. He liked to drive around while he reflected on cases, an unsafe but effective habit he developed in law school. He passed street after street of historic row houses. By now, many of the homes were completely dark, though a few of them were still well lit, revealing the grandeur of their interior decor.

Illuminated by floodlights, a redbrick house with black shutters caught David's eye. As he passed the home, he noticed a side garden that added nice color to the home's yard. Then, casually looking back to the road, he saw a college student dart out from behind a parked car and into the street in front of him. His muscles tensed as he braced for impact.

He slammed on his brakes with both feet, and his car's tires screeched as his luxury BMW came to an abrupt stop just a couple of feet from the young man. The student shot him a drunken wave as he continued to the other side of the street to meet his friends. David's adrenaline was pumping, realizing he had come dangerously close to a horrible accident.

He pulled the car over, turned the engine off, took a few deep breaths, and closed his eyes.

*That's all I need*, he thought, *a wrongful death lawsuit…*

Suddenly, he had an epiphany and opened his eyes. He couldn't believe he hadn't thought of it earlier.

*That's it! It's a wrongful death case!*

David grinned and slapped his steering wheel in excitement. He would file a wrongful death lawsuit against the federal government, citing the Division Act as the primary cause of Samuel Mercer's death.

*The idea was brilliant!* He nodded in self-affirmation.

His "thinking-while-driving" exercise had proven to be successful, yet again. As he pulled a U-turn in the middle of the street to head back to his apartment, he knew this approach was likely unprecedented. David would call Sarah the following morning and ask permission to file the lawsuit on her behalf. He hoped she would be on board.

As David continued to drive back to his apartment and think more about his grand idea, he began to feel nervous. Wrongful death suits were generally taken on a contingency basis, where the attorney would receive a portion of the amount recovered, if any. David would not get his traditional three-hundred dollar per hour fee, and he wondered how he would pay for the litigation if it lasted for months, or even years.

He also wondered how the press would cover the case and how this lawsuit could tarnish his sterling reputation with other high-end law firms in town. After all, he needed a job, and plenty of firms would be interested, but maybe not if they perceived him as an "ambulance chaser."

David also knew if he moved forward with this plan, he would be under the federal government's microscope, possibly creating personal problems for himself. Most importantly, David liked to *win*, and with this fight, he would probably lose.

He made a left-hand turn onto Wisconsin Avenue and drove down into his apartment's private underground garage. After parking his car, David headed up to his apartment on the third floor. He went straight to bed, knowing he would need to be well-rested if he was going to move forward with this case.

# Chapter 17

In 1954, then-Senator Lyndon Johnson introduced an amendment to the U.S. tax code, which prevented all non-profit organizations, including churches, from participating in, or promoting, political campaigns. This amendment became known as the "Johnson Amendment," scrutinized for decades for directing the actions and activities of religious organizations. Senator Stephen Smythe used the Johnson Amendment as his inspiration for the Division Act.

However, he took it one step *further*. Both pieces of legislation used a church's tax-exempt status to regulate its activity. Yet, the Division Act sought to regulate *specific acts of worship*, which Senator Smythe found especially distasteful. He even tried to sneak in a few restrictions he had hoped would go undetected. He was wrong.

Of course, while he suspected hundreds of members of Congress barely read the bill, right-wing activists scrutinized every word and immediately filed lawsuits arguing the Act was unconstitutional. Senator Smythe didn't care. He anticipated that response and was ready for the fight.

It was early in the morning, and the Senator had just finished his first cup of coffee in the private conference room connected to his office. He was reviewing his notes for the speech he had to give in the Capitol's famous Rotunda to a local progressive think tank that had donated a large sum of money to the Capitol's recent restoration project. Apparently, a million-dollar donation is enough to get you breakfast in the most famous room on Capitol Hill.

Senator Smythe was the keynote speaker and planned to offer a few remarks at the end of the breakfast event. He had ten minutes before he needed to head that way and decided to take one final look over the speech his aide, Tim, had prepared.

Tim walked into the room with a cup of water and poured it into the large green plant that sat nestled underneath the conference room's only window. Senator Smythe glanced up from his notes. Tim was tall but looked slight compared to the conference room's half-circle groin-vaulted ceiling accented with gold trim.

"Stop watering those things!" the Senator barked as he looked back down at his notes. "Don't we have people who do that stuff?"

He found the trickle of the water distracting as he highlighted phrases in his speech he wanted to emphasize with a yellow highlighter. Tim set the cup down and approached his boss.

"Sir, I'm sorry to bother you, but it's time to go."

"Get this stuff and put it in my portfolio. I have to take a leak," the Senator said as he rose from his chair, dumped a pile of papers in Tim's arms, and hurried toward his private restroom.

Tim dutifully compiled the notes on the table while Senator Smythe took care of his business. Finally, after a couple of minutes, the Senator emerged, wiping his hands with a cloth hand towel he casually discarded on the conference room table. Tim picked up the hand towel, shoved it in his pocket, and followed his boss down the hall toward the Rotunda.

"I hate this crack of dawn speech crap!" Senator Smythe said aloud as if he were talking to himself. Tim was a few steps behind with the Senator's portfolio, trying to keep up.

The Rotunda always impressed Senator Smythe. It was magnificent and full of history. As he entered the room, he looked up at the ornate ceiling. The painted pictures in the eye of the Rotunda's highest point, called *The Apotheosis of Washington*, carried the images of gown-wearing figures staring down at the Rotunda's waxed Seneca sandstone floor below.

As the members of the think tank noticed Senator Smythe enter the room, many of them stopped eating, laid down their utensils, and gave him robust applause. By the time he reached the podium, all forty attendees were giving him a standing ovation.

"Just five minutes with a brief Q&A, right?" The Senator confirmed with Tim as he put his hand over the podium's microphone. Tim nodded.

Senator Smythe then turned his attention to the audience, and putting both of his thumbs in the air, shined his bright, beaming smile. The crowd roared even louder.

"Thank you…thank you, very much. Thank you, please be seated."

The crowd quieted and resumed their seats.

"I always wondered what a million-dollar donation to the Capitol restoration effort would get me…it looks like it would get me breakfast in the Rotunda and a short speech from… well…*me*," Senator Smythe joked. The crowd laughed.

Over the next several minutes, Senator Smythe described the need for greater government regulation for tax-exempt organizations, explaining that the Johnson Amendment laid the groundwork for this theory decades earlier. Signs of approval throughout the crowd signified he had a sympathetic audience. After he finished his remarks, he opened the floor to questions.

A portly gentleman with a thick mustache sitting at the front table raised his hand. Senator Smythe pointed at him.

"Yes, sir?"

"Do you think the Division Act will hold up against legal claims that it's unconstitutional, especially from right-wing religious special interest groups?" The man finished his question and nervously took a sip of his coffee as he kept his eyes trained on the Senator.

Senator Smythe knew he would get this question. He always did, and he was prepared.

"Absolutely! The Establishment Clause of the U.S. Constitution is clear – the federal government cannot financially support religious organizations. And, their water is about to get cut off. So, of course, they're pissed." More laughs came from the crowd.

He continued, "In all seriousness – it's time we stop hanging on to the archaic religious biases which have divided us for hundreds of years. We finally have a chance to hit the restart button and build our country on a neutral foundation. Religious organizations can still exist; we're just not going to subsidize them any longer without additional regulation." Senator Smythe nodded after his comment – it was an old political trick he learned to get people to agree with his statements. Often, audience members would nod along with him.

Another hand shot up from one of the middle tables. An Asian woman with graying hair spoke up.

"Beyond the financial support issue, how have you handled criticism related to restricting certain actions and activities of religious organizations? Singing in churches, for example." The question drew annoyed glances from members of the crowd. Senator Smythe tried to mask his irritation.

"Well, it's pretty simple. Certain activities of some religious sects increase the risk of spreading infectious diseases, and it's just not something we're willing to risk again. Look what happened during the COVID-19 pandemic. A number of states restricted attendance and activities at churches, synagogues, and mosques. No doubt that brave action saved hundreds, maybe thousands, of lives."

Senator Smythe decided to drive his point home.

"It's government's first job to protect the American people from harm and, as we have seen time and time again, places of worship can be hotbeds for the spread of infectious diseases."

"What about sports venues?" Came an interjected question from someone at the back of the room.

"That's a good point, and I have a simple answer...the government does *not* subsidize or offer tax breaks to professional sports teams the same way it subsidizes *religious* organizations. If we funded sports teams, then we would apply similar restrictions to them," Senator Smythe confidently responded.

Tim appeared on the side of the podium and signaled it was time to wrap it up.

"Well, folks, I appreciate the questions, and I appreciate your support. Thanks for your financial contribution, and we look forward to a similar donation next year." Senator Smythe smiled and waved to the applauding crowd. He and Tim quickly retreated to the side hallway from which they came. Senator Smythe's smile turned into a scowl.

"Tim, I don't want to answer *any* questions next time. These clowns are on my side and still try to blow holes in the Division Act. Unbelievable!"

"I didn't think any of their questions were unfair, sir. Your answers were solid." Tim responded.

Senator Smythe rolled his eyes and slammed his office door in Tim's face, flopped down on the couch, and closed his eyes for a quick nap before he started the workday.

# Chapter 18

Rita Valore showed up at David's apartment at half-past eight with coffee in hand. She banged on the door for ten minutes until she roused David from his deep sleep. He slowly meandered to the door with his black hair sticking up on one side and his green eyes bloodshot and half open. He rubbed his right eye with the back of his hand as he swung the door open to invite Rita into his cluttered apartment.

"Good to see you're ready to start working," she brushed past him and put the coffee on his kitchen table.

Despite the clothes piling up on the couch and the empty pizza boxes casually tossed on the kitchen counter, David's apartment was one of the finest in the area. He chose this particular three-bedroom apartment on Wisconsin Avenue because he wanted to be in the heart of Georgetown, one of the most historic neighborhoods in Washington. It cost David a small fortune, but, at the time, he could afford it.

He made the third bedroom a plush home office, complete with a large desk that sat in the middle of the room with a green banker's lamp placed neatly on one side. The walls were covered with large bookshelves with books about politics, poetry, and the law. An oversized leather chair, similar to the one he had at Johnson Allen, was behind the desk. The light from the window behind the desk silhouetted the furniture, casting angled shadows on his white carpet. In the corner nearest to the door was a yoga mat near a few spare dumbbells, in case David wanted to sneak a moment of meditation, or a quick workout, into his weekend workdays.

David pointed Rita toward his home office and instructed her to log in to his computer, to start researching the Division Act's nuances, and pull copies of the lawsuits that had been filed against the Act. After giving his instructions, David realized he was still in his pajamas and needed to clean up before jumping into the research.

He hopped in the shower. The warm water felt pleasant on David's unshaven face. For the first time since he had moved in, he wondered how he would pay for that soothing warm water without his high-profile job. After a few minutes, he turned the water off and turned his thoughts to his case; he had work to do and needed to focus.

David emerged from his bedroom twenty minutes later wearing athletic shorts and a wrinkled Georgetown Law T-shirt. While Rita was dutifully reviewing documents on the computer, David decided to call Sarah Mercer. After all, he needed her permission and complete cooperation to move forward with the lawsuit.

David located his cell phone on the couch and dialed. Sarah picked up after the second ring and seemed surprised to hear David's voice so soon. David explained it was simply his nature to follow up when he felt passionate about an issue. He described how he believed the government should pay for what they did to her son and why he believed she had a case. While Sarah seemed hesitant at first, David's suave salesmanship convinced her to move forward with the first steps in the legal process.

"Okay, Mr. Stoneman, if you think we have a case...but..." Sarah stopped mid-sentence.

"But, what?" David inquired.

"I don't have any money to pay you, and I don't want to ask you to do this for *free*."

There was a momentary silence on the phone. David knew, deep down, what his response should be.

"Sarah, I want to help you. And, I can't promise I can work for free forever, but I can get this process started for you free of charge."

"I'm very appreciative, but why are you doing this for me?" Sarah questioned.

"Right now, I just need to do something good, honest, and right. I need to clear my head for a couple of months. Believe it or not, this will be just as therapeutic for me as taking a vacation." David felt bad he was not being *entirely* truthful concerning his motives, but he was sincere when he said he wanted to help.

"Well, thank you, Mr. Stoneman. I really appreciate it!"

"No problem. I've got your email address, and I'll send you a quick message to confirm I am officially acting as your attorney for this case. After that, all communications between you, me, and my paralegal will be covered by the attorney-client privilege and remain confidential. Sound good?"

"Sounds good. Thanks again!" As the call ended, David joined Rita in his office.

"So, what are we doing, Dave? I heard bits and pieces of your phone call. You planning on filling me in anytime soon?" Rita asked as she clicked through online articles.

David smiled, "Rita, I'll pay you half your usual rate out of my severance payout. And, I know you're getting severance too, so, let's just pretend we're back in Norfolk, and you're working directly for me again." David took a sip of his coffee and looked over Rita's shoulder at the computer screen.

Rita raised an eyebrow and looked up at David. David realized he would have to give her a bit more information to convince her this project was worth her time. So, he then explained the situation to Rita and elaborated on why he felt they should take the case.

"Let me get this straight…you agreed to take this case pro bono? The guy who won't wear a tie that wasn't made in Italy is going to work for *free*? Dave, I know you too well, babe! What's the *real* reason you're taking this case?" Rita knew there was more to the story.

David shrugged his shoulders and walked into the kitchen without responding. Rita suspected David's motive was publicity and decided to bait him into a confession.

"Well, okay, you got me, Dave…but there is a good chance the press will pick this case up, and that could put a nice spotlight on us…right?" She looked up from the computer and toward the office door. David popped his head in with a large grin.

"Yea, I guess that's possible," he said as he disappeared back into the kitchen.

Rita smiled, knowing she had unveiled David's real motivation behind taking the case. Sensing her judgment, David hollered from the kitchen, "…but that doesn't mean it's not the right thing to do, Rita. Quite frankly, I was moved by Sarah's story."

"Sure, sure. Whatever you say, Dave." Rita yelled back sarcastically.

David and Rita spent the next several hours researching, printing, reading, and highlighting salient portions of existing lawsuits against the Division Act. Their case needed to be unique from the others and, with the wrongful death angle, David felt confident it would be. They ordered pizza and immersed themselves in legal research. For David, it was just a typical workday.

Surprisingly, due to an apparent administrative oversight on his last day at Johnson Allen, the firm had not yet canceled David's online legal research subscription. So, he was able to download dozens of cases, statutes, and articles on the firm's subscription account, and his printer was nearly smoking after an entire afternoon of paper printing.

David had saved complaint templates for all of the state and federal courts in and around Washington. He decided to file this lawsuit in the federal court that would generate the most media attention – *the United States District Court for the District of Columbia*. He pulled the appropriate template and was able to quickly add the required boilerplate language. Now, it was time to lay out his argument.

David's argument would need to be clever, concise, and compelling. The last thing he wanted was for the court to either dismiss his case, make him jump through administrative hoops, or worse, force him to join the other lawsuits, which would draw the case out for years. That's not what he wanted. Simply stated, David wanted the immediate spotlight directed on Sarah Mercer's case and, by default, himself.

After hours of reviewing existing case documents, he and Rita confirmed that a "wrongful death" claim had not yet been argued in any of the cases filed against the Division Act. As such, this would be a case of first impression, and David knew he would have to get creative with his argument to impress a federal judge. Using the tenets of the Federal Tort Claims Act as a starting point, and with an insistence that immediate action be taken to ensure the public's health and welfare, David began building his case, block-by-block.

----

After nearly twelve hours of non-stop work and numerous cups of coffee, David's complaint was complete. David and Rita called Sarah Mercer to walk her through the document to ensure all relevant facts were included. After Sarah confirmed the information, David felt emboldened and reassured Sarah they were ready to move forward.

"Sarah, I know this stuff is difficult to understand, but everything is ready to go, and we feel confident we have a solid argument." David yawned, tired from a long day's work, and waited for her response.

"Mr. Stoneman, after thinking about it, I don't want any news cameras or reporters hounding me about this. Mark and I have been through too much."

David was frustrated by her comment, and sensing she was going to renege on her willingness to move forward, David quickly interjected.

"Exactly, Sarah," David responded in a comforting tone, trying to mask his annoyance.

"You *have* been through a lot, and you should be compensated for that struggle. That's why I will list your damages at ten million dollars for the loss of your son. How's that sound?" David's experience had taught him that throwing out large numbers generally garnered a positive response from clients.

"Ten million?" Sarah replied in disbelief.

"Yes, ten million. Although it's hard to put a price on Samuel's life, I have to put something down for damages and, after adding up the medical bills and treatment costs and evaluating damages in similar cases, ten million dollars is fair."

"Okay…" Sarah said hesitantly as her voice cracked, and she choked up.

She continued, "let's do it for Samuel!"

David hung up the phone, took a deep breath, and exhaled.

Rita grabbed her red faux-Louis Vuitton purse and headed home. It had been a long day. As David sipped his cup of cold coffee, he knew that the media would hit him like a hurricane when he filed the complaint the next morning. In fact, he counted on it. He planned to leak the story to a few friendly contacts at major news outlets, as he had done many times before. David would be back in the spotlight in no time, and law firms all over the country would be begging him to come work for them after this case made national headlines.

His moment of euphoria was disrupted by the realization that this case could drag on for months, even years. So, his only hope would be to create a big bang from the outset to encourage the government to settle the case quickly. He finished his coffee and headed to bed, satisfied that he had put in a full day's work.

# Chapter 19

The following morning, Greg Thomas was in the office early at 10:00 a.m. As he walked past Stacy, she smiled and greeted him as usual.

"Good morning, Mr. Thomas," Stacy said in a chipper tone.

"Yea, hi…I want my large coffee with *two* sugars this morning," Greg Thomas ordered as he walked through the large wooden door and into his office, barely acknowledging his assistant.

"Sure thing, Mr. Thom—" Stacy's response was cut short by the large wooden door shutting in her face.

As Greg Thomas settled in, he received an unusual call on his private phone line. Only a handful of people had that number, and it was rare for that line to ring during office hours.

"Hello?" he answered curiously.

"Greg?" the voice responded.

"Speaking," he said cordially, not knowing whether he was talking to a lowly associate or the President of the United States.

"It's Alex Mitchell at the Department of Justice; how you doing this morning?"

Truthfully, Greg Thomas felt terrible. He had been at The Palm in Tysons Corner the night before and thoroughly enjoyed a bottle of red wine and a full-bodied Cuban cigar which left a charcoal taste in his mouth. He had also indulged a bit too heavily in their high-end bourbon selection and was paying the price. The two aspirin he took that morning were set to kick in any minute.

Alex Mitchell was in his late thirties and was a rising star at the Department of Justice. He was of average height with an athletic build and looked like he dressed out of a Brooks Brothers catalog. His long, wavy brown hair was neatly parted to one side, making him look much younger than his age. He had cut his legal teeth working at the Fairfax County Commonwealth's Attorney's office on the outskirts of Washington out of law school and was making a name for himself in D.C. legal circles.

Alex was a career public servant but was beginning to understand the "real way" the legal world worked and played the game well. Accordingly, his all-American charm and idealism were giving way to the monotony of the vast, unchangeable government justice system. Despite all of that, he still had lofty goals of holding a high political office, so he tried to be poised and professional in his interactions with private sector attorneys. Today, however, he was dealing with a potential crisis.

"I'm doing great, Alex; how are things over at DOJ?" Greg Thomas pretended to care.

"Not so good, Greg, that's why I'm calling you."

"Okay, what can I do for you?" Greg Thomas inquired.

"Well, I received a call from the District Court Clerk's office about an hour ago, and they told me that a lawsuit was just filed against the government by a Mr. David Stoneman…he's one of your guys, isn't he?"

Greg Thomas chuckled into the phone, which caused his hangover headache to intensify.

"We just fired him, Alex, so, whatever he's doing, he doesn't represent Johnson Allen. He's not our problem anymore." The other end of the phone was silent for a few seconds causing Greg Thomas to glance down to make sure he hadn't been disconnected.

"It actually *is* your problem, Greg. If you fired him, then you must have done something to piss him off. Stoneman swung for the fences with the lawsuit he filed this morning, and the media will be all over this story by lunch."

"Come on, Alex, it can't be that bad…"

Alex lowered his voice, almost to a whisper, and put the phone close to his mouth.

"Greg, Stoneman filed an *unprecedented* lawsuit against the Division Act. This could be very bad for our mutual friend, Senator Smythe. I know you go way back with the Senator, and I'm sure he would be *very* grateful if you would help us on this one."

Greg Thomas knew what he was implying – this lawsuit could have devastating effects for the Senator if left unaddressed.

Greg Thomas ran his hands through his silver hair and leaned back in his oversized leather chair as he considered the request.

"I'll help, but I want to know what's in it for me!"

For the next five minutes, Greg Thomas learned how financially and politically profitable his support would be. Promises of tax-free beach homes, money in off-shore accounts, and exclusive event invitations had his mind spinning.

"Okay, what do you want *me* to do?" Greg Thomas finally asked.

"Well, first, you need to contact Stoneman and convince him to drop the lawsuit, and if that doesn't work, then we can pull you in as a litigation consultant, or maybe even special counsel, and use your status to muscle Stoneman."

"Alright, let's get the little jackass," Greg Thomas bellowed with enthusiasm.

The call ended, and Greg Thomas knew he would have to pull out all of the stops to keep David quiet. It may even get to a confidential payout to both Stoneman and his client. Unfortunately, Greg Thomas knew David loved the spotlight, and it would take a substantial number to get him to drop the case, especially if it created a media frenzy.

*But why was the DOJ so concerned about this case?* Greg Thomas wondered. *What clever argument had David made that was so newsworthy?*

Greg Thomas hit his conference call button and beckoned Stacy into his office. She hurried in with a notepad and a pen.

"Hey, sweetheart, I need you to pick an associate and have them pull a copy of the Division Act and the lawsuit David Stoneman just filed this morning in the D.C. District Court."

"Any particular associate, Mr. Thomas?"

"Yea, give me that cute associate who just started on the second floor. I always like to see more of her," Greg Thomas said as he turned around in his chair to look out his floor-to-ceiling window. He noticed Stacy was still in the room and turned back around.

"And, I'm still waiting on my coffee!" He reminded her with a condescending tone.

Stacy hurried her pace as she disappeared behind the large wooden door to do what she was told.

Greg Thomas twiddled his thumbs as he thought about his next move. He knew he would have to play dirty to get David to comply. Greg Thomas folded his arms in his big leather chair and seemed okay with that approach. After all, he had done it in the past; why not do it again?

# Chapter 20

Sarah Mercer was having second thoughts. David Stoneman had been compelling when he insisted on taking her case to federal court, but, after the benefit of a good night's sleep, she was wondering if moving forward with a lawsuit was a good idea.

Sarah and Mark had just settled into a small, modest condominium in Fairfax, Virginia, near the bustling campus of George Mason University. Sarah was able to secure inexpensive housing while working as a waitress at The Greene Turtle, a local watering hole near the Fairfax County Courthouse. Sarah was earning enough to keep a roof over her son's head in a safe neighborhood, and that was good enough for her.

Occasionally, on her way home from work, Sarah passed through George Mason's campus, half-tempted to stop and pick up an enrollment application, but she never dared to follow through with that inclination. Sarah had started college, but after she became pregnant with the boys, she felt that entering the workforce was the only viable option, especially with her then-husband's poor track record of consistent employment. She persisted and did what she had to do to support her family.

From time to time, she wondered what a better life would look like. Perhaps sending Mark to private schools and eating at expensive restaurants was a lifestyle she would enjoy. However, raising her son to be a man of good character was more important to her than the bells and whistles of life in high society. Sarah cared much more about principles than material things.

That's what she hoped would be the result of her lawsuit – some kind of moral justice for her son, Samuel. Still, she was so taken with David's corporate good looks and silver tongue that she quickly agreed to jump into a process about which she had very little knowledge. Her only experience with the law was bailing her former husband out of jail. And, even then, they always used a public defender's services and not a fancy lawyer, like David. So, she was drawn to David's top-shelf persona and blindly followed him down, what could be, a deep legal rabbit hole.

It started to sink in that she may have to relive all of those horrible days and nights in the hospital with Samuel, watching him go through such pain. David told her she might have to testify if the case went to trial but assured her he would take whatever time was needed to coach her to be an effective witness.

Sarah was quiet by nature, and her girl-next-door attractiveness always drew the attention of the opposite sex. Growing up, she welcomed that kind of attention; however, being a plaintiff in a major lawsuit against the federal government was not the kind of attention she would enjoy. Sarah shuddered at the possibility of being peppered with questions by a pit bull government lawyer with an entire courtroom watching her squirm on the witness stand.

However, it was too late now. David had filed the lawsuit that morning and would call her within the hour to discuss the next steps in the case. All she could hope for is swift justice for Samuel and a straightforward legal process for her and Mark to endure. Unfortunately, Sarah didn't know just how important this case was to the government. Its implications went well beyond her son's death and, this time, the government would not go down without a major fight.

# Chapter 21

David Stoneman was seated on the steps of the federal courthouse when his cell phone rang. He immediately recognized the number; it was Johnson Allen. David screened the call, assuming it was just the human resources department calling to tie up loose ends. After a moment, he felt the phone buzz, indicating he had a voicemail. Curious, he pressed the voicemail button and put the phone up to his right ear. David almost dropped his phone when he heard Greg Thomas's voice thundering through the speaker.

"Stoneman, it's Greg Thomas. I need you to call me right away. This cannot wait until the end of the day." The message ended abruptly.

David smiled when he realized Greg Thomas had *never* left a voicemail on his cell phone the entire time he worked at Johnson Allen. Greg Thomas always had one of the secretaries handle that task. However, he had a sneaking suspicion he knew why Greg Thomas was so eager for David to call him back. It had to be about the lawsuit.

Greg Thomas had many friends in the government and he, no doubt, received a call from one of his VIP contacts who searched David's name and saw him still listed as a Johnson Allen attorney.

*Wow, good news travels fast in this town*, David thought as he dialed Johnson Allen's main office number. The receptionist answered in her usual pleasant voice.

"Greg Thomas, please. This is David Stoneman returning his call."

"One moment, let me see if Mr. Thomas is available."

A few seconds later, David was connected.

"Stoneman?" The gruff voice barked.

"Hey, Greg. To what do I owe the honor of your call?" David sarcastically asked. Greg Thomas was not interested in small talk; he jumped right in.

"What in the world do you think you're doing with this ridiculous lawsuit? You haven't been gone from this place a week, and now you're grandstanding with a sham lawsuit?" David could tell Greg Thomas had no clue what the case was about; the purpose of his call was to ridicule and intimidate.

"What are you talking about, Greg?" David asked, playing dumb.

"You know *exactly* what I'm talking about, you little snake. That nonsense you filed downtown. I'm getting calls about it, and it's jacking up my morning."

"Sorry to hear that, Greg, but I don't work for you anymore, remember? And, in case you didn't know, it's a *wrongful death lawsuit,* and it's the real deal." David felt good telling off his former boss. He had wanted to do that for a long time.

"So, filing this suit is your idea of some glorified act of public service? Or are you some scum-sucking ambulance chaser now?!" Greg Thomas shouted into the phone.

"Actually, no, this is about a woman who lost a child, Greg. Perhaps, if you did some pro bono work yourself, you too could understand the concept of helping other people." That comment drew stares from a couple having lunch on a nearby park bench. David switched the phone to his left ear and away from eavesdroppers as Greg Thomas responded.

"Well, Dave, if you knew what was good for you, you would drop this lawsuit *today*."

David could tell by his responses that Greg Thomas had more invested in this case than just bad publicity for a friend in the government. David had been in the room when Greg Thomas tried to shake down opposing attorneys in the past, and he simply didn't get this flustered. This case seemed critical to him, and David was going to find out why.

"Greg, I don't know what to say, except I'm moving forward with the suit, and I'm afraid I can't discuss this issue with you any further."

The phone was silent.

"Listen, Stoneman, you're in *way* over your head. You know I'm the best litigator in this city, and you've seen what I can do to people's reputations. If you move forward with this, I will make it my personal mission to destroy you. You got that?"

"I'm glad to hear your concern, Greg, but I have to get back to work," David remarked as he hung up the phone.

Although David was proud of himself for standing his ground against the great litigator, he suddenly grew nervous about the enemy he had just made. But there was no turning back now. David got up from the courthouse steps and ordered a fully-loaded taco from a nearby food truck. As he waited for his lunch, he scrolled through his email, looking for media requests for interviews to discuss the lawsuit. None had come through yet. It was still early, and the news outlets were probably just learning about the case. David expected a flurry of email activity by mid-afternoon.

As he stood by his car and ate his crunchy taco, David had no idea he was gambling with more than just his career – he was gambling with his life.

# Chapter 22

Senator Stephen Smythe did not receive bad news well. He was enjoying a casual lunch at Congressional Country Club in Bethesda, Maryland, after an excellent round of golf. *Congressional*, as it's called, remains one of the most exclusive clubs in America, serving as a regular destination for Washington's political elite. Opened in 1924 by political powerhouses such as William Howard Taft, Woodrow Wilson, Warren G. Harding, Calvin Coolidge, and Herbert Hoover, Congressional offered a temporary, secluded respite, for a select few, from the chaos of Capitol Hill.

Senator Smythe was not a member, but, as a sitting Senator, he secured a guest pass for a quick round of golf on Congressional's world-class course. The Senator was on his third gin and tonic at the corner table in the club's Founders' Pub and enjoying a bacon cheeseburger when his aide, Tim, raced into the room out of breath and looking disheveled.

Tim slowly and respectfully walked over to Senator Smythe's table. Senator Smythe gave him a look that indicated he was not interested in being disturbed. However, this was an emergency. Senator Smythe's muscles tensed as Tim leaned down to whisper the bad news in his ear. With his drink in hand, the Senator quickly excused himself from the table and stepped into the adjacent library. He sat down on one of the library's velvet couches with his legs crossed and his arms folded as Tim briefed him on the new lawsuit filed against his Division Act.

"They've taken a new angle," Tim said, still trying to catch his breath.

"This one is bad, Senator. It's likely going to get a lot of media attention." Tim was pacing back and forth, running multiple public relations scenarios in his head.

Senator Smythe was angered by the news but angrier that Tim had ruined his pleasant afternoon.

"Does our legal team think we can get it tossed out?" Senator Smythe asked as his heel repeatedly tapped the carpet in a nervous cadence.

"I called Greg…I mean, our *outside legal resource*, and he said he thinks the Court will let this suit stand alone because it focuses on a kid's death, and not the constitutionality of the Act."

Now that it was clear this case was likely not going away on its own, Senator Smythe knew he needed the best legal mind in Washington to weigh in further on the matter. The Senator accepted the fact that his social time was over and that he now needed to snap into damage control mode.

"Set up a call in ten minutes with our outside legal resource. We need to learn more about how we can fight this thing," Senator Smythe instructed as he waved Tim off and took another sip of his drink.

The Senator felt his alcohol buzz deepen, which should have calmed his nerves. But he was anything but calm.

*Could FARCO take care of this?* He wondered.

*It may be too late for that if the media is already focusing on the case.*

He took another sip as he evaluated his options.

*Perhaps the major media outlets could be paid off to buy some time and minimize the negative press. Less press, less mess,* Senator Smythe thought as he glanced at his Rolex watch and realized he needed to head back to Capitol Hill.

He hurried down to the club's entryway, outside past the putting greens, and then instructed his driver, waiting outside with Tim, to retrieve his black sedan from the parking lot. Senator Smythe continued walking a few hundred feet until he was under the shade of the large trees which lined the road leading to the club's entrance.

Tim was lagging a few feet behind, knowing he needed to keep his distance. Senator Smythe pulled his phone from his pocket and began scrolling through his many influential contacts.

Over the next several minutes, he made phone calls to a number of key executives at major news outlets and strongly encouraged them *not* to cover the new lawsuit against the Division Act. All of them had heard about the case, and it took Senator Smythe promising to share important secrets with them in the future to convince them to bury the story.

Shortly thereafter, the driver collected Senator Smythe's golf clubs and swung around Congressional's circle driveway to retrieve the Senator and Tim, who had wandered over to the driving range.

Once they were in the car, Senator Smythe asked Tim to call their outside legal resource, Greg Thomas.

"You let him know I would be calling, didn't you?" Senator Smythe asked expectantly as he put on his seatbelt.

"Sure did, sir. He's expecting your call on his private line."

The Senator had Greg Thomas's private office number for emergencies such as this. The phone rang twice.

"Hello, this is Greg Thomas."

"Greg, it's Stephen Smythe. How are you today?"

"I'm doing good, Senator…better than you, from what I'm hearing."

Senator Smythe tried not to respond defensively to the antagonistic comment. Instead, he decided to play it off like a minor annoyance.

"So, you heard about the case?"

"Yes, I did. And, I know the attorney who filed it."

Senator Smythe raised his eyebrows and nodded in optimism as he looked at Tim, who was sitting next to him in the back seat.

"Is there anything you can do to persuade this attorney to drop the case?"

"I don't think so, Senator…you see, we just fired him, and when I spoke to him this morning, he told me to piss off. Perhaps, you would have better luck reasoning with him. But a word of advice…I'm not sure this one can be bought," Greg Thomas cautioned.

"Well, Greg, we do have *other* ways to persuade folks, as you well know," Senator Smythe responded as his tone grew more sinister.

"I understand, Senator. We'll either get him to drop the suit or bleed him dry in court. Let me work with my team at Johnson Allen, and I'll be in touch within the next couple of days," Greg Thomas said confidently.

The call ended, and Senator Smythe handed the phone to Tim. He glanced out the car's tinted windows at the large, palatial homes which lined the streets of Bethesda. Senator Smythe often wondered why he ever bothered to leave his cushy private sector life in Massachusetts to enter the political fray. Sometimes, it didn't seem worth it.

"What are the next steps, sir?" Tim asked.

"Let's call the DOJ attorneys when we get back to the Hill. Surely, they'll have a plan."

The rest of the car ride was quiet as Senator Smythe continued to stare out the window, thinking about how he could use his considerable resources and power to crush this lawsuit and the lawyer who filed it. He also knew he needed to raise the stakes, so he decided it was time to bring FARCO's leader, Sergeant James Henderson, into the discussion as well. This issue may have to be dealt with "off the books."

# Chapter 23

I t had been a week and a half since David filed Sarah Mercer's lawsuit. The case had garnered *some* media attention, but not nearly as much as David had hoped. He suspected that was probably due to a number of substantial checks written to keep the media quiet on the issue, at least for now.

Shortly after filing the complaint, David requested an emergency hearing to get the case "fast-tracked" and have the typical administrative and procedural prerequisites waived, claiming not doing so would be detrimental to the public's health and safety. It was a long shot, but he had to try. David assured Sarah she didn't need to attend the hearing, and, accordingly, she gave him her blessing to carry on without her. David preferred it that way.

On the day of the emergency hearing, only one low-level Department of Justice attorney attended on behalf of the government and put forth a dismal and canned opposition argument. David suspected the DOJ's top brass assumed the case would either quickly move forward or be immediately dismissed; there would be no middle ground. Consequently, they were back at their offices getting a head start building a staunch defense, if needed.

The judge presiding over the case was the Honorable Michael Callaway. Judge Callaway was known for his willingness to let cases move fast and in non-traditional ways. This case would be no exception. Unfortunately for the government, Judge Callaway also had a reputation for pushing the limits of established legal precedent if such action generated a more equitable result.

As such, just minutes into the hearing, Judge Callaway recognized David did not want this lawsuit to fall into the tedious litigation cycle with the other Division Act lawsuits. Seeing his concern as legitimate, the Judge conveyed to the parties he was disinclined to bundle this case with the other suits because of the claim's unique nature. Further, he agreed with David that this case could pose a threat to the public's health and safety and waived the traditional administrative and procedural requirements for this type of lawsuit. Not surprisingly, Judge Callaway did not grant the government's half-hearted request to have the case dismissed. The case would move forward.

However, before the proceedings concluded, Judge Callaway suggested an alternative to the long, drawn-out federal litigation process. He recommended the parties enter the Court's Mediation Program. The Mediation Program could resolve the case in a matter of weeks, and all of the proceedings would remain *confidential*.

Judge Callaway agreed to give the parties two weeks to consider this option. In the meantime, both parties were instructed to begin an expedited discovery process which required both sides to exchange relevant case documents right away. The low-level DOJ attorney was dumbfounded by the decision and hurried out of the courtroom to alert his superiors.

David walked out of the hearing beaming and thinking about his case strategy moving forward. On the one hand, the Mediation Program could garner a settlement within the month, which would be great for Sarah. However, due to the Mediation

Program's confidentiality requirements, David would lose, what he believed to be, his greatest ally – the national media attention.

He had a lot to think about, and, of course, he planned to discuss the options with Sarah. Judge Callaway's clerk gave each party a brochure that explained the Court's Mediation Program in detail. David sat on a bench outside of the courthouse and quickly skimmed the Program's description:

> *The District Court Mediation Program allows litigants to confidentially discuss – with a specially trained, neutral third person – the possibility of settling their dispute. Mediation offers many advantages over formal litigation. Mediation can lead to faster, less costly resolutions and may better address all parties' interests than a judicial remedy. The District Court offers mediation without any fees or charges to the parties.*

David folded the brochure and put it in his right coat pocket. He would read the rest later. In the meantime, he had document requests to send out. David was eager to see if the government was going to be cooperative or play hardball.

----

A few days later, David received the government's first production of case documents at his apartment. There were hundreds of thousands of files to review – including any document remotely related to the Division Act, how it came to pass, the legislative history, multiple red-lined iterations of the bill, and even scribbled drawings. All had been categorized as "relevant" to the case. Clearly, the government had produced every piece of paper in Washington, trying to bury David in overwhelming, unnecessary paperwork.

The DOJ attorneys knew David no longer had the considerable resources or support staff to efficiently and effectively review all of the produced documents before Judge Callaway's deadline. David assumed the government strongly preferred the Mediation Program in order to get this case concluded *quickly* and *confidentially*. For the government, the less press, the better. So, they buried David in paperwork so he would be more likely to accept the mediation option.

However, David was hesitant to make that call just yet. He still dreamed of standing in front of dozens of cameras on Capitol Hill, with Sarah by his side, shaking his fist and demanding justice for the whole world to see. Nevertheless, David had to face reality. In a couple of months, he would run out of money and would have to dip into his savings and retirement account to finance this case. And, David also suspected the government would employ stall tactics to ensure that he did.

Rita Valore paced fiercely back and forth in David's living room, holding an orange mug half-filled with cold coffee. She was exhausted and venting her frustration.

"Dave, I've gone through at least fifty thousand documents so far and I've barely made a dent. And, just to be cute, the DOJ included a copy of the freaking Constitution in the documents they produced." She sighed and shook her head.

David had delivered fewer than two hundred documents to the government, including Samuel Mercer's medical reports, hospital bills, and other relevant documentation David was able to dig up from the other Division Act lawsuits. The government would be able to review his submitted documents before the sun went down.

He was finally concluding that, perhaps, this case was simply too big for him to handle. In his mind, David was already considering other attorneys who might be willing to take Sarah's case pro bono.

He had limited time before he had to let Judge Callaway know if they wanted to move the case into the Mediation Program. David wasn't sure they had much of a choice. Over the next couple of hours, David asked Rita to focus on the *Division Bill* as it was being debated in Congress to see if any member of Congress raised concerns about its tortious implications – a stretch. Still, maybe there was something there that could bolster their case.

David focused his efforts on the bill's foundational research conducted through a series of government grants. In his research, David kept seeing one particular scientist's name connected with the Division Bill's earliest research reports.

Out of curiosity, David Googled his name. When he saw the search results, he called Rita over to his computer.

"Rita, take a look at this!" David said curiously. Rita read the headlines out loud.

*Government Scientist Murdered in Apartment Near Eastern Market.*

"Look at the date on the article, Rita," David said, waiting for her to connect the dots.

"It was just a few weeks ago. But how is this relevant to us?" Rita asked, taking a sip of cold coffee.

David pointed to Dr. Francis Pietrov's name on one of the research grants.

"This is the man who was killed." David tapped his finger on Dr. Pietrov's name and continued.

"He also happens to be the *original lead researcher* behind the Division Act. Don't you think it's a little suspicious that he ends up getting murdered in his apartment as lawsuits begin to pile up against the Act?"

"I don't know, Dave. It's D.C. People get killed here every day," Rita responded incredulously.

"Maybe…but maybe it's *not* a coincidence," David said as he continued to read the newspaper articles covering Dr. Pietrov's death.

Rita ignored her boss's last comment as she talked aloud, trying to confirm her understanding of the Division Act.

"So, let me get this straight," Rita said as she ambled around the living room.

"The Division *Bill* was drafted based on government-funded studies that showed Church and State were becoming too interwoven in America. Therefore, if the government continued to offer tax breaks to religious organizations, it would, in turn, demand more oversight and regulation of those organizations. Is that right?"

"That's my understanding," David reflexively replied as he continued reading newspaper clippings.

"Only the federal government would conduct excruciatingly detailed research on a piece of legislation that ends up being unconstitutional anyway…more wasted tax dollars," Rita said sarcastically as she shook her head, walked into the kitchen, and placed her orange coffee mug in the stainless-steel sink.

David was barely listening, but Rita's last comment caused him to look up from his computer.

"What did you just say, Rita?"

Rita walked over to where David was seated and shrugged; not sure what David was referring to.

"What did I say? I just said that the government wasted tax dollars on unnecessary research."

David stood up and aggressively shuffled around his kitchen table for a notepad and a pen. He found a legal pad under his old, worn-out First Amendment law book.

"Rita, you're a genius!" He said as he scribbled down notes on the yellow sheet of paper.

"Okay...but how?" Rita was confused.

"You said two things that make complete sense – first, government-funded grants always have a narrow focus and a strong element of oversight, especially if there is a politically motivated interest in reaching a certain conclusion. Meaning, if they were researching a *specific issue*, it's definitely relevant to our case."

"Alright..." Rita responded as David continued.

"Second, what if the drafter of the Division Bill *wanted the focus* to be on the Bill's constitutionality? What if that was the plan all along?"

"Dave, I'm sorry, babe, but I'm just not tracking," Rita said as she put her hands on her hips and shook her head.

"Don't you see? They teed up an obvious constitutional issue so that the real issues would get buried or overlooked! There's something more here..."

Rita shrugged, still not understanding his point. David put down his pen and took a deep breath.

"Rita, it may be possible that the government *wanted* the public to focus on the Division Act's constitutionality simply to draw people's focus away from something else that they didn't want to get out or be publicized. And what if Francis Pietrov was killed because he knew that secret reason?"

"What do you think they're trying to hide?" Rita asked, intrigued by David's conspiracy theory.

"I don't know…I have to think about it…and I have to find out more about Francis Pietrov."

A few moments earlier, Dr. Pietrov was just another scientist on a government-funded research grant, but now, David realized he might be *the key* to winning the case.

# Chapter 24

Sergeant James Henderson did not have difficulty gaining access to highly secured locations in Washington. Despite his checkered military past, he could simply make a phone call to those in his debt and get top-level security clearance for any government building. Consequently, as Sergeant Henderson walked down First Street NE and headed toward the Northwest entrance of the U.S. Supreme Court building, he felt confident he would cruise through security with a simple flash of his badge. He was right.

Inside the building, he made his way through the Great Hall, which resembled a Roman palace, and shot a glance into the courtroom at the ionic columns and red velvet curtain, which served as the backdrop for the nine black leather chairs reserved for the nine Supreme Court Justices. He continued to the arranged meeting spot – the West Conference Room. As he turned the corner, he saw Senator Smythe's driver standing outside the conference room door.

"Go on in, sir; the Senator is waiting for you," the emotionless man said with his arms folded neatly in front of him.

Sergeant Henderson had never been in the West Conference Room. He and the Senator preferred to change their meeting locations often to avoid being detected or followed. Today, the meeting place was just a couple hundred feet from the most powerful court in the country.

The West Conference Room was grand with two large chandeliers, each affording a golden hue as the lights bounced off the ornate golden-boxed patterns on the high ceiling. The massive, stately blue carpet rested regally on the wooden floors, extending the spacious room's length.

Sergeant Henderson looked to his right and saw Senator Smythe standing and facing the room's dark wood fireplace. Its mantle stood taller than most men and carried a small circular clock, which sat on a perfectly balanced frame. Above the clock was a portrait of a robed man with white facial hair.

Senator Smythe glanced over his shoulder and realized Sergeant Henderson had joined him. He turned back to the portrait on the wall above the fireplace.

"This is Chief Justice Charles Evans Hughes – do you know anything about him?"

"No, Senator, I don't." Sergeant Henderson responded as he squinted to re-examine the robed figure on the wall.

"He was a man of many accomplishments and, despite being a Republican, he is a man I deeply admire. In 1906, he beat famous media mogul, William Randolph Hearst, to be Governor of New York, and in 1910 he was appointed to the Supreme Court by President William Howard Taft."

Senator Smythe pointed to the wall on the opposite side of the room toward the portrait of a trim Chief Justice Taft. Then, he turned his attention back to Chief Justice Hughes and continued.

"In 1921, he was appointed Secretary of State by President Warren G. Harding. After all that, in 1930, he was nominated by President Herbert Hoover to be *Chief* Justice of the Court. And, here he is, immortalized in a frame for only a handful of people to admire!" Senator Smythe was silent for a few seconds as he continued to stare at the portrait.

"That's an impressive resume, sir…can we get down to business now?" Sergeant Henderson's past military experiences taught him to be judicious with his time.

Senator Smythe smirked as he turned and walked toward the single table in the center of the room.

"I thought a man of your military background would appreciate some history," Senator Smythe commented as he unbuttoned his pin-striped suit jacket and approached the meeting table.

"I do appreciate history, sir. And, forgive me for saying this but, I prefer to study leaders like Grant or Eisenhower over career politicians. If they can handle a foxhole and a gun, they're okay in my book." Sergeant Henderson sat down and folded his hands neatly in front of him on the table. He continued.

"No offense to you, of course, Senator." He lifted his palms toward the ceiling and slightly bowed his head, in deference to the politician, not wanting to offend him. Senator Smythe dismissed the comment and the gesture.

"Fair enough! Let's get down to business…we may have another situation, in addition to our *South Carolina* problem. Another lawsuit was filed against the Division Act. It's different from the others. The lawyer is some do-gooder cowboy who can't be bought or reasoned with."

"Well, sir, we have an answer for those types of folks. Do you want him to disappear, or do you want him to have an accident?"

"I don't want to do anything yet," Senator Smythe said as he leaned into the conversation and put his elbows on the table.

"As you know, we have an outside legal resource who helps us with these types of sticky legal issues. He told me that if this case goes into the Court's Mediation Program, we're in the clear because everything discussed in that mediation will be confidential. However, if this cowboy attorney does not agree to mediation and moves forward with litigation, we will need to take care of him. I'll give you a status update in a day or two."

"Sounds good, Senator. I'll wait for your word," Sergeant Henderson nodded in agreement.

"While we're here...what's the status of the *South Carolina* problem?" Senator Smythe leaned back in his chair and crossed his arms.

"Unfortunately, sir, it's still unresolved." Sergeant Henderson said sheepishly, anticipating that was not the answer the Senator wanted to hear. Predictably, Senator Smythe's demeanor changed, and he raised his voice.

"What do you mean, *unresolved*?! He's a minister, for crying out loud! You're telling me your men can't kill a *minister*?!"

"Well, sir, he evaded local police in Charleston, and cell phone tower tracers indicate he could be here, in Washington. But we can't be sure – he may have ditched his phone to throw us off. He has a daughter in Oklahoma, and I have a couple of my operatives monitoring her. However, my main guy in the field is back in town and trying to track him down."

"We don't have room for errors here, Sergeant. We need to finish that job right away, do you understand?" Senator Smythe was staring daggers at Sergeant Henderson.

"Consider it done, sir," Sergeant Henderson said as he confidently stared back at the Senator.

With that, Senator Smythe abruptly rose from his chair and left the room, escorted by his driver. Sergeant Henderson lingered for a couple of minutes and decided to make a phone call.

When the man with the slicked-back hair answered, Sergeant Henderson knew he had to be brief.

"I just met with *Eagle*, and we may have another problem in D.C. with an ambitious lawyer. If so, can you handle it?"

"Of course," the man responded.

"Roger that, standby for further instructions on that issue. What's the status of *South Carolina*?"

"Still searching, sir. I have local friendlies helping me with surveillance and intel. He'll resurface soon."

"10-4. Keep me updated." Sergeant Henderson hung up the phone and planned to head back to FARCO headquarters, where he would brief the rest of his team on the possible new target. As he walked outside, he turned to admire the magnitude and magnificence of the Supreme Court building. He read the words "Equal Justice Under Law," etched into the pristine marble.

*If only that were true*, he thought as he put on his military-grade sunglasses and a black cap and disappeared into a crowd of tourists.

# Chapter 25

David and Rita sat on the drafty floor of David's living room, surrounded by papers. It had been hours since David realized Dr. Francis Pietrov could be a pivotal piece to his case puzzle. He kept a worn-down yellow highlighter nestled behind his left ear, which was nearly out of ink.

"Dave, you have to tell me *why* we're going down this rabbit hole." Rita was growing frustrated as she thumbed through pages of David's handwritten notes.

"You've been like a crazy person flipping through thousands of pages and furiously scribbling on your legal pad, but I still have no clue why this guy's important."

Rita knew once David became laser-focused on an issue, he would tune out everything else, sometimes for days.

"Dave?"

"Huh? I'm sorry, Rita, what did you say?" David was irritated by the interruption.

"We've pulled tons of documents that reference Pietrov...why?"

David sat upright, stretched out his arms in front of him, and yawned. He knew if he was going to get any more help from Rita, he would have to give her some additional insight into his suspicion. After compiling a few select documents, he began his explanation.

> When a bill is proposed in Congress, there's usually considerable research to support a desired conclusion, and that research is often discussed in committees before the bill goes to the House or Senate floor for debate. Most of this research is included in a variety of reports and memoranda that no one reads. In fact, some members of Congress don't even read *the bill* before they vote on it. Then the bill moves to the other house for review, debate, and a vote. If the bill passes both houses, it goes to the President's desk for approval or veto. Or, with this President, a rubber stamp.

David smiled at his attempt to make a political joke, but Rita looked unamused, so he continued.

"Regardless, in the initial research for the *Division Bill*, there are numerous references to a Dr. Francis Pietrov. However, he abruptly vanishes from any of the later reports, and there is no mention of his name in any documents or legislative history. There's plenty of commentary about *constitutional issues*, but Francis Pietrov simply disappears."

"Is that uncommon?" Rita questioned.

"Big time...these researchers are often funded by blank-check government grants, Rita. No way someone would just walk away from an opportunity to be one of the lead researchers on a groundbreaking piece of legislation. Further, these guys are often called in to testify before Congress to support their research."

David continued, "Dr. Francis Pietrov is omitted from all records except for the *first* phase of the research studies. Also, I couldn't find any evidence he had been terminated from his position or was removed from the Division Bill research team. So, this just doesn't add up. I think he knew something that was excluded from the final report. We have to figure out what it is."

"So, how do we do that?" Rita asked.

"I'm not sure, but if there is a missing piece of information that the government wants to keep buried, they're probably watching our case *very closely*. That explains why Greg Thomas called me the day I filed the lawsuit. We're onto something…"

"What?! What does that mean?" Rita nervously questioned.

"It means we're not going to get any help from the media, and if this case drags on, there's a good chance you and I, and maybe Sarah won't live to see the trial – I don't mean to be dramatic, but we have to get the government to settle this case right away."

"So, what are you saying, Dave?"

David looked at Rita, pursed his lips, and ran both of his hands through his thick, black hair.

"I'm saying, I think we have to do the Mediation Program."

David realized his dream of a trial in the public eye was no longer attainable and certainly not safe. He suspected they had stumbled upon an issue that was meant to be kept secret and which may have unintentionally put them in grave danger.

David pulled his cell phone out of his pocket and called Sarah. He planned to keep the conversation brief.

"Hello?" Sarah answered.

"Sarah?" David could barely hear her over the bar noise in the background.

"Hi, David. I'm at work. Do you need something?"

"Just a quick minute – Rita and I think the Mediation Program is the best option for your case at this point. Otherwise, it could drag on for years, and we don't want that."

"Okay, David, whatever you think. That's fine. Hey, I'm sorry, I have to run. Do whatever you need to do." Sarah hung up, and David was left tapping his cell phone against his forehead.

"Rita, email opposing counsel and tell them we would like to mediate. We'll send formal notice to the judge's clerk in the morning. Believe me, they will agree to mediation to keep this thing out of the press."

----

After Rita sent the requested email, David gave her a hug and sent her home for the night. At that exact moment, Greg Thomas was on the phone with Senator Smythe telling him the good news – the case would be mediated. After their conversation, Senator Smythe texted Sergeant Henderson, *Second threat no longer an issue. Focus on finding South Carolina.*

# Chapter 26

It had only been a couple of weeks since Tommy Felton met Jerry Hatfield at the Fellowship Presbyterian Church in Washington, D.C., but they were quickly becoming friends. They had a mutual friend in Francis Pietrov but didn't talk much about him. Jerry thought his death was untimely and suspicious but said he only knew what happened by what he had read in the newspapers.

Tommy, on the other hand, was a fugitive in hiding. He told Jerry he was in town for a short while on sabbatical from his church. Tommy didn't tell Jerry about his wife's death or that his home had been burned to the ground.

Tommy suspected sharing too much with Jerry too soon was dangerous. After all, he didn't know if he could trust him. Perhaps, Jerry was the person who had Francis Pietrov killed in the first place. It was hard to know.

Consequently, Tommy's plan was simple: he would casually get to know Jerry without raising any flags, and determine whether or not Jerry was a man he could trust. After that, he would solicit Jerry's help to search for answers.

Tommy had been sleeping in his car in a nearby park, keeping his cell phone turned off to stay off the radar. He suspected he had dozens of voicemails from his daughter, Jenny, and the police, but he knew he couldn't risk calling *anyone* – just one call could give away his location.

Tommy visited the Fellowship Presbyterian Church every few days to see Jerry. And, after two weeks and several casual lunches, Tommy finally mustered up the courage to deepen the conversation about Francis Pietrov. Up until that point, all Jerry knew was that Tommy and Dr. Pietrov were friends and nothing more. It was time to change that.

The two men were sitting on a bench in a public park near the Foggy Bottom-GWU metro station, less than a quarter of a mile away from the church, enjoying the nice weather and a mid-afternoon snack when Tommy started the conversation.

"Jerry, I know we've talked a bit about Francis, but I have to confess, I haven't been *completely* honest with you…"

Jerry turned his head to look at Tommy and raised his eyebrows.

"No?"

"No…you see…Francis called me on the day he died. He told me a secret and I suspect he may have told you as well. That's why I'm here in Washington – to see if you can help me."

Jerry smiled and took a sip of his soft drink.

"Tommy, I knew you had an agenda with our conversations. I'm not an idiot; I was just waiting for you to bring it up."

"You did?" Tommy asked, genuinely surprised that his attempts at concealment had been ineffective.

"Of course. I read people for a living, remember? The night we met, you told me the cut on your arm and the burns on your neck were from a *cycling accident*. But Tommy, I've never seen a bicycle catch on fire."

Jerry looked Tommy up and down and continued.

"Also, you've been wearing different combinations of just two outfits since I met you. You wear that cheap, knock-off Washington Nationals ballcap that you, no doubt, bought from a street vendor because you haven't had a decent shower in the last few weeks. Not to mention the fact that one of our church ushers saw you washing your hair with hand soap in the church bathroom last week."

Tommy was embarrassed. But, after all, he was a pastor, not a spy. The men sat in silence for a moment until Jerry continued.

"Oh, and another thing. You said you were in town as a tourist on sabbatical, but you show up at the church nearly every other day to talk to me? Come on. I'm not *that* interesting. So, what's the *real* story, Tommy?"

Tommy took a deep breath and let it out slowly. His eyes welled with tears.

"I'm in trouble, and you may be in trouble too."

"In trouble, how?" Jerry's usually casual demeanor changed into one of concern.

"Did Francis ever talk to you about his work? Specifically, the research he was doing before he died. His research on the Division Act." Tommy waited for Jerry's response with bated breath.

Jerry looked up at the blue sky, thinking about how he wanted to respond.

"Yes…we discussed his work, but I really can't share the details of our conversations, Tommy." Jerry said as he looked back at his new friend. Tommy leaned in and lowered his voice.

"It seems you and I are the only people who know about Francis's work on the Division Act…and the day Francis died, a man showed up at my house, killed my wife, and burned my house down. He left me for dead." Tommy couldn't hold back his tears any longer. After he composed himself, he continued.

"I got out alive and came to D.C. to find *you*. I've been living out of my car, trying to figure out if I could trust you or not."

Jerry put his hand on Tommy's shoulder.

"Tommy, I'm so sorry for the loss of your wife…and, for what it's worth, I haven't seen any assassins hanging around the church, so I think we're safe at the moment."

Tommy managed a smile through his tears, appreciating the levity Jerry brought to the conversation. Still, Tommy decided to inquire further.

"Can you tell me *anything* about what Francis told you relative to the Division Act?"

"You know I'm bound to keep all information I learn in my counseling sessions private, right?"

That was not what Tommy wanted to hear. He was no closer to finding answers if Jerry wasn't willing to share *any* confidential information with him.

"But…in light of what you just told me, and since this appears to be a matter of life and death, I feel comfortable sharing a few things with you. For starters, I think I know what research you're referring to."

Tommy felt relieved but didn't know what to say next.

Jerry continued with his explanation, "No one knew I was counseling Francis. He didn't want a paper trail of our conversations for obvious reasons. When I first started seeing Francis professionally, many years ago, when he moved to D.C., I saw he was hurting and decided to help. Our weekly sessions became more like a casual conversation between friends rather than formal counseling sessions. Still, I maintained the confidentiality of what we discussed."

Tommy gulped and asked the bombshell question again, "Jerry, please...what did he tell you about the Division Act?"

"It's not what he told me; it's what he *gave* me," Jerry replied as he looked around the park for bystanders who could be eavesdropping on their conversation. When he didn't see anyone, he continued.

> I told him I didn't need to know the details of what he was working on. So, we agreed I would keep copies of his research in a safe place, and I would not read them unless he permitted me to do so. The copies were his insurance policy against some pretty powerful people. He told me to hide the documents and deny all knowledge of their existence if government agents came looking for them. I agreed. However, I never dreamed Francis would be killed because of those reports. I just thought he worked for the CIA or NSA or something.

Tommy realized there might be a chance, after all, to bring Marie's killer to justice. First, he had to get his hands on those documents.

"Can I see the reports?" Tommy eagerly asked.

Jerry was silent for a few seconds as he stared at the ground, obviously struggling with this decision. He cupped his hand around his mouth and turned to Tommy.

"Under the circumstances…I'm okay with it. I hid them in a vacant office in the basement of the church. So let's head back, and we can review them together."

# Chapter 27

As Jerry Hatfield and Tommy Felton left the park, Jerry admitted Dr. Pietrov had been giving him copies of research reports for *months* prior to his death. However, Jerry claimed Dr. Pietrov never divulged the magnitude of the reports and only casually mentioned they were related to the Division Act and had to be preserved.

As Jerry and Tommy walked through the front doors of the Fellowship Presbyterian Church and then down the concrete stairs that led to the basement, Tommy wondered whether he should explain the importance of the reports to Jerry. He decided it wasn't the right time.

As they snaked through the old, musty, dimly lit basement hallways, their conversation turned to Jerry's work.

"You know, my counseling career has been more than I bargained for," Jerry said as he flipped on several overhead fluorescent lights.

"What do you mean?" Tommy inquired as he stopped to take a drink from the vintage porcelain water fountain.

"I was so focused on work for the last thirty years; I didn't have time to start a family of my own."

"Never took the plunge, huh?" Tommy questioned as he wiped his mouth with the back of his hand.

"I was close once. She gave me an ultimatum – it was either her or my career. You can guess which one I chose," Jerry said with a chuckle as he continued down the hall.

Tommy could sense Jerry's relationship history was not a favorite topic of conversation. The two men walked through the fellowship hall, through its dated kitchen, and into another dark hallway. Jerry turned on a beige light switch which illuminated the floor's faded gray carpet.

"Besides me, who else are you counseling these days? Anyone as interesting as Francis?" Tommy asked jokingly.

"Yes, actually. Over the past year, I've been working with a young lady with a tragic story. She recently lost one of her sons." He paused for a second and turned to Tommy.

"I believe she was here, at the church, the night you first came to see me. I heard she just filed a pretty big lawsuit against the government related to her son's death."

Jerry and Tommy came to a door at the end of the hallway which carried, what appeared to be, a shiny bronze padlock.

"Hmmm…this is *new*. I'm not sure I have a key for this." Jerry was puzzled as he gripped and twisted the locked doorknob.

"No?" Tommy asked as he studied the lock.

"The offices are on the other side of this door. I've worked here for a while now and have never seen a lock on *this door*. We'll have to go back outside. There's a side door in the alley which goes directly into the office suite. I think I have the key to that door in my car."

The two men headed back down the hallway toward the fellowship hall. Jerry was turning off lights as they walked. As he flipped the switches, he was curious about something.

"Tommy, what did Francis tell you on the phone the day he died? What are you hoping to find in these reports?"

Tommy didn't respond immediately.

"I can't answer that right now, Jerry. I'm sorry."

Jerry stopped in his tracks in the middle of the fellowship hall kitchen and turned to Tommy.

"You're sorry? Tommy, you're going to have to do better than that. If I'm going to dig into these reports with you, I deserve to know what I'm getting into." Jerry's stern look indicated he was serious.

Tommy knew Jerry had a valid point but felt he needed more information before sharing the whole story.

"Jerry, look…it's nothing personal, but Francis told me something about those reports, and I have to read them myself to see if it's true. There's a reason Francis didn't tell you when he had the chance."

Jerry sighed, flipped off the kitchen lights, and kept walking.

"Okay…but if you find what you're looking for, *then* will you fill me in?"

"Absolutely…I'll have to. At that point, I'll need your help. If there's nothing there, then I'll head back to Charleston this afternoon."

Jerry led Tommy out the church's front doors, down the steps, and into the long narrow alley adjacent to the church. When they were halfway down the alleyway, Jerry realized he forgot to retrieve the key to the side door.

"Oh, shoot. Let me run to my car and grab the key. I'll be right back." Jerry jogged back toward the parking lot, which was across the street from the church.

Tommy walked another thirty feet to the side door and was surprised to find it was unlocked. He glanced back to inform Jerry, but he had already turned the corner and was out of earshot. So, Tommy casually opened the door, walked down the three concrete steps, and into a small hallway that contained two tiny offices.

Meanwhile, as Jerry approached his car, he was startled by a police officer advancing towards him suddenly from the sidewalk.

"Good afternoon, sir." The officer offered.

"Can I help you with something, officer?"

"There's an urgent matter that requires your attention; please come with me." The cop beckoned as he grabbed Jerry's arm and led him toward the alley he had come from.

"Uh, okay, can I ask what this is regarding?" Jerry was confused and growing nervous, but he tried not to show it.

"I don't have all of the details, sir; I was just sent to retrieve you," the officer coldly responded.

"*Who* sent you to get me? And for *what?*"

The cop remained silent, and his grip on Jerry's arm grew stronger as he quickened his pace across the street and into the alley.

"Um, sir, this is a dead end." Jerry knew something was wrong and was trying to figure out what to do next. He looked around for Tommy, but he was nowhere in sight.

At that moment, the officer slammed Jerry into the side of the brick church building with brutish strength. The man looked around to make sure there were no witnesses.

"Where is he?"

"Who?" Jerry asked.

A punch hit Jerry in the stomach and caused him to fall to his knees.

"I'll ask one more time, where is Tommy Felton?"

Jerry realized Tommy had been telling the truth. He knew if he lied to the man, Tommy might have a chance to escape.

"I just dropped him off at the metro station. He said he was going back to South Carolina." Jerry said as he winced through the pain.

"You're a terrible liar…" the man said as he drew a silenced pistol and shot Jerry twice in the chest.

The man removed his fake police hat to reveal his slicked-back hair. He tossed his uniform in a nearby dumpster, grabbed Jerry's cell phone, keys, and wallet, and ran to an adjacent building and out of sight. Jerry felt his chest getting warm with blood as he fell face down on the pavement. He closed his eyes and passed away.

Once out of sight, the man with slicked-back hair pulled Jerry's driver's license out of the stolen wallet and called the FARCO headquarters.

"*South Carolina's* companion has been identified as...*Jerry Hatfield*. Run a full friends-and-family trace. Companion has been neutralized, but *South Carolina* is still in the wind. I'll provide a status update in short order. Over-and-out."

# Chapter 28

Sarah Mercer finished her shift at The Greene Turtle restaurant and was walking down the sidewalk toward her home. Mark was at a friend's house, and she had some time all to herself. So, even though Sarah usually took the bus to work, she decided to enjoy the lovely spring weather and walk the nearly two-mile trek back to her modest condo. The flowers were in full bloom, and she could smell the newly cut grass as she strolled along on the sidewalk on Chain Bridge Road.

She strode past the Historic Fairfax Courthouse. The red-brick building was full of history, and Sarah took a moment to admire the beauty of the structure. After Samuel's death, Sarah began to take time to appreciate the small things in life. She never used to "stop and smell the roses." Now, she understood the importance of observing the colorful details in the world, like the architecture of historical buildings or enjoying the simplicity of walking home from work. She had always been too busy or distracted, but Samuel's death taught her that life could change in an instant, and the small things should not be taken for granted.

As Sarah meandered past the modern Fairfax County Circuit Court building, she began to see how much the legal system had changed in the last century. She glanced back and compared the old Fairfax Courthouse's look with the newer, grandiose modern building.

She didn't know much about the law. But, now that she was the plaintiff in a multi-million dollar lawsuit against the government, she increasingly appreciated its complexities the further she immersed herself in the case.

Just then, her cell phone rang. It was David.

"Hey, David. How are you?" Sarah answered as she continued to walk.

"Things are good. Do you have a minute?"

"Absolutely, what's up?"

"I just want to let you know I received notification that Judge Callaway granted our request for mediation. So, it looks like things are going to move fast from this point on."

"Okay, what does that mean?" Sarah asked as she looked both ways and crossed the street.

"Well, the good news is we are likely to settle the case, but we probably will not get the full damages amount we requested. However, I would be very surprised if the case doesn't settle for at least seven figures."

"Wow, that's great." Sarah was elated by the news. David sensed her excitement and continued.

"The government may try to evaluate the weaknesses in their case in the mediation to assess what 'silver bullets' we may throw at them if it isn't settled and goes to trial. Still, assuming our argument is compelling, they *should* settle quickly. Fingers crossed!"

"Do we have anything that would cause them to want to settle?"

Sarah asked as she stepped up onto the sidewalk near the edge of George Mason University's Fairfax campus.

"Sort of… I'm still working on that. Don't worry, just leave that part to me. I'll keep you updated but just wanted to give you the heads up that we'll likely begin the mediation process *this week*. Judge Callaway likes to push cases through this program with breakneck speed."

"Thanks for the phone call, David. Anything else you need from *me*?"

"Nope. I'm good. I just wanted to let you know."

"Great, I'll talk to you soon! Goodbye!" As she hung up the call, Sarah realized she was growing more comfortable with David, and he wasn't hard on the eyes either.

However, she quickly dismissed the idea of getting into a relationship at this point in her life. She was sure a guy like David had hundreds of dating prospects, and a single mother who worked at a bar probably was not at the top of his list. Plus, she had casually dated a couple of men since her husband's death, but nothing serious. It would take someone exceptional to take the place of the boys' father. Nevertheless, she thought David was kind, engaging, and handsome. So, she would continue to work with him on this case and see where things went from there.

Sarah was approaching her condominium complex and, as she made her way through the parking lot, she saw a black sedan suspiciously parking under a line of tree cover, about a hundred feet away. The car backed in to the parking space, and the two men sitting in the front seat were staring at her. When they realized she noticed them, the men got out of the car and began walking toward her. Sarah quickened her pace and pretended not to see them.

"Excuse me, ma'am. Are you Sarah Mercer?" One of the men hollered at her.

Sarah was taken aback by how quickly the men approached her.

"Yes, I'm Sarah. Who are you?" Sarah asked as she put her hand on her purse.

The men stood tall with impeccable posture, close-cropped haircuts, athletic builds, and chiseled jawlines. Sarah suspected they were military.

"You're the same Sarah Mercer who filed the lawsuit, right?"

A tingle flew down Sarah's spine.

"I'm sorry, *who are you?*" Sarah insisted, growing more irritated by their lack of response.

"That's not important, Ms. Mercer. We just wanted to see where you live, that's all," one of the men said in a menacing tone as he looked up at the condo complex. The other man chimed in as well.

"We're really sorry about your son, Ms. Mercer, but riding along on an attorney's quarter-life crisis isn't the best way to express your grief, is it?" His tone was crude and condescending.

Sarah looked around the parking lot in search of potential witnesses in case the situation escalated. The man continued.

"You know Stoneman's just using you, right? Once he gets his spotlight, he'll be gone. And where will that leave you? Embarrassed, broke, and on the government's blacklist."

At that moment, Sarah saw Mark walking up the sidewalk with a couple of his neighborhood friends. She turned her attention back to the men.

"Listen…if I ever see you around here again, I'll call the cops, or better yet, I'll get a gun and deal with you myself."

One of the men smiled and pulled up the front of his army-green shirt to reveal his six-pack abs and a handgun nestled neatly in a holster on his belt.

"I'm not sure that's a good idea, Ms. Mercer. You see, we tend to shoot back." The man said as he smirked at his partner.

Sarah quickly turned and ran to meet Mark and his friends before they got too close to the men. When she reached them, she was out of breath and panicky. She pointed over her shoulder as she spoke to the boys.

"Mark, if you ever see those two men, I want you to call the police. You understand me?"

Mark looked past his mother.

"Mom…who are you talking about?" Mark asked, confused by his mother's instruction.

Sarah turned to see the black sedan pull out of its parking spot and speed away.

"That car…if any of you boys see *that car*, you call the police, okay?"

The boys nodded and continued to walk toward the complex. Sarah was too flustered to follow them immediately. Instead, she spent the following minutes walking around the parking lot to see if she could identify any other nefarious characters in the vicinity. She didn't see anything else that looked suspicious, so she pulled her phone out of her purse and called David back.

"Hello?" David answered.

"David...I need to tell you something." Sarah was distraught as she circled the parking lot one last time.

"Okay, Sarah, you sound upset. What's going on?"

"Two men, David. Two men just approached me at my condo, in front of Mark. They had guns and threatened me. They even mentioned you!"

"Okay, okay, just calm down. I'm sure it was just a scare tactic. I've seen this before. What did they look like?" David grabbed a pen and a notepad to capture Sarah's description.

Sarah's attempt at a physical account was futile. The only discernable trait she could explain was that they "looked like military men," a phrase which she repeated multiple times.

David put his pen down and knew his chance of finding the men was basically zero. Sensing the fear in Sarah's voice, he tried to calm her down.

"I'll tell you what...why don't you and Mark come and stay with me for a week until the mediation is over. I have a big apartment with a spare bedroom. Will that make you feel better?"

Sarah appreciated the gesture but was hesitant to leave her home and move in with a man she had just met, even if the offer seemed entirely platonic. However, she concluded David's apartment would likely be much safer and more secure than her place. Consequently, she decided to accept the offer.

"That's very nice, David. Are you sure it wouldn't be too much trouble?"

"Absolutely not. Get some stuff together and come down anytime this evening. I'll text you my address and make sure the guest room is made up and ready for you."

When Sarah hung up, relief flooded over her. At least she and Mark would be safe. However, the temporary reprieve was repressed when her thoughts turned to the news that her case would be fast tracked. Everything was happening so quickly and she felt ill-prepared.

Sarah headed upstairs to her condo to dismiss Mark's friends and start packing.

# Chapter 29

Inside the basement of the Fellowship Presbyterian Church, Tommy sensed something was wrong. It had been over ten minutes since Jerry went to retrieve his keys, and he had not yet returned. Tommy poked his head into the two dark offices in the office suite, both of which looked basically dormant. He could barely walk through the door of one of the offices because the room was filled with old, broken church furniture. There were cobwebs throughout the room, signaling no one had been in that space for years. He shut the door and walked across the hall to the other office. It smelled musty, but dustless books and new magazines sitting on the metal desk indicated the room had been recently used.

Natural light cascaded in from a small rectangular window in the room's upper-left corner near the ceiling. Tommy could see the alley through the window from his tiptoes, so he pulled the rickety desk chair to the outside wall and climbed up to look for Jerry.

He nearly fell off the chair when he angled his head to look further down the alley and saw his friend lying face down on the pavement in a pool of blood. He jumped off the chair and immediately ran to the office door and slammed it shut.

*What did this mean? Had the man who killed his wife also killed Jerry? Was he still in the alley?*

Tommy's head was swirling, and he thought he was going to faint.

His first inclination was to race outside to help Jerry. But Tommy suspected Jerry was already dead, and the culprit could be waiting outside to finish the job he started in South Carolina.

*What should he do? The files!* Amid the chaotic situation, he had a moment of clarity.

*He had to retrieve Pietrov's files – maybe he could turn them over to the authorities in exchange for protection.* Tommy knew that without Pietrov's files, he had no leverage and would be dead before the weekend.

Tommy didn't have the key to the locked desk drawers, and he didn't dare go out into the alley to search Jerry's dead body for it. So, he took a heavy, green marble paperweight from the corner of the desk and began smashing it against one of the drawer's locks. After the fourth hit, it opened to reveal a three-hole punch and yellowed computer paper. He moved over to the drawer on the other side of the desk and began pounding. He was afraid the loud noise of the paperweight hitting the metal desk would alert Jerry's killer to his location, so he had to move fast and hit hard.

After his fifth hit, the drawer opened, and files poured out onto the floor. There were about half a dozen thick manila folders, and he saw Dr. Pietrov's name on one of the folders in the middle of the pile. Tommy didn't have time to sift through all of the documents to determine which ones were relevant, so he threw all of the files into an empty trash bag and planned his next move.

He knew he couldn't leave through the alley. Instead, he planned to break through the padlocked basement door and exit out the church's front doors. At least he would be on a public street and could scream for help if trouble found him. Tommy realized it was only a matter of time before someone saw Jerry's body, and the police would be on their way. And, he didn't want to be around when they arrived. After all, Tommy was likely a suspect in his wife's death, and, no doubt, there would be a warrant out for his arrest. Tommy had to get out of the building fast and undetected.

----

Outside, the man with the slicked-back hair positioned himself on the roof of a nearby building and watched through military-grade binoculars as a pedestrian stumbled upon the gruesome scene and erratically called 911. The police arrived in a matter of minutes. The man smirked at the confusion on the officers' faces upon arrival. Experience told him the crime scene would be active for several hours, and more police would be on their way.

He was willing to wait. If Tommy was still in the church, the police would find him and take him downtown for questioning. Once in custody, it would be easy for the man to get to him and make it look like an accident.

Sirens rang out as two first responders entered the unlocked alley door to the church's office suite. At that same time, Tommy hurried out of the front doors and onto the sidewalk. The police had not yet secured the scene, so Tommy was able to retreat unnoticed and, with a trash bag full of files in hand, he quickly walked down the sidewalk away from the sirens and blended in with other passing pedestrians.

The man with the slicked-back hair witnessed Tommy's departure from his rooftop perch. The police had not seen Tommy, and shooting him on the open sidewalk, even with a silencer, would alert the police to the man's location. He had to pursue Tommy on foot if he was going to have a chance to catch him.

As Tommy walked toward the Foggy Bottom-GWU metro station, he saw additional police cars fly past him. Within the hour, the police would likely pull the street's surveillance footage, showing Tommy racing from the church just moments after Jerry's murder. Consequently, he knew he couldn't go back to his car which was parked near the church; it was no longer safe.

Tommy walked past a restaurant across the street from The George Washington University Hospital. He was anxiously waiting for the crosswalk's walk sign to illuminate so he could enter the metro station and swiftly leave the area.

In the thirty seconds he was waiting for the walk signal, Tommy realized that even though he had escaped detection by the police, the killer could still be following him.

As he stood on the crowded corner, he casually glanced around to see if he noticed any suspicious characters. Most of the people appeared to be students or hospital workers. However, as the lights changed and he began to stride across the busy intersection, he looked over his left shoulder to see a familiar face about fifty feet behind him. It was the man with the slicked-back hair. Before he had time to think, his feet were already running toward the entrance to the metro station. The man knew he had been recognized and took off after his target.

Tommy barreled through a T-shirt stand and ran under the checkered canopy entrance to the metro station. He hustled onto the escalator, which led down into a concrete chasm to the train platforms. He shoved past dozens of people as he made his speedy descent. Tommy then tripped near the bottom of the escalator and tumbled onto the concrete floor. Luckily, none of the files spilled out of the trash bag.

He looked up to see the man about halfway down the escalator rapidly making his way toward him. Tommy rose to his feet, grabbed the trash bag, sprinted past the ticket bank, and jumped over the entry gates. He heard the sound of a train boarding on the deck below and pushed his way down another set of escalators. The smell of the train's fuel became more pungent as he raced down to the platform.

The platform was dimly lit, and the white-gray wall and ceiling patterns added an eerie dungeon ambiance to the dire situation. Tommy heard the pre-recorded voice indicate the train was departing, and he was only about ten feet away when the doors began to shut. He knew if he didn't make this train, he was dead.

So, with every ounce of strength left in him, he leaped toward the train's closing doors. He barely pulled the garbage bag into the car before the doors closed tightly behind him. Tommy quickly stood up and walked to the back of the car as it began to move. He looked out the window toward the platform and saw the man with the slicked-back hair staring at him, and then he turned and ran back toward the escalators.

Tommy saw a metro map on the train's wall and noticed his next stop was Farragut West. He would exit there and lay low until he found a safe, private place to review Dr. Pietrov's files. He was running out of time.

# Chapter 30

According to the U.S. District Court Mediation Program's local rules, the mediation proceedings are administered by the Office of the Circuit Executive for the United States Courts for the District of Columbia Circuit. Their mediation staff is responsible for assigning cases to volunteer mediators vetted and trained by the Court. In Sarah Mercer's case, the staff selected Mr. Charles Morison as the mediator.

David was familiar with Charles, and, from what he had heard, he was a solid choice.

Charles Morison was a retired former partner at a boutique law firm in Rockville, Maryland. He made a name for himself by standing up against large drug companies. Charles was fair but tough. As an African-American growing up in a tumultuous time in a notoriously rough part of Atlanta, he had learned how to stand up to bullies and, when necessary, fight them. Charles saw the value of education and recognized it as his ticket to a better life. So, he studied hard and earned full-tuition scholarships to both college and law school.

As an adult, the only fighting Charles did was in the courtroom, and he was good at it. His style was subtle, and his stoic persona caused his opponents to let their guard down – that's when he would hit them the hardest. However, after Charles beat you in court, he was the type of person who would also invite you out for a beer to bury the hatchet.

In the Mercer case, an order was issued specifying that the mediation should be concluded within thirty days. However, both parties were eager to get started and lobbied to begin the mediation proceedings as soon as possible. Charles agreed to the expedited schedule – he, too, was anxious to start the process.

David was thrilled to learn Greg Thomas would be special counsel for the defense, which meant he would be going head-to-head with Johnson Allen's finest litigator. David knew adding Greg Thomas to the defense team was an intimidation tactic. In actuality, what they didn't know is that David wanted nothing more than a pound of flesh from his former boss and was excited to have a chance to take it from him.

The first step in the mediation process was for each party to draft a confidential mediation statement, which could be no more than ten pages, and send that document to Charles. No later than seven days after the mediation statements were submitted, Charles would host an in-person meeting with both parties, followed by separate, individual sessions with each party, as needed. Thereafter, hopefully, a settlement offer would be discussed.

While the process would be much faster than litigation, David loathed the fact that all aspects of the mediation would be *confidential.* Sarah could get her payday, but the world would never hear about her struggle. Judge Callaway wouldn't even know the details of the proceedings. Once again, the government would be able to buy its way out of this tight spot.

David was sitting alone in his kitchen. Rita had gone home and, after unpacking their things at David's apartment, Sarah and Mark went down the street to get a bite to eat. David drafted his initial mediation statement, but a large hole remained in his argument. He simply did not have enough information about Dr. Pietrov's research to draw the conclusion he needed. David knew there was a lot of smoke, but he could not produce evidence of the fire.

At that moment, David's cell phone rang. It was Greg Thomas.

"Hello?"

"David, it's Greg Thomas. I've got some good news!"

David was skeptical that the news was, in fact, *good*, but he decided to play along.

"Oh, yea? What's that?"

"Despite my objections, the government would like to make your client a settlement offer." David could tell by Greg Thomas's tone that he was in "deal-making" mode. David decided to take the wind out of his sails right away.

"Really? Before the mediation even begins? Well, we're not interested, Greg."

"You know you're obligated to take our offer to your client, and how can you do that when you don't even know what it is?"

"I'm listening…" David said unenthusiastically.

Greg Thomas told David he wanted to explain the offer in person and gave David an address by the Georgetown Waterfront where they could meet. He told him to come alone.

This was unusual, and David had no intention to accept a settlement offer at this early stage. Nevertheless, he was curious. In an abundance of caution, he pulled an old Glock 26, 9-millimeter handgun out of his sock drawer. David's father was a decorated military veteran who died when David was younger. But he remembered his father telling him to always carry a loaded gun if he was heading into trouble. And, with this meeting, David suspected that could be the case. He tucked the gun into the back of his suit pants, left a brief note for Sarah on the kitchen counter saying he would return shortly, and headed for his car.

----

The navigation feature in David's BMW indicated he had arrived at the meeting place. He parked his car and got out. David heard voices of people enjoying their evenings in the bars and restaurants that lined Washington Harbor. For a second, he thought about darting into one of the bars to take a few shots of courage before this meeting, but he concluded it would be best if he were completely sober, just in case he needed to use his gun.

As he paced back and forth near the docked boats along the water in the location Greg Thomas gave him, he noticed a large, stout man with an earpiece approaching him.

"Mr. Stoneman?" the towering man said in a hulking voice.

David nodded.

"Right this way, they're waiting on you." The man turned and began walking in the other direction.

David cautiously followed the giant man into what looked like a closed barbershop under one of the overpasses. The man walked past the barber chairs, into a back storage room, and through a narrow wooden door. David grew more nervous the further back into the shop the giant man took him. He put his hand behind his back, reached under his suit coat, and gripped the gun's handle with his right hand. If the giant man drew a weapon, he would be ready.

As David was about to turn and run out, he heard chatter coming from a back room.

What appeared to be a closet door wasn't a pantry at all. David couldn't believe his eyes as he walked past old cleaning equipment and into a *private club*.

It was a single large room with elaborate and ornate wooden fixtures climbing the walls. The room was roughly fifteen hundred square feet and was full of oversized dark green leather chairs and poker tables. Cigar smoke limited the room's visibility, but through the smoke near the back of the room, David could see a bronze bar that sat next to a large billiards table.

By a quick headcount, David guessed there were over two dozen men in the room, all of whom were staring at him as the giant man took his place next to the door and left David silhouetted in the doorway. David recognized most of the men. They were titans of industry, judges, local celebrities, and politicians. David knew he was in way over his head and debated whether or not to leave. However, curiosity caused him to linger.

*What is this place?* he wondered.

One of the men rose from his chair and extended his hand to David for a handshake. David recognized him immediately.

"David, glad you could join us. I'm Senator Stephen Smythe – welcome to The Senator's Club. Please have a seat."

David shook the Senator's hand and sat down in one of the large green leather chairs without saying a word.

"Can I get you a drink? Cigar? Anything?" Senator Smythe inquired.

"No, I'm fine, thanks." David was still looking around the room to determine if he was about to get whacked, mafia-style. Then, he noticed Greg Thomas in the back corner of the room taking a shot at the billiards table with the editor of one of Washington's major newspapers. Greg Thomas glanced at David, smirked, shook his head arrogantly, and went back to his game.

Strangely, Greg Thomas's presence made David feel more at ease in the mysterious room. Greg Thomas was a lot of things, but he was not the type of person who would be around if they were planning to kill David. He was too smart for that.

"Go on, have a scotch," Senator Smythe insisted as he grabbed a half-filled decanter and a glass from a side table, poured David a stiff drink, and handed him the full glass.

Senator Smythe took his seat in front of the room's crackling fireplace, lit despite it being springtime. The members of The Senator's Club insisted on the fire blazing year-round. The red and orange embers at the base of the flames added to the room's ambiance, and the smell of burning wood mixed with the cigar smoke gave the space a rich, hazy aroma. The walls were covered by expensive artwork displaying scenes from Greek and Roman mythology. The room's largest painting was of a muscular lightning-bolt-wielding deity, which hung directly above the fireplace. It was obvious the room was meant to exude power, influence, and intimidation to invited guests.

"Dave, let me get right to it. We want this little lawsuit to go away, and *everyone* in this room will contribute funds to make that happen. Off the books, of course."

David was shocked at the audacity of the illegal request.

"How much?" Again, David was curious.

Senator Smythe realized his cigar had gone out and snapped his fingers at the giant man and waved his cigar in the air. Within seconds, the man approached with a butane lighter and held it carefully as the Senator puffed and twirled the cigar back to life.

"Two million dollars." Senator Smythe said as he exhaled smoke into the air.

"That's not going to get it done, Senator." David raised his eyebrows and shook his head at the political juggernaut.

Senator Smythe glanced at the fire and leaned forward to place his cigar on an ashtray which sat atop a side table.

"I wasn't finished…two million for your client, and one million, in cash, for *you*." Senator Smythe pointed both of his index fingers at David, then folded his hands and sat back in his chair and crossed one leg over the other.

"It's a generous offer, sir, but I'm going to have to decline. I'm not big on bribery."

Senator Smythe did not appreciate David's sarcasm and his demeanor changed.

"David, I'm going to be your friend for a minute. Do you know where you are?"

"Not really…" David responded as he glanced around the room once again.

"The Senator's Club is a special place where a *very* select group of folks hang their hats from time to time. We don't invite many guests. You are an exception."

"It's a nice place…but really, Senator, I must be going." David tried to stand up, but the giant man with the earpiece forcefully pushed him back down into the chair. David realized he wasn't allowed to leave until he was dismissed.

"You see, Dave, the men in this room were invited here for a reason. It's not just to get away from our wives and girlfriends, although that is a benefit. We have a purpose here, Dave. You could say we're on a mission!"

"And what mission is that?" David asked as he looked up at the giant man and then back at the Senator.

Senator Smythe chuckled as he repositioned himself in his chair.

"Right now, it's to make you a settlement offer and cause this case to disappear. But, if you are unwilling to comply with that request, every man in this room will do their best to destroy you. And, by the time we're done, you'll be lucky to get a job at a free legal clinic."

Senator Smythe leaned forward, lowered his voice almost to a whisper, and glared at David with his cunning eyes.

"You know it would be devastating if you had some kind of accident. Perhaps, Sarah Mercer could have an accident too. You never know what kind of danger lurks around every corner here in Washington."

David scowled at Senator Smythe as his blood boiled with anger. The Senator broke the staring contest with another question.

"What would it take for you to drop the case, Dave? Name your price."

"Well, Senator, as I said before...I'm not big on taking bribes, and I really get pissed when I'm threatened. So, before we had this little chat, I probably would have come up with a pretty good number for you. But, after this meeting, there's no amount of money on this planet that could make me drop this case. I guess your buddy over there, Greg Thomas, didn't tell you – I'm a pit bull, just like him." David said in a razor-sharp tone.

Senator Smythe waved Greg Thomas over to the discussion.

David's former managing partner casually walked over in his three-piece suit with pool chalk on his left sleeve and a grin on his face.

"Don't worry, Senator," Greg Thomas roared, "Dave's not dumb enough to pursue this lawsuit with me as co-counsel. He's seen me in action many times and knows I'm the best."

"To the contrary, Greg. It appears our Davey-boy isn't backing down. In fact, he's talking tough." Senator Smythe said mockingly.

David rose from his chair, and the Senator waived the giant man back to his position by the door. David looked Greg Thomas right in the eye. He was just inches away from his face.

"Remember, Greg, I've beaten Johnson Allen before…that's why you hired me. I'm happy to do it again. And, especially happy to do it to *you*."

"You haven't beaten *me*…and you *can't* beat me…and you know it!" Greg Thomas's arrogant disposition turned to hostility.

The giant man grabbed David by the shoulders and pulled him back away from Greg Thomas before the verbal altercation turned physical.

Without thinking, David pulled the gun out from under his jacket and pointed it at the giant man's forehead. The room grew deathly silent, and everyone stopped what they were doing and looked at David.

The giant man was stunned.

"Touch me again…and I'll make sure it's the last thing you do. Got it?"

The giant man nodded, frozen in his tracks. Senator Smythe began to laugh.

"Pulling a gun in a room like this is an awfully dangerous move, Mr. Stoneman." Senator Smythe announced.

"I was just leaving, Senator," David replied as he backed toward the exit and directed the giant man to open the door, which led back to the barbershop. David quickened his pace as he left, repeatedly looking over his shoulder to ensure he wasn't being followed.

Once he was safely outside, David doubled over and put his hands on his knees.

*What did I just do?* David wondered. *It was instinct; I was never going to shoot anybody.* His knees were shaking.

He found solace knowing that no one in that room would report his actions to the police because that would require them to give up their club's secret location. David knew he was safe for now, but he shouldn't make it a habit of pointing guns at people's heads.

David hobbled back to his car and put the gun in his glove compartment. He was still shaking. He was a pro at putting on a tough exterior persona, but that interaction had been terrifying. David took a couple of deep breaths and started the car's engine. He half-expected it to explode. But despite his unsteady nerves, David felt proud he had stood his ground against Senator

Smythe and Greg Thomas. At least now they knew he wasn't going to back down.

Back in The Senator's Club, Greg Thomas stood shocked. He didn't think David had it in him.

"I got to say, the kid has spirit. I saw him do a lot at the firm but never saw him stick a gun in someone's face…that's a first." Greg Thomas laughed as he refilled his scotch glass.

Senator Smythe was less amused. If David were armed, it would be too risky to send FARCO to try to take him out. If, by some miracle, David killed one of the operatives in self defense, the trail would lead directly back to FARCO and then back to the Senator.

Senator Smythe would have to find another way to get to David. He had an idea and took a long drag on his full-bodied cigar as he stared into the roaring fireplace.

# Chapter 31

It had been several days since Senator Smythe and Greg Thomas ambushed David at The Senator's Club. He had received calls from other people at the club that night, who either threatened him or attempted to bribe him to drop the case. The pressure did not deter David. On the contrary, he was emboldened after pointing a gun at the club's security guard. David was not going to lie down for anyone.

He spent most of the day continuing to draft and polish his mediation statement though there were still massive gaps in his argument related to Dr. Pietrov and his research. Sarah, Mark, and Rita were at David's apartment going over the final version of the mediation statement before it had to be submitted to Charles Morison the following morning.

Sarah and Mark were still staying with David, and Rita might as well have moved in, given the amount of time she had spent at David's place over the last week.

While Rita was intricately involved in the details of the tedious mediation preparation, Sarah was generally disinterested. She seemed content sitting on the couch watching television with Mark while Rita and David huddled at the kitchen table, hard at work.

David hadn't told Sarah about Francis Pietrov. At that point, there simply was not much to tell. All David had was a theory but zero evidence to back it up. And, he didn't want to get Sarah's hopes up in case his theory turned out to be incorrect.

David could sense life had been especially hard on Sarah and Mark since the lawsuit was filed. They were receiving strange hang-up phone calls, and, to makes matters worse, the IRS just notified them that it was auditing Sarah. There was no chance this was a coincidence.

David tapped his hand on the table as Rita reviewed his mediation statement for the seventh time that evening. He was growing impatient.

"Well?" David couldn't wait any longer.

Rita put her index finger in the air, signaling she would only be another minute.

David stood up, took a sip of his iced tea, and looked out his living room window at the bustling Georgetown street below. He was startled by the sound of Rita clapping her hands together.

"It looks good, Dave. Clean and simple. Of course, you're missing a major portion of your argument." David put his finger to his mouth to quiet Rita as he moved back to the table. Rita was stating the obvious, but David didn't want to alarm Sarah. Unfortunately, Sarah overheard the comment and inquired further.

"What argument is missing? What does that mean for the case?" Sarah asked over the noise of the television.

David gave Rita an annoyed look and turned to respond to Sarah.

"It means we have a choice…whether to bluff or not," David then added more context to his cryptic statement.

"I've been practicing law for nearly a decade and have been up against the government many times. I have *never* seen them this nervous about a case. I mean, the fact that I have United States Senators trying to shake me down tells me we're close to the truth."

"You have Senators doing *what*?!" Rita questioned. David realized he had not yet shared his experience at The Senator's Club with Sarah or Rita. His comment even caused Mark to glance up from his show. Unsatisfied with David's diversion response, Sarah asked her question a second time.

"Rita said something is missing from our argument. What's missing?"

David sighed and knew it was time to bring Sarah into the strategic fold.

"We strongly suspect that a scientist, a guy named Francis Pietrov, conducted research related to the Division Act and that research may be damaging to the government's case."

"That's a good thing, isn't it? Can't we just find this scientist and ask him about it?" Sarah looked at David, then at Rita, wondering why the situation was so complicated.

"Unfortunately, no…he's dead." David saw Sarah's face drop in disappointment.

Rita ran her boney fingers through her graying hair and decided to prod the conversation along.

"Okay, David, so what are you going to do?"

David turned to Rita and shrugged his shoulders as he resumed his seat at the kitchen table.

"I'm going to bluff and pray it works," David said as he took another sip of his drink and leaned back in his chair.

David could tell Rita was not comfortable with that answer – she began to pace in the kitchen.

"Sarah, can you ask Mark to go into the bedroom for a minute?" David knew the discussion could get intense.

Sarah gave Mark his game tablet and asked him to give the adults some privacy. Mark began scrolling through the available sports games on his device and was happy to oblige as he strolled into the spare bedroom and shut the door.

Once Mark was gone, David lowered his voice and continued.

"You need to know something, Rita. If I add this information to the mediation statement, our lives will almost certainly be in danger."

Sarah and Rita looked at each other and then back at David. He continued.

"Right now, the government doesn't know we have this information, and we don't even know if we're right. However, *if we are right*, I believe they may try to kill us to keep the information secret – I suspect that's what they did to Francis Pietrov."

Sarah became frightened. Reality set in, and she began to panic. She stood up, visibly distressed, and objected.

"No, no, no…it's not worth it, David. I can't risk Mark's safety. I won't do it!"

David tried to calm her down.

"Don't worry, Sarah, if they come after anyone, it will be me. I'll make sure it's only me. The mediation is currently set to only last two days, so we just have to stick together until this thing is over, and we're in the clear, alright?"

Sarah was non-responsive as she resumed her place on the couch. After a few seconds, she began crying into her hands and shaking her head. Rita sat down at the kitchen table and was staring at the floor, thinking through alternative options.

"It'll be okay, Sarah. I won't let anything happen to you or Mark. Believe me when I say that."

Sarah briefly looked up at David and wiped her tears as she tried to compose herself. David understood that losing Samuel had nearly put Sarah over the edge, so even the thought of losing Mark as well was simply too much for the young mother to bear. However, he didn't know what to say to comfort her – they had to bluff about the Pietrov evidence, or else they would lose the case. It was that simple.

"We should go to the cops!" Rita exclaimed as if she had an epiphany.

David shook his head. "Good thought, but we don't know who we can trust over there; some members on the force could be in on this too. It's not safe to go to the police, or anyone else, at this point."

Sarah believed she could trust David's judgment in this matter, but she was still upset.

Rita seemed less concerned as she yawned and glanced at her watch. She had been through many tumultuous cases with David, and, by this point, she was practically numb to the risks.

"Hey, Dave, whatever you decide is good with me. You add the info to the mediation statement, and I'll format it and submit it to Charles Morison first thing in the morning. But I'm wiped out and am leaving now."

"Okay, thanks, Rita."

Rita picked up her oversized purse and shot David and Sarah a quick wave goodbye as she left the apartment. Sarah retrieved Mark from the bedroom, and they sat back down on the living room couch. Sarah put her arm around Mark, and he nestled up next to her – David could tell they were close. After some reflection, Sarah turned to David, who was still sitting in the kitchen, skimming through his mediation statement.

"Are you sure about this, David?" Sarah asked in a soft, broken voice. David kept his head bowed toward his papers but cocked his head to the side and looked at Sarah.

"*Pretty sure*...but if we don't try it, we're going to lose this case and still may be in the government's crosshairs. So, I think we have to try." Sensing his answer didn't do much to calm Sarah's nerves, he set down his mediation statement and moved to sit next to Sarah on the couch.

"Look, I'm just as scared as you are, but I'm in this fight with you, and I'm not going to let you down." Sarah smiled and nodded.

David hoped he was doing the right thing. If he was wrong about Dr. Pietrov's research, not only would he lose the case for Sarah, but he would lose his reputation, and maybe even his life, along with it.

# Chapter 32

Sergeant Henderson was standing in his secluded glass-walled office at the secret FARCO headquarters in Northern Virginia when his phone rang.

He immediately recognized the familiar voice on the other end of the line.

"We're outside; what's the code?"

Sergeant Henderson changed the base's entrance code daily to make it impossible for anyone other than FARCO operatives or invited guests to access their secret headquarters.

"122-675." Sergeant Henderson heard the beep from the keypad, followed by a loud clicking sound signifying the inconspicuous door had unlocked and was opening. He left his glass-walled office and walked down the metal stairs into the heart of the FARCO war room. Like a NASA command center, FARCO's war room had multiple large monitoring screens continuously tracking the many FARCO operations around the globe.

Sergeant Henderson glanced up to the main screen to see drone footage of a cattle farm in the Middle East. He suspected that activity represented the anti-terrorist operation they were supporting in the region. Several FARCO operatives were wearing headsets and stationed in front of their computers, laser-focused on their tasks.

The external war room door opened to reveal Senator Smythe and Greg Thomas.

"To what do I owe the honor of this visit, Senator?" Sergeant Henderson asked as he moved toward his guests.

A handful of FARCO operatives glanced up from their computers. It wasn't often a sitting United States Senator visited the facility – or any outside guests, for that matter. But, after a few seconds of curious stares and hushed side-commentary, the operatives returned their focus to their missions.

Sergeant Henderson had met Greg Thomas before, and he didn't like him. He viewed Greg Thomas as more of a mercenary than himself, using his fancy education and silver-tongue to fight his opponents from an ivory tower. Consequently, Sergeant Henderson barely acknowledged Greg Thomas as the three of them stepped into the glass-walled conference room on the far side of the war room for a private conversation.

"Your operative has failed, Sergeant," Senator Smythe barked as he took a seat at the head of the long, metal conference table.

"He got Pietrov, but the pastor is still just roaming around Washington. He could be walking up the steps of Capitol Hill right now, for all I know! What kind of shoddy operation are you running here?" Senator Smythe yelled in frustration as his face reddened.

The glass door of the conference room was still ajar, and the Senator's accusatory comment drew the attention of two former Navy SEALs seated within earshot. Their gaze was enough to cause Senator Smythe to retract his comment and stand up to shut the conference room door to prevent further eavesdropping.

"Look, I'm sorry! I know your guys are good, but I can't have any loose ends here, Henderson." The Senator loosened his blue paisley tie and unbuttoned the top button of his crisp, starched shirt as he resumed his seat at the conference table.

Sergeant Henderson was furious but held his tongue and his temper. He reminded himself the Senator was consistently and quietly flowing money to his organization, so he wouldn't deal with him as he dealt with others.

"We're working on it, Senator. My operative has been hot on his target's heels for days now. It won't be long before he completes his mission." Sergeant Henderson calmly replied.

Sergeant Henderson knew as long as the funding remained steady, he would only have to work a bit longer before disappearing to a remote island for his retirement. But, today, the hand that feeds him was upset, and he was going to make it right. He continued.

"Senator, I assure you, the man on this op is one of my best, and he always hits his mark."

Greg Thomas chimed into the conversation.

"Good, because our mediation starts *tomorrow*, and if any information comes out, it's because you and your men didn't get the job done." Greg Thomas immediately regretted his comments – very few people intimidated him, but Sergeant Henderson was one of them. Greg Thomas had heard terrifying stories about Sergeant Henderson and knew him to be an elite killing machine. His ink-stained palms began to sweat.

Sergeant Henderson took three steps toward Greg Thomas, clenched his fists, and stared daggers at the high-powered litigator.

"Mr. Thomas, thank you for your insight into this matter. But if you ever speak to me like that again, I promise you I will personally send you out of here in a body bag."

Sensing his life was in danger, Greg Thomas took a small gulp, nodded, and looked down at the ground. Senator Smythe attempted to break the tension.

"Okay, enough of this testosterone nonsense. You have twenty-four hours, Henderson. After that, this thing may be too big to quash. Luckily, I'm working on another angle to shut this down, but you need to pull your end of the deal. I have folks to report to as well, you know…"

"We do have *another option*, which is a bit more…ominous," Sergeant Henderson said with a sly grin as he turned back to the Senator and crossed his muscular arms.

"I'm listening." Senator Smythe responded as he leaned forward and put both elbows on the cold, metal conference table.

"The woman in this case – she has a son, doesn't she?" Sergeant Henderson inquired.

"Yea. So, what?"

"We could *pick him up* for a few days and use him as leverage."

Senator Smythe was quiet for a moment, considering whether kidnapping the boy would be worth the risk. He finally broke the silence.

"Okay, get the boy. I'll work my angle too. This ends now!"

Greg Thomas didn't agree with the decision but didn't dare object.

"Good, I'll make the arrangements with my guy; we'll bring the boy here and put him in the holding cell in the basement. That should get his mother's attention." Sergeant Henderson jotted a few notes down on a small, black notebook he pulled from his pocket. He had his orders.

The meeting concluded, and Senator Smythe and Greg Thomas left quietly amidst the loud, fiery explosions captured in high-definition on the primary war room monitor. Jeers and cheers from the FARCO operatives caused Senator Smythe and Greg Thomas to quicken their pace as they headed toward the exit. The less they knew, the better.

As they left the war room, Sergeant Henderson called the man with the slicked-back hair.

"Slight change in plans – I want you to hold off on finding *South Carolina* for now and pick up a boy named Mark Mercer. He's the son of the plaintiff in the case. I just spoke to *Eagle*, and he approved the op." The phone was silent for a second.

"You got it." The man with the slicked-back hair responded. He was excited to have a new target, a more important target, and this time, he was not going to fail.

# Chapter 33

Rita staggered out of David's apartment after a long day. She walked down Wisconsin Avenue planning to grab a late dinner in the heart of historic Georgetown. After the work she put in, an ice-cold beer and juicy cheeseburger sounded great, and the pleasant culinary aromas that wafted through the Georgetown streets caused her mouth to water as she mentally shuffled through close potential dining options.

The mediation started the following morning, and since school was out for the summer, Rita offered to watch Mark at the apartment while David and Sarah attended the mediation.

Rita passed The George Town Club, which she and David frequented many times for elegant client meetings and formal firm happy hours in years past. The chic club's bright corner bar room was crowded, no doubt filled with politicos, prominent members of the press, and D.C. socialites. The George Town Club was the epitome of historical sophistication. There even were rumors George Washington and Pierre L'Enfant frequented the same building as they were developing the layout of the nation's capital.

As Rita walked past the club's veiled entrance, she wondered if she would ever darken those doors again. Life had changed dramatically for her, and, even though she would never admit it to David, she considered floating her resume to a few other firms in town. After all, she had to think about her future as well.

As Rita continued down Wisconsin Avenue, she would soon pass Martin's Tavern on her right. She sometimes patronized Martin's with her firm friends for a casual pint after work. But those days were over. She had gone all-in with David, and her fair-weather friends at Johnson Allen stopped taking her calls after she was let go.

As she crossed over N Street, a passing figure brushed her shoulder. She turned to see a young man wearing a coat and tie. He couldn't have been more than twenty-five years old.

"Rita?" The young man asked as he took a few steps closer.

"Yes…do I know you?" The man was just a couple of feet from her, and she didn't recognize him on the dark street.

"No. You don't know me, but I know *your brother*." The man's tone and demeanor turned solemn.

Rita knew this encounter was not an accident.

"How do you know my brother? Who are you?"

"I know he's a crack addict and currently in prison. I also know that you're going to come into Martin's Tavern and talk with me unless you want him to get hurt." With that, the young man turned and began walking toward Martin's, confident Rita would follow him.

Rita was speechless; she couldn't believe what this mystery man had just said to her. Regardless, she followed the young man into the bar. She was nervous but equally curious and agitated, worried that something terrible might happen to her brother.

The hostess sat them in the *Proposal Booth*, where John F. Kennedy proposed to Jackie. On other nights, the bar's history and nostalgia would be pleasant, but this conversation was anything but enjoyable for Rita.

"Okay, who are you, and what do you want?" Rita asked sternly as she shuffled into the booth.

"My name is Tim, and I work for someone very powerful on Capitol Hill."

"Okay…so what?" Rita inquired as she glanced around the bar, curious to see if this young man had an entourage.

"He wants the case you're working on to go away, Rita." The young man's tone was curt and rehearsed.

"What does that have to do with my brother?" Rita asked angrily as she glared back across the table.

"My boss can help reduce his prison sentence, but only if you play ball with us."

Rita's brother, Tony, had been convicted of dealing drugs five years earlier. David tried to help him, but the district attorney had a mountain of evidence against him and jail time was inevitable. The best David could get for him was ten years if he helped provide information on rival drug dealers. It was a good deal, and David suggested Tony take it.

The young man continued, "I understand it's tough to be a snitch in jail. You constantly have to watch your back, never knowing if a moment will be your last. It would be a shame if the guards weren't watching when something tragic happened…" Tim let his voice trail off, implying the worst.

Rita couldn't bear the thought of Tony getting hurt, and she became emotional.

"What do you want me to do?" She sniffled, holding back the tears with her head down.

"We want to know where the holes are in your case," Tim whispered as he leaned forward and put his thin, bony elbows on the table.

"Surely, there has to be a soft spot in your mediation statement."

Before he could continue, the waitress approached to take their drink order.

"Hey, Tim! Good to see you again! Will Senator Smythe be joining you tonight?" The waitress quickly realized she had walked into a tense situation.

"We need a minute, please," Tim responded, annoyed by the interruption and especially aggravated the waitress inadvertently unearthed who he worked for.

The waitress nodded dutifully and retreated.

"You work for *Senator Smythe*? Of course, you do. David has all of you figured out. He was right; there is a conspiracy related to the Division Act! Otherwise, why would you be here blackmailing me?!" Rita raised her voice which drew glances from nearby bar patrons.

Tim scanned the room and lifted his hand to the side of his mouth to prevent onlookers from reading his lips.

"One more word like that out of your big mouth, and your brother gets tossed in solitary confinement," Tim threatened in a raised whisper. He was not used to playing this game of hardball, and his hands shook as he slung threats at Rita. Rita looked at his demeanor and could tell Tim was flustered. She considered getting up and walking out, but she still wasn't sure whether or not he was bluffing about access to her brother. She didn't want to take any chances with Tony's life.

Tim frowned at Rita. He didn't dare return to Senator Smythe without any answers or a promise of cooperation. He was planning on starting law school in the fall and knew one false move could get his acceptance letters revoked. So, he pushed even harder.

"One last chance, Rita. Otherwise, I'm going to tell my boss you were uncooperative. You may not get another chance to help your brother – give me *something*!" Tim slammed his fist on the table. The sudden loud bang startled a few patrons, and Tim could see the waitress talking to the bartender and pointing his way. He suspected another outburst might result in the police being called, which was the last thing he wanted. Fortunately for Tim, Rita cracked.

"Fine – just please don't hurt Tony. Please. Please." Rita whimpered as she wiped her eyes with a napkin. She continued.

"There's a part of our argument we can't substantiate…we don't have Francis Pietrov's research report, but we're claiming we do. It's a bluff; there – are you happy?" Rita began crying quietly in the booth.

"Now, what assurances do I have that my brother will be unharmed?" She asked through her tears.

The young man stood up, threw twenty dollars on the table for the waitress to forget she had seen anything, and smirked.

"Thank you, Rita. If this information is true, your brother will be just fine. However, if you lied to me or if you mention anything about this meeting to anyone, especially Stoneman, your brother will suffer the consequences." Tim walked out of Martin's Tavern and disappeared into the night.

Rita managed to make it outside before she completely broke down on the sidewalk. She leaned against a storefront window, slid down to the sidewalk, and wrapped her knees in her arms as she sat alone in the darkness. The reality was setting in that she had just betrayed David and Sarah.

----

As Tim walked to a black, parked car waiting near the Georgetown Cupcake shop on M Street, his emotions were bittersweet. He knew Senator Smythe would be happy with the information and the result, but he felt horrible about the pain he had caused Rita. Tim was just a kid from Boston who was smart and interested in politics. But tonight, he was the thuggish enforcer for a crooked politician. Tim didn't know how he felt about that.

As he opened the car door, smoke flooded out. He hopped in the backseat to find Senator Smythe enjoying a full-bodied cigar and eating a salted caramel cupcake.

"Well?" Senator Smythe asked with his mouth full of sugary delight.

"I did what you told me, and she gave up a weak point in their argument. It seems they are bluffing about having some report research."

"For which report?" The Senator asked with irritated anticipation.

"She didn't go into detail, but it was a report by someone named Francis Peehh…" Tim had already forgotten the last name. Senator Smythe finished his sentence.

"Pietrov…Francis Pietrov?"

"Yes, that's it. Who is she?"

Senator Smythe smiled as he consumed the last morsel of his delicious cupcake.

"Francis Pietrov was a *man*. A scientist who conducted preliminary research for me on the Division Act."

"Was?" Tim asked, obviously confused.

"He's deceased...and hell will freeze solid before anyone finds that report. I had all the copies destroyed months ago. We're good, thanks, Tim."

Tim smiled, knowing that a kind word from Senator Smythe was rare.

"Anything else I can do for you, sir?"

"Yea, go get me another cupcake."

# Chapter 34

At the same time that Rita was being blackmailed in Georgetown, Tommy was locking himself in a dusty broom closet at the Good Samaritan Homeless Shelter in downtown Washington, near Capitol Hill.

He had laid low for a week, bouncing from shelter to shelter in an attempt to evade the man who was hunting him. Fortunately, he finally found a completely isolated, private place to review Jerry Hatfield's counseling files. Tommy suspected Jerry knew more about Dr. Pietrov's Division Act research than he had let on, but, it didn't matter anymore. Jerry was dead.

Tommy checked into the homeless shelter under a false name. He picked a shelter close to the Capitol because he knew the heightened security measures taken by the Capitol police, ironically, could offer an extra layer of protection for him. Those who were looking for him would expect him to be hiding off the grid. Instead, he was hiding in plain sight in the heart of the city.

Tommy thought it best not to make any calls from his cell phone or the landline at the shelter. If he needed to make a call, he could use an old payphone bank around the corner. He didn't want to do anything that would give away his location.

As he nestled into a corner of the shelter's dimly lit broom closet with his garbage bag full of Jerry's files, Tommy knew he had limited time before someone realized the closet door was locked, and he was barricaded inside. Still, it was the only place in the shelter where he would have complete privacy and could really dig into the files.

Tommy pulled out the manila folders one by one until he saw the file carrying Dr. Pietrov's name. He opened the folder and shuffled past documents with the word DRAFT written in red ink at the top of the page. He stopped when he saw, what appeared to be, a final draft of a government report. The document was bound, relatively thin, and its cover page was formal. Dr. Pietrov was listed as the author at the bottom of the page. As Tommy folded back and creased the cover page, he began to read the report's introduction:

> INTRODUCTION: The purpose of this research study is to support the conclusion that mass religious gatherings and, specifically, close proximity "corporate prayer" and "indoor, interactive religious activities," like singing and chanting, can, and should be, limited by the federal government. Because the government subsidizes non-profit organizations, including religious institutions, the federal government must regulate activity that may pose a serious health risk to the public at large. This study is meant to prove that such religious activities provide no scientific or medical benefits to practitioners and only increase health risks. This conclusion would lend credibility to certain portions of new proposed federal legislation limiting such activity, working title: "the Division Bill."

The report's second page delved into relevant historical precedent and context for the Division Bill's proposed restrictions. It cited the 1954 Johnson Amendment as justification for the government's ability to regulate religious institutions that receive government subsidies and included numerous references to states limiting certain religious activities during the COVID-19 pandemic.

Specifically, the report mentioned California's 2020 Executive Orders N-33-20 and N-60-20, which prohibited in-person worship services in California due to the threat of COVID-19. Further down the page, the report also cited the July 2020 California Department of Public Health directive that required places of worship to discontinue "indoor singing and chanting activities" and encouraged congregants to physically distance themselves from non-family members. Dozens of similar examples were cited, including references to mandatory vaccination requirements. Tommy understood the purpose of the section was to connect the dots between worship activities and the spread of viral diseases.

As he continued to skim the report, Tommy observed a plethora of graphs and charts with explanatory paragraphs under the images. He briefly glanced at one of the notations:

> The information herein expands on previous research conducted on this subject including, but not limited to John A. Astin et al., "*The Efficacy of 'Distant Healing': A Systematic Review of Randomized Trials*"; Wayne B. Jonas, "*The Middle Way: Realistic Randomized Controlled Trials for the Evaluation of Spiritual Healing*"; and the published works of Dr. Caroline Leaf.

Nearly a dozen sources were cited on the bottom half of the page. Tommy turned the page. The final portion of that section caused his jaw to drop:

All of the above research addresses a possible link between prayer and physical healing. Based on the use of new state-of-the-art technology, my research conclusions remove any speculation or doubt as to whether there is an actual scientific connection between corporate, hands-on prayer and in-person worship and physical healing. Please note that in addition to the quantitative evidence described herein, these conclusions are also supported by key scripture verses in the Christian Bible (*See*, for example, Mark 16:17, 18, "[a]nd these signs will accompany those who believe… they will place their hands on sick people, and they will get well.").

Tommy's eyes were glued to the report. Then, as his fingers found the last couple of pages, he read the Conclusion paragraph out loud:

CONCLUSION: The data included in this report overwhelmingly supports my conclusion that large groups of people (i.e., fifty or more test subjects) actually *can* influence the biological composition of a human being's diseased cells through corporate, hands-on prayer meetings and religious worship services. This phenomenon transcends the concepts of science and religion because, in fact, the evidence now shows those two concepts are not entirely separate, as has been previously suggested. Consequently, corporate prayer meetings and in-person worship should not only be allowed, but *encouraged*, for patients who are willing to participate in non-medicinal therapies to enhance, and perhaps expedite, the healing effect and transformation of diseased cells into a state of cell-regeneration and, hopefully, achieve total healing for diseased patients. I understand the potentially negative impact my findings may have on the passage of the Division Bill. Nevertheless, I must report my findings wholly and accurately. As such, it is my scientific opinion that the portions of the Division Bill restricting religious gatherings and, specifically, corporate prayer meetings and in-person worship should be removed from the legislation until further studies can be conducted to affirm or refute the evidence included herein.

Tommy turned to the very last page, and he saw something he knew was out of place in a research report – an errant "Author's Note" after the Conclusion paragraph. Tommy couldn't even blink as he read the fateful words.

AUTHOR'S NOTE: As the author of this report, I feel compelled to address an issue that has been burdening me since Senator Stephen Smythe recruited me to lead this research effort. In short, I believe Senator Smythe is trying to eradicate religion from America and attempting to use science, and the Division Bill, to support that goal. My communications with Senator Smythe over the last several months decisively affirm my suspicion that he wants this report to conclude that religion has no positive effect on critically ill patients so that he can advocate increased governmental regulation of American religious institutions and thereby dilute the religious freedom and autonomy guaranteed in the U.S. Constitution. As a person of Russian descent, I can tell you from first-hand experience, this kind of religious censorship, oversight, and overregulation *will* undermine the fabric of American society, and I believe the American people deserve to know the true purpose behind the passage of the Division Bill. As such, this Author's Note is a formal objection to the Division Bill's passage, in its current form, for the reasons stated above.

Tommy could barely breathe – what Francis Pietrov had told him the morning he died was true! He realized he had just read, arguably, the most significant scientific breakthrough and cover-up in American history. A sitting U.S. Senator trying to eliminate religion from America? The U.S. government trying to cover up scientific proof that religious practices can cause physical healing in terminally-ill patients? A chill ran down his spine.

He composed himself and dug through the trash bag to locate the file with the most recent date stamp. Perhaps there was additional relevant information in one of Jerry's newer case files that could be helpful. According to the date on the file tabs, Jerry had only one active case after Dr. Pietrov's report was developed.

Tommy opened that file and began to read. As he sorted through Jerry's handwritten notes detailing the situation, he realized he was reading another person's confidential counseling information. He located a name at the top of one of the pages.

*Sarah Mercer*, he read as he jogged his memory.

As he glanced back at the file, Tommy noticed something curious on the second page of Jerry's notes which caught his eye: *Connection to the Division Bill? See Pietrov report.*

*What did Sarah Mercer have to do with the Pietrov report?* Tommy wondered.

As Tommy continued reading Sarah's file, he realized Jerry had suggested the death of one of Sarah's twin boys could be evidence of the concerns raised in Dr. Pietrov's report. However, it was clear from the sporadic notes that Jerry had not yet fully drawn that conclusion.

Tommy spread all of the papers from Sarah's file onto the cold cement floor. Then, he took a spare notepad and pen he found on one of the nearby closet shelves and began capturing the synergies he saw between Sarah Mercer's file and Francis Pietrov's report. He spent the next twenty minutes focused on this exercise and came up with half a dozen pages of notes.

As he scribbled down his findings, he had mixed emotions. As a minister, he was elated to see scientific evidence that prayer worked. This research was groundbreaking and would convert millions of people around the world. However, it was undeniable that there were influential people actively trying to keep this information a secret. So, Tommy realized he needed a plan to get these files quickly into the right hands.

A loud banging at the closet door disrupted his moment of introspection.

"Who's in there?! You can't be in there; come on out!"

Tommy swiftly gathered the files, tossed them into his garbage bag, and opened the door.

A stern-faced night custodian confronted him.

"Were you doin' drugs in here, man?" The custodian sniffed the air a few times.

"No, sir, just needed a moment alone," Tommy said as he walked out of the closet and down the hallway. He planned to escape to the nearby payphone bank and call the number he pulled from Sarah Mercer's file. After all, she may know something that could help him. Instead, however, he was met at the door by one of the shelter's no-nonsense security guards.

"I'm sorry, sir, but we don't let folks leave after 8:00 p.m. if they plan on staying here for the night." The guard was cordial but firm in stating the policy.

"Not even to make a phone call?" Tommy asked.

"You're welcome to use the phone here, or the computer in the common area is available until 10:00 p.m. if you want to send an email." She pointed him back to the common area.

Tommy had to get in touch with Sarah Mercer as soon as possible but didn't dare make the call from the shelter's landline. He wasn't sure if Jerry mentioned the Pietrov report to Sarah or not but, if so, her life could be in danger as well.

Given his limited communication options, Tommy decided to log onto the shelter's internet to see if he could learn more about Sarah. He wouldn't be surprised if he found out she had been murdered within the last month.

However, as he searched Sarah's name online, he found a few short articles discussing a lawsuit she recently filed against the federal government. After reading one of the articles, his heart sank. The Division Act was mentioned several times – it may be too late. However, he didn't see an obituary posted, so he could only assume she was still alive. He had to get in touch with her.

Tommy repeatedly saw her attorney's name in the article and realized it might be safer for Sarah if Tommy contacted her lawyer instead of her directly. So, he wrote down the name "David Stoneman," and another quick internet search highlighted the phone number for his last listed law firm, Johnson, Allen, Peters & Branson.

Tommy logged off the computer, climbed into his assigned bunk with the trash bag filled with files tied securely to his ankle under the blanket. Tommy was exhausted and, even though there were dozens of other men snoring in the room, he was asleep in seconds.

# Chapter 35

Senator Smythe was sitting in the antique barber's chair, reading the front page of the local newspaper as the barber slathered white shaving cream on the nape of his neck. The cream had a rich aroma and felt warm on his skin. The barber unsheathed a straight razor from his drawer, which carried an ivory handle made from an elephant's tusk. He then surgically slid the sharp razor blade in a careful parallel pattern along the Senator's neck, providing a clean, smooth culmination to his overpriced haircut.

At that moment, the giant security guard entered the barbershop with Alex Mitchell and Greg Thomas. The barber was wiping Senator Smythe's neck with a hot towel and casually brushing spare hairs from the Senator's shoulders. Greg Thomas was wearing his customary three-piece suit, and Alex Mitchell donned his usual blue jacket, oxford shirt, khaki slacks, and striped tie.

"Gentlemen, welcome to the barbershop!" the Senator said as he studied his hair in the large mirror in front of him.

Alex Mitchell was confused and turned to Greg Thomas.

"I thought we were meeting at a *private club*," he remarked as he sidestepped the piles of hair on the floor.

"Greg, show Mr. Mitchell into The Senator's Club. I'll join you in a minute." The Senator didn't like to discuss business in the barbershop.

The giant man walked to the back of the room, and Greg Thomas and Alex Mitchell dutifully followed him into the closet. The barber removed Senator Smythe's apron and handed him a small mirror to review his haircut more closely.

"Looks good, Martin!" The Senator exclaimed as he handed the man a fifty-dollar bill and joined the group in the back.

Upon entering The Senator's Club, Senator Smythe noticed Greg Thomas had already treated Alex to a cigar and a scotch. They were sitting in the big green leather chairs in front of the crackling fireplace. Senator Smythe took a seat across from them and asked the giant man to bring him a drink as well.

"Wow, Senator, this place is great. Are you accepting new members?" Alex ignorantly asked as he looked around the room, like a kid in a candy shop. Senator Smythe and Greg Thomas locked eyes, and Greg Thomas spoke up.

"It's not really like that, Alex. We don't do applications here. You see, this place is financed by a group—" Senator Smythe cut off Greg Thomas mid-sentence.

"The details aren't important, Alex. What's important is that we are very generous with guest passes, for *friends*." At that moment, the giant man arrived with the Senator's three fingers of dark brown liquor in his usual monogrammed, crystal scotch glass. Senator Smythe raised his beverage to Alex. Alex returned the gesture.

"Cheers! Here's to a slam dunk victory in the Mercer case," the Senator bellowed as he took a hearty sip.

Alex winced after gulping his stiff scotch. He was not a big drinker and especially not accustomed to the bite of decades-old, imported spirits. It took him a minute to regain his composure as his nose started to run from the sting.

"Slam dunk? I'm not sure it's a slam dunk," Alex responded skeptically.

"Surely you don't think this case has any merit, do you, Mr. Mitchell?" Senator Smythe inquired.

"Actually, Senator, this one is making the DOJ sweat a bit. It's a clever angle, and it's unprecedented. We're just lucky we convinced them to mediate to keep all of the information quiet for now!"

"Meaning what?" The Senator wanted more information.

"Well, we would never tell Stoneman, but this case could be *groundbreaking*. If he had the resources to back his litigation costs, we would be screwed..." Alex could tell his answer didn't sit well with Senator Smythe, so he decided to clarify.

"Look, Senator, it's like I was telling Greg earlier, this case is the potential death knell of the Division Act. If this thing goes back to litigation, the press will cover it more closely, and other vulture ambulance chasers will just find other Sarah Mercers to file similar claims. This case *has* to be settled, and settled quickly and quietly."

Senator Smythe looked at Greg Thomas, whose head was turned toward the roaring fire.

"Well, Greg...do you agree?"

Greg Thomas snapped out of his momentary hypnosis and rejoined the conversation, "I think I do, Senator. Throw some more money at Stoneman, and he'll probably go away."

"Oh, and one more thing…" Alex chimed back in.

"What is this research Stoneman keeps referring to in his mediation statement? I had my team scour the discovery files, and they found the researcher's name but couldn't locate the final version of his report."

Greg Thomas and Senator Smythe locked eyes again.

"The report doesn't exist, Alex. Francis Pietrov was pulled off of that research study long before it was completed." Senator Smythe lied.

Alex nearly spit out a mouthful of scotch in laughter. He took another gulp and responded. Both Greg Thomas and Senator Smythe were taken aback by his brazen response.

"You expect me to believe that? So, I guess it's just coincidence that this guy was recently found murdered in his apartment here in town? I may not have gray hair, but I wasn't born yesterday, gentlemen!" Alex set down his glass on a sidetable and continued.

"Look…I don't need to know all of the details. In fact, I don't want to know all of the details. All I need to know is how the report affects us." He glanced at Greg Thomas, hoping to get some support for his request.

"The report is bad for us, but Stoneman won't find copies of the report anywhere. All copies of that document were destroyed," Greg Thomas confidently replied.

"Well, I don't want to get disbarred for this, so I'll let you hound him about the report in the opening statement at the mediation.

Sound good, Greg?"

"Fine by me." Greg Thomas responded.

Senator Smythe sat calculated and slumped into his large green leather chair, like a snake, coiled and ready to strike. He was reading the situation and social dynamic between Alex Mitchell and Greg Thomas.

*Is Alex going to talk?* he wondered. *He'll keep his mouth shut and his head in the sand if he knows what's good for him.*

Senator Smythe looked down at his scotch as it swirled in the pricey glass.

"Okay, Greg, what's the game plan for tomorrow?" The Senator asked.

"Simple, really. Alex will open with general statements about setting negative precedents, and I'll bring it home by calling Stoneman out for relying on evidence he can't produce. If we can embarrass Stoneman enough, I think he'll settle the case for pennies. Either way, we win. Like you said, slam dunk."

Senator Smythe shifted in his chair and turned his full attention to Alex. He wanted to confirm Alex's alignment with that strategy.

"Does that sound good to you?"

Alex paused for a moment and took another drink of his scotch.

"Yea, I can get on board with that."

"Good!" Senator Smythe felt confident the plan would work. He waved the giant man over.

"Can you call our lady-friends and ask them to meet us here in a half hour? I want to introduce them to my *new friend*, Alex." Senator Smythe said with a nasty smile.

The giant man nodded and disappeared to make a phone call. Alex grinned, knowing what that meant for him.

"You see, Mr. Mitchell. I've decided you're a friend of ours – and we take good care of our friends."

Senator Smythe leaned back in his green leather chair and lit a cigar, which he pulled from his left jacket pocket. Finally, he could rest easy; this whole chaotic ordeal would be over within forty-eight hours.

# Chapter 36

The next morning, David was up early. He performed the same, tried-and-tested ritual before every first day in court. He would wake up at 5:30 a.m. and go for a long jog at a fast pace, winding through the cobblestoned Georgetown side streets. He would then grab a hot shower, put on his expensive, tailored navy-blue suit, crisp white shirt, and carefully selected silk tie, which was usually light blue. After that, he enjoyed a quiet cup of black coffee as he casually gazed out his apartment's third-floor window at the traffic below. Interestingly, there was something about traffic that calmed David. It reassured him to know other people were busy as well and had places to go and things to do.

However, this morning's ritual was cut short by Mark turning on cartoons in David's living room at 7:30. David was adjusting to having roommates and, while Sarah and Mark were not a nuisance, the apartment was simply more crowded than David was used to.

Sarah emerged from the guest bedroom wearing a knee-length black skirt and a white blouse. David noticed she had put on make-up and straightened her hair. She looked nice.

Sarah walked into the kitchen and grabbed a red apple from the refrigerator's bottom drawer.

"You about ready, Sarah? Rita should be here any minute." David asked as he turned his attention to Mark.

"Hey, bud, you sure you're cool staying with Rita today?"

Mark nodded his head without looking up from the television. By now, David knew any response from Mark when he was glued to a screen was a monumental communication victory.

There was a soft knock at the door. David opened it to find Rita looking exhausted and disheveled.

"Rita...are you okay?" Rita could barely make eye contact with David.

"I'm fine, Dave." She brushed past him, sat down on the couch with Mark, and crossed her arms without acknowledging anyone else.

David knew something was wrong, but a quick look at his watch revealed they were running late and needed to leave immediately. As fate would have it, the meditation location was moved, at the last minute, of course, from a conference room at the courthouse to the Johnson Allen offices. David knew this venue change tactic was meant to throw him off his game. No doubt Greg Thomas thought it would provide a home-field advantage for his side.

David and Sarah rode the elevator down to his apartment's parking garage, got in his car, and headed for the mediation.

----

Upon arriving at the Johnson Allen offices, David and Sarah were escorted to the large conference room with which David was all too familiar. When they first filed the lawsuit, David envisioned dozens of eager reporters, bright lights, and news cameras flooding the courtroom's crowded halls on the litigation proceedings' first day. However, that was disallowed because of the Mediation Program's confidentiality requirement, so there were no reporters or news cameras. The only people in the room were Sarah, David, Charles Morison, Alex Mitchell, and Greg Thomas.

The smell of freshly-brewed coffee and toasted morning bagels wafted from a carefully placed beverage cart, which remained untouched in the corner of the room. Charles was seated at the head of the large ebony wood conference table, and the parties were on opposite sides, sitting across from one another. Once everyone settled into their seats, Charles began his opening remarks.

> Welcome! This is the first day of mediation pursuant to the rules of the United States District Court Mediation Program. The plaintiff, in this case, Ms. Sarah Mercer, through her counsel, Mr. David Stoneman, will present an opening statement, and the United States, represented by Mr. Alex Mitchell, with special counsel, Mr. Gregory Thomas III, will also be given time for an opening statement. Thereafter, each party will be escorted to a separate room. I will spend a reasonable amount of time with each party throughout the day to more fully understand each side of the argument and offer my suggestions to each party based on the facts I have available to me. I have reviewed the mediation statements submitted by both sides and will use the information and arguments in those documents to frame my initial conversation with each party. Due to the fast-tracked nature of these proceedings, this mediation is only scheduled to last two business days, today and tomorrow. If the parties have not reached a mutually agreeable settlement at the end of those two

days, I will then inform the Court, and this case will proceed through the normal litigation process. Are there any questions at this time?

Seeing that neither party had any questions, Charles invited David to present his opening statement.

David stood up, buttoned his navy suit jacket, and cleared his throat. He could feel the judgmental gaze of Alex Mitchell and Greg Thomas bearing down on him as he took one final look at his notes and began to speak.

Mr. Morison, unlike other lawsuits which cite the Division Act to challenge its constitutionality, Sarah Mercer's case is *different*. It's different because we allege the restrictions set forth in the Division Act, sponsored in Congress by Senator Stephen Smythe, specifically those restrictions related to mass religious gatherings and corporate prayer, withdrew a proven therapeutic treatment from Ms. Mercer's now-deceased minor child, Samuel Mercer. Our mediation statement highlights research conducted by the lead scientist for the Division Act, that raises a number of questions and concerns about the legislation as well. As such, the wrongful act of denying the Mercer family's right to engage in hands-on, corporate prayer was a proximate and direct cause of Samuel Mercer's untimely death. My mediation statement's attachments contain multiple medical reports that indicate Samuel's illness was identical to the disease of his twin brother, Mark. In fact, they were identical twins, with identical conditions and identical therapies, except for *one* treatment. Mark received the benefit of corporate prayer, and Samuel did not. Samuel was deprived of that therapy because such activity was rendered illegal by the federal government in the Division Act. As such, our claim is not directly contesting the Division Act's *constitutionality*, as others have done, but rather citing its illegal restrictions as the primary reason and proximate cause of why Samuel Mercer is not with us today. Consequently, we believe the government should be found liable for the wrongful death of Samuel Mercer and, his mother, Sarah Mercer, is entitled to no less than ten million dollars in damages for his wrongful death. Thank you."

David sat down and glanced at Sarah. She was teary-eyed, but a nod and slight smile relayed her approval of his opening statement.

Charles turned to Alex.

"Mr. Mitchell, your opening remarks?"

"Yes, sir, I have a few brief statements, but I would like to reserve a couple of minutes for Mr. Thomas to speak as well."

Charles agreed, and Alex began.

This lawsuit is frivolous. It's based on hypothesis and hyperbole and would set a highly dangerous precedent for cases against federal legislation in the future. The American public's ability to challenge federal legislation through the court system is a right afforded to us under the concept of separation of powers. However, the founding fathers certainly did not envision that our court system would be used by ambulance chasers trying to earn a quick buck. While the loss of Plaintiff's son deeply saddens the government, we must blame *cancer* for his death, not federal legislation, which was primarily developed to keep people safe. If plaintiffs are allowed to prevail in these types of suits, the federal government would be facing billions of dollars in litigation settlements each year. As mentioned in our mediation statement, this case is truly unprecedented and does not neatly fall within the purview of the Federal Tort Claims Act. Regardless of the creativity employed in Plaintiff's mediation statement, Plaintiff cannot show, beyond a preponderance of the evidence, that the Division Act affected her son's health *at all*. So, while Plaintiff's counsel may categorize this as a trailblazing lawsuit, the government considers it a meritless, self-indulging, wild-goose chase. And, while the government may be willing to entertain some form of settlement, we are not in the habit of caving to baseless claims, even in the face of public pressure. So, if this mediation is unsuccessful, we are fully prepared to put all of the Department of Justice resources behind this case to prevent it from setting an unfair and dangerous precedent in our country. I yield the remainder of my time to Mr. Thomas."

Greg Thomas was sitting back in his chair with a self-righteous smirk. He winked at David before standing up and finished the government's opening statement.

As Mr. Mitchell mentioned, this lawsuit is baseless. It's tragic, really. It's tragic that Plaintiff's son passed away; it's tragic that Plaintiff's counsel is dragging her through this nasty lawsuit, and it's especially appalling that Plaintiff's counsel *has lied* about the evidence in the case.

Charles was taking notes, but Greg Thomas's last comment caused him to stop and look up at the silver-haired litigator.

It's true, Mr. Morison. I have it on good authority that Mr. Stoneman lied about research that allegedly contains *proof* of the Division Act's connection to Plaintiff's son's death. Please ask Mr. Stoneman to present such evidence to support his claims regarding the research he cites in his mediation statement. I think you'll find he is unable to do so. How tragic it is that this young lawyer would lie about evidence just to get an easy payday. So, if Mr. Stoneman insists on moving forward with these proceedings by basing his core argument on research reports *which don't exist*, then I'm going to be forced to file a motion for sanctions when this case inevitably ends up back in litigation. Shame on you, Mr. Stoneman, for turning this woman's pain into your self-promotion.

Greg Thomas's admonition lingered in the air as he stood stoically, allowing his accusations to sink in like a thousand sharp knives. After a few seconds, he sat down, and Alex grinned at David, knowing they had backed him into an inescapable corner. The room was silent for a minute. David didn't know what to do or say – his gamble had just blown up in his face massively and catastrophically.

Greg Thomas thought it fitting to add one more underhanded jab at David as he leaned forward and put his hands on the table. "Sorry, son…maybe this case will teach you a lesson on what *not* to do in the future…Ms. Mercer, I'm sorry Mr. Stoneman put you in this unfortunate position."

Anger boiled up inside of David as he glared at his former boss. It was true, David initially took this case for his own self-glorification, but he had come to believe Sarah's theory had merit. Further, over the last month, he began to care for Sarah and Mark, and it pained him that Sarah had to endure his haughty opposing counsel characterize him as a disgruntled, self-serving, scum bag. He couldn't hold his tongue any longer.

"That's a load of crap, Greg, and you know it!" David yelled as he slammed his fist on the table, losing his temper. Greg Thomas sneered back at David, knowing he had gotten under his skin.

Charles quickly spoke up. "Okay, gentlemen, take it easy. Mr. Thomas and Mr. Mitchell, you can stay in this room, and Mr. Stoneman and Ms. Mercer, please follow me to another room."

Charles took Sarah and David to an adjacent conference room, and, as they entered, Charles shut the door behind them and invited everyone to sit down.

"I'm going to speak frankly. If I discover that portions of your mediation statement are based on falsified or fraudulent information, I will end this mediation today, and I, too, will recommend that you be sanctioned by the Court. Do I make myself clear, Mr. Stoneman?" His tone was stern.

"Mr. Morison, I—" David was interrupted by the loud buzz of his cell phone in his pocket. He had silenced it but not turned off the vibration feature.

"I'm so sorry; this could be my paralegal. Do you mind if I take a quick glance?"

Charles was annoyed but acquiesced.

When David pulled out his phone, all he saw on his screen were twelve terrifying words:

*I have the boy. Call me. Don't tell anyone, or he dies.*

Sarah must have read the horror on David's face.

"What's wrong, David?"

Mark was in trouble, and David and Sarah had to leave immediately.

"Mr. Morison, I'm terribly sorry, but an emergency has come up, and Sarah and I have to leave right away. I apologize, but this will have to wait a few hours. I'll call you when I know more. Again, I'm so sorry." Charles was speechless as he threw his hands up in the air, venting his frustration and disbelief.

David didn't wait for permission to be excused. He quickly rose from his chair and aggressively hand gestured for Sarah to follow him. David and Sarah flew out of the Johnson Allen parking lot, and David called the number on the text message as soon as they hit the highway. The phone rang twice, and an ominous voice answered.

"Hello, David Stoneman. Don't talk; just listen. I have the boy, and I've taken him to a secret location. I will send you an address – you and the boy's mother will go to that address *when I tell you*. You two better come alone, and if you tell anyone about this, especially the police, the boy will die. Your choice."

The line went dead. Sarah was hounding David for more information because he hadn't told her anything. Still, she sensed something was horribly wrong.

"Sarah, it's Mark…he's been kidnapped. I'm waiting on instructions on how we can get him back."

Sarah broke down in the car's passenger seat.

David didn't know if Rita was alive or dead. So, he decided to race back to his apartment and wait for the kidnapper to send further instructions.

# Chapter 37

David and Sarah sprinted into David's apartment and found Rita unconscious on the floor. A chemical stench on Rita's face indicated the kidnapper had snuck up behind her with a soaked rag and rendered her unconscious. As David leaned down to check her pulse, she began to stir.

"David?" Rita said in a weak voice as she rolled over onto her back and opened her eyes.

"Yes, Rita, I'm here. Are you alright?!"

"David, what happened?" Rita seemed to have no recollection of the event.

"Rita, where's Mark?!"

"He was sleeping on the couch, and I was sitting in the chair. That's the last thing I remember." Rita realized Mark was not in the room and began to panic.

"Oh, my goodness, is Mark okay?! Where is he?!" David knew he had to give her some of the bad news.

"Rita, I want you to stay calm." David put his hands on her shoulders; her eyes darted wildly around the room looking for the boy, and her breaths became fast-paced and shallow. She began hyperventilating. Through her belabored breathing, she managed a question.

"Just tell me, David…where is he?" Rita begged. David sighed and responded.

"He's been kidnapped, Rita. I got a text message from the kidnapper. He's going to provide instructions soon." It took a few seconds for Rita to appreciate the gravity of the fragile situation. Sarah was at the kitchen table sobbing inconsolably.

"Do you remember seeing anyone suspicious around the apartment complex? Any strange characters?" David hoped Rita would remember *something*.

Suddenly, Rita realized her comments at Martin's Tavern might be connected with Mark's kidnapping. She could barely utter a clear word but managed a couple of coherent sentences.

"It's my fault, Dave… I sold you out! It's my fault." Rita confessed as she fell into David's arms, weeping. Sarah overheard Rita's comments which triggered her maternal instinct. She grew angry at Rita's half-confession and prodded heatedly.

"What did you do to my son, Rita?! Where is he?!" Sarah screamed as she rose from her chair, grabbed Rita, and shook her. David stood by helpless, not knowing what to do and trying to make sense of Rita's confession.

"I didn't do anything to him, but I sold you and David out! That may be why *they* took him. They threatened to hurt my brother, Dave…" Rita continued as she dropped her head into her hands. Sarah let go of the sobbing woman and took a step back, realizing there was more to the story.

"*Who* threatened you? Tell me, Rita! Please!" David pleaded.

"One of Senator Smythe's cronies threatened to hurt my brother if I didn't give them information about our case. They made me tell them about Pietrov's missing research, and they know you don't have it. But I didn't know they would take Mark... I swear I didn't know!" Rita broke down again and sunk to the floor, distraught.

David was fuming, but he wasn't just upset with Rita. He knew her brother meant the world to her, and any threat to his life would be too much for Rita to bear.

*It all makes sense,* David thought, as his face reddened.

*This explains Greg Thomas's statements at the mediation. Senator Smythe's people informed him we didn't have Pietrov's research.* David's mind was racing.

His heart sank in his chest when he realized his bluff had backfired, and Sarah and Mark were the collateral damage. He had lost his job and likely lost this case, probably his law license too, and, most importantly, he lost Sarah's only remaining child. All David could do now was sit in his living room, console Rita and Sarah, and wait for further instructions from the kidnapper. He didn't think the day could get any worse – he was wrong.

# Chapter 38

The man with the slicked-back hair had accomplished his mission. He took the boy, and no one was following him. As he navigated the busy streets of Georgetown, the dark tinted windows on his black sedan prevented onlookers from possibly catching a glimpse of Mark asleep in the backseat.

As he stopped at a red light, he evaluated the pick-up just a few minutes earlier. It was a straightforward and uncomplicated operation, compared to his usual missions. He had simply scoped the apartment complex to determine the security level he was up against. The man concluded the sole unarmed security guard in the apartment's lobby would not pose a serious threat.

The rear of the building made the most sense for his entry point, so the man temporarily parked in a handicapped spot near the building's key-coded back door and picked the silver lock leading to the apartment's emergency stairwell. He then made his way to the third floor. The man was surprised to find no cameras outside the building, in the staircase, or on the third floor. For a luxury apartment complex, the security was minimal. Consequently, for him, gaining entrance was child's play.

He strode onto the third floor and located David's front door. It was a workday, and the floor was quiet, aside from the sound of a small dog barking down the hall. The man picked the lock, cracked the door, and peered inside. He saw Mark sleeping on the couch and the babysitter casually sitting in a chair with her back to the door.

He snuck in undetected. Quickly putting a chemical agent wipe over the babysitter's mouth, she fell to the floor, unconscious in seconds. Fortunately, the boy was still asleep, and the man was able to gently place the damp rag over his open mouth to ensure he would remain sleeping for another fifteen minutes until he could make his getaway.

The man picked up Mark and escaped down the back stairwell he had emerged from. He laid Mark in the backseat of his car and peeled out around the front of the building. It was one of the easiest kidnapping missions of his career. He didn't even have to shoot anyone.

The light changed to green, and his daydream replay of the operation was cut short as he turned his attention back to the road. As the man carefully crept out into the intersection, an SUV from the adjacent lane was trying to beat the red light and barreled out into the intersection, coming inches from hitting the man's front bumper. The man slammed on the breaks, and the reckless SUV swerved sideways and hit a truck in oncoming traffic.

A police cruiser parked on a nearby side street witnessed the incident and quickly flipped on the red and blue lights. The female officer jumped out of her cruiser to manage the scene. She raised her hand as she ran across the intersection, signaling to the man to keep his car stopped. The man considered speeding away but knew it was wise to oblige the cop, at least for now. The officer ran to the accident to ensure everyone involved was unharmed and did not need immediate medical attention. After a few brief comments with each driver, she then started walking back toward the man's black sedan to give him further instructions and take his statement of what had occurred.

The man only rolled down his window halfway to hear the officer's instructions, but not enough for her to see the bottom-half of his face or inside the car.

"Did you see what happened?" the officer questioned, stopping roughly twenty feet from the man's driver-side door as she waved another car past her.

"No, ma'am, I was focused on *my* light. Didn't really see anything." The man hoped the cop would buy his story and let him go.

"Well, we need to get a formal statement from you for the report, so please pull your vehicle over to the side of the road, and I'll come to talk to you in a minute."

The man interrupted the officer, "Ma'am, I *really* need to be somewhere and, like I said, I didn't see anything."

The man put his hand on his sidearm, which was resting in a holster on his hip. He could not risk Mark waking up in the car, and he knew he had less than five minutes before the chemicals began to wear off.

The policewoman was irritated by the man's uncooperative response and began walking toward his car. When the officer was just a few feet away from his door, the man put his hand on the gun's trigger. He would wait a couple more seconds, and then he would try to take the cop down with one clean shot to the head and flee the scene. But before he unholstered his weapon, the officer turned around to find the drivers of the two vehicles involved in the accident screaming at each other and getting physical in the middle of the busy Georgetown street.

The officer quickly turned back to the man.

"Okay, you can go," the policewoman said as she hurried to break up the altercation.

The man breathed a sigh of relief and pulled out his secure cell phone as he rolled up his window and carefully continued through the intersection.

"Call Henderson," the man said, triggering the phone's voice dial function.

"Henderson, here," the voice answered.

"Sir, I have the package in tow, and I'm headed to HQ pronto. ETA is ten minutes."

"10-4, we'll be waiting," Sergeant Henderson said as the line went dead.

Mark began stirring in the back seat. The man looked in the rear-view mirror and saw Mark sit up and rub his eyes.

"Hey there, Mark!" The man exclaimed in a phony pleasant tone.

"I work for Mr. Stoneman, and I'm taking you to a place to meet him and your mom. Is that okay?"

Mark was still groggy and seemed confused about why he was in a moving car, but nodded his head in approval and laid back down in the backseat to sleep.

The car's GPS defaulted to the FARCO headquarters and began recalculating when the man took an odd turn. Neither the GPS nor Sergeant Henderson knew that the man was not going to FARCO's headquarters as he had been instructed to do. Instead, he was going to Ivy City, on the Northeast side of town.

The man knew it would be approximately twenty minutes before Sergeant Henderson and the FARCO team realized he had disobeyed direct orders. However, the man had his own plans for Mark, Sarah, and David.

After several minutes of driving, he pulled into an old abandoned warehouse in Ivy City, sat in the parked car, and texted David the address with specific instructions for him and Sarah to come alone. He told them to come quickly because he knew the other FARCO operatives wouldn't be far behind.

# Chapter 39

David's cell phone buzzed loudly and illuminated on the kitchen table to alert him to a text message. Rita and Sarah were comatose on the couch, numbed by the realization Mark had been kidnapped. David was in the kitchen drinking a glass of distilled water and discarded his cup in the sink and retrieved his vibrating phone.

"We have the address!" David eagerly announced as he grabbed his car keys from the counter and headed toward the door. Rita and Sarah sprang up.

"Did the text say anything about Mark?!" Sarah anxiously asked as she hurriedly gathered her purse from a nearby end table.

"No…just the address. Sarah and I have to go alone, so, Rita, stay here and keep your phone turned on in case we need something."

Rita nodded dutifully, resumed her place on the couch, and began to bite her fingernails nervously.

David and Sarah raced down to David's car and plugged the address into the car's navigation system.

"Ivy City?" David questioned. "Why would he take Mark to Ivy City?"

"What's Ivy City?" It was apparent Sarah was unfamiliar with the location.

"It's an old area of town with a lot of abandoned buildings…
open that glove compartment for me and pull out my handgun."
David buckled his seatbelt and opened his right hand to receive
his firearm from Sarah.

Sarah did as she was instructed. She was not a fan of guns and
held the holster with just her thumb and index finger as if the
weapon were a venomous snake. David put the gun under his
driver's seat, where it could be easily accessed, if necessary. He
turned to Sarah, who was clearly unsettled by the entire situation.

"I don't think I'll have to use it, but I want it out, just in case."
Sarah gave David a half-smile and turned to look out the
window with her arms crossed.

As Sarah and David sped to the given location, the car ride
was calm, but both of them were mapping out possibilities in
their mind of what *could* happen next. And, since some of those
possibilities were unpleasant, neither person was eager to chat.

Sarah spent most of the ride reciting silent prayers for her son's
safety, and David, true to his personality, was generating several
alternative plans depending on how the situation unfolded.

As they pulled up to the short driveway leading to a large, faded-
brick warehouse, David noticed many of the building's windows
were broken, with multi-colored graffiti covering much of the
foundation. The warehouse was three stories tall, and there was
no evidence of any inhabitants.

The dilapidated building looked abandoned and was falling into
disrepair, with spotty green and brown grass with weeds crawling
up into the shattered ground-floor windows. In an abundance of
caution, David drove past the building and parked on the side
of the old road. If this were a trap, he wanted to ensure he and

Sarah could escape quickly.

"Okay, let's go. But remember – stay behind me, and if something should happen to me, grab my keys, get back to the car, and get out of here. Got it?" David unholstered his gun and turned off the safety.

"But what about Mark?" Sarah asked as she unbuckled her seatbelt.

"We can't help Mark if we're both dead…" David realized his last comment was harsh, so he clarified.

"What I mean is, we don't even know if Mark is here. So, if this situation gets dangerous, we should regroup and wait for additional instructions. Make sense?"

Sarah nodded.

As David slowly exited his vehicle, he quickly looked around to make sure he wasn't being surrounded or potentially ambushed. The afternoon sun was beating down on him, and a droplet of sweat raced from his dark hairline to the edge of his lightly stubbled chin. He clutched his weapon tightly in his right hand as he shut the driver's-side door with his left. Sarah retreated from the passenger seat and circled the back of the car to stay close behind him, as instructed. The smell of sulfur was pungent, which had, no doubt, wafted over from nearby manufacturing plants. The odor added to the situation's unpleasantness.

As they crept down the warehouse's cracked driveway, David realized there wasn't an identifiable front door. So, he continued around the side of the building until he saw a backdoor with a single light shining in a small entryway.

As they cautiously approached the rusted metal door, David's muscles tensed and his shoulders raised. He was now clutching the gun with both hands and half-expected to see a face pop up in the metal door's small rectangular window. He used his left hand to turn the rusty metal knob, which was unlocked, and pulled the squeaking door toward him. The entryway was shadowy, with a single lightbulb hanging from the ceiling. David was unsure whether or not they should enter. He couldn't see more than a few feet in front of him and didn't feel comfortable stepping into the darkness. Then he heard a voice.

"Come in, Mr. Stoneman."

The sound of the voice in the darkness sent a chill down David's spine, and he used his left leg to prop the door open as he, again, clasped his weapon tightly with both hands.

"Where are you?! Show yourself!" David shouted as he pointed the gun in multiple directions.

David heard the sound of footsteps in the distance and, in seconds, he began to see the outline of a figure wearing a dark suit emerging from the shadows.

As the man with the slicked-back hair came into the light, David trained his gun on the man's chest to ensure he would hit him if he had to fire his weapon. The man did not appear to be armed, but David wasn't taking any chances.

Suddenly, David heard a loud gasp from over his right shoulder and felt Sarah tightly squeeze his right arm. David turned to look at her – she was white as a ghost, with her eyes fixated on the man in front of them. Her jaw dropped, and her eyes began to well with tears. David darted his head back and forth between Sarah and the figure, unsure what was happening.

"Terry?! Is that you?!" Sarah uttered in disbelief.

The man with the slicked-back hair smiled warmly.

"Yes, Sarah…it's me." he calmly replied.

Sarah ran past David and embraced the man with a massive hug. Sarah drew back and looked at the man and began touching his face with tears of joy running down her cheeks.

David was confused.

"Sarah, do you know this guy?" David realized he was now pointing his gun at both Sarah and the man. Sensing the threat was not imminent, he lowered his weapon.

Sarah turned to David, full of emotion.

"Yes…he's my husband!"

# Chapter 40

The man with the slicked-back hair's name was Terry Gutierrez, and he was Sarah's allegedly deceased husband. Terry grew up on rough streets in D.C. and became involved in gangs at an early age. Even as a teenager, he was skilled at efficiently extinguishing the lives of rival gang members. The only reason Terry bothered to attend high school was to spend time with his then-girlfriend, Sarah.

Sarah showed him there was more to life than street violence, and Terry slowly began to curb his wayward trajectory. After high school, Sarah enrolled in the local junior college, and, unbeknownst to her, Terry joined the Army Reserve while trying to hold down multiple part-time jobs. He didn't want Sarah to worry about him possibly getting deployed, so he decided to secretly join the Reserve to get a taste of military life before fully committing.

Terry's commanding officer learned of his checkered past and solicited his involvement in a special anti-gang task force the military was developing in collaboration with the FBI. Terry was a natural in the role and began infiltrating gangs in many major cities. He would then filter valuable information back to the bureau, which led to dozens of high-profile arrests.

Terry eventually told Sarah about his military service but was instructed to lie about the details of his position. So, all Sarah knew was he was in the Army Reserve and was called out-of-town for "training" for weeks at a time. After all, any leaked information, even to Sarah, could jeopardize the entire covert operation – that was not a risk the FBI was willing to take.

By then, Sarah learned she was pregnant and expressed concerns about Terry's ability to support their growing family. Terry was in too deep with the gang-infiltration operation to easily extract without landing on the gangs' hit lists, which, in turn, would put his family in danger. He was heartbroken by the reality he would not see his twin boys grow up, but he knew his number one job as a father was to keep them safe. Consequently, there was only one way to ensure their safety and anonymity – he would have to fake his own death.

A simple falsified story about an old gang feud was a logical cover story, and the government-planted corresponding article in the local newspaper gave his cover legitimacy. The fake funeral was small and sparsely attended. Terry watched from a couple hundred yards away as the love of his life wept and draped herself across his empty, American-flag-covered casket.

After the funeral, Sarah recognized Terry's volatile past could also pose a threat to her boys, so she changed their last name back to her maiden name, Mercer, to protect them.

With no more family tethers, Terry became a full-time contractor with the FBI. He was deployed worldwide and injected into a variety of gang-related incidents on multiple continents.

He was one of the bureau's best deep cover resources until he took a witness interrogation too far and stabbed a Japanese gang leader in the back, paralyzing him. After that, his cover was blown, and the government disavowed any relationship with him. In his mind, the bureau left him hanging out to dry to save themselves from embarrassment in a Congressional hearing. As a result, he became a mercenary, providing his services to the highest bidder, and business was good. FARCO found him in

West Africa on an operation for some unsavory characters and gave him an offer to join their growing team in Washington.

Until that moment, Terry had successfully avoided any contact with his wife or his son for nearly a decade. All he had to do was stay away, and they could live a happy life. Nevertheless, Terry had rehearsed what he was going to say if they were reunited. Now that moment was here, he was speechless.

"Sarah, I'm so sorry…" was all Terry could manage as he held her tight.

"I want you to know I did it to keep you and the boys safe. It was the only way."

"Did you know about Samuel?" Sarah asked through her tears as she clung to Terry.

"Yes, I knew. But, because you changed your last name, no one in my organization made the connection between you and me. I'm shocked that slipped through the cracks, but I'm glad it did."

Terry glanced at David and nodded. David put his gun back in his waistband.

"Listen, Sarah, I've done many bad things, and I'm stuck in this life forever. When I realized you and Mark were targets, I kidnapped him so another operative wouldn't take him instead."

"Where is he? Where's Mark?" Sarah eagerly asked as she looked around the shadowy space.

"He's watching television down the hall." Terry pointed down the dark hallway.

"This place is my personal hideout. Not even my organization knows about it. But when they realize I didn't bring Mark to their headquarters, as I had been instructed, they will use their considerable resources to hunt me down, and they *will* find us. You and Mark can't be here when they do."

"What organization do you work for?" David asked as he peeked down the dilapidated hallway.

"I'm sorry, Mr. Stoneman, but the less you all know about my organization, the better...trust me on that." Terry put his hand on Sarah's back, prodding her to follow David down the hall toward the sound of the television as he locked the back door.

"Terry, I don't understand...why can't you come with us?" Sarah asked as her red eyes looked back at him.

"You're in danger when you're near me, Sarah."

"But, I—" Terry cut her off before she could finish.

He stopped her midway down the hall, leaned in, and kissed her. Sarah wished that kiss could last forever, but it was brief. Terry knew they didn't have much time.

It had been years since Sarah had kissed her husband, and she let the joy of that moment slowly wash over her. Her happiness turned to relief when she saw Mark and ran to give him a big hug.

"Are you okay, baby?" Sarah studied Mark's face to ensure he didn't have any cuts or scratches.

"Yea, mom, I'm fine. Terry has been great! He gave me soda and chips and let me watch the baseball game."

David studied the small dingy room they had entered. It was

musty and roughly the size of a walk-in closet. Two metal folding chairs sat upright in the middle of the room; an Army-green sleeping bag was packed neatly in one corner, and a small portable refrigerator was oddly placed on the floor near the door. An old television sat on a wooden box in another corner of the room next to a cheap, plastic side table, upon which was a black backpack and two long rifle bags. As David looked up, he saw a single, unshielded light bulb nestled tightly against the ceiling, which carried years of brown and black water stains that crept down the walls. Needless to say, David didn't want to stay for long.

Terry turned to David and lowered his voice to an intense whisper.

"He was asleep on the couch when I arrived at your apartment. He woke up in my car on the way here. I told him I was a friend of yours. I didn't tell him who I am. It's easier like that. By the way, is the babysitter alright?" Terry removed his suit jacket and put it on top of the black backpack.

"She's a little shaken up but seems fine." David was still uncertain how to handle the situation. He wasn't sure if Terry could be trusted. David decided to prod a bit further.

"Just tell me this, are you working for Senator Smythe? Why do these people want us dead?"

"I'm working for the people Senator Smythe works for. The Senator thinks he's in charge, but he's just a puppet. This game is much bigger than him." Terry picked up one of the rifle bags and unzipped it, revealing an automatic assault rifle.

"How long have you been tracking us?" David wasn't finished with his interrogation.

"You were a *secondary* target. A scientist was the primary target. That's what started this whole thing; some scientist wrote something that pissed off Smythe."

David's face turned white.

"Are you talking about Francis Pietrov?"

Terry looked at David, surprised to hear him say that name.

"Yea, how do you know that?" David had Terry's undivided attention.

"Our case. Well, Sarah's case, needs the information he had. Did you collect any reports or documents from him by any chance?"

"No, I was just sent to kill him. They didn't tell me much, but whatever he knew must have been *very* important." Terry returned his attention to his weapon and looked through its scope.

A chill ran down David's spine. He was right! Francis Pietrov did have secret information that was buried.

Again, David grew uneasy when he realized he was just feet away from Dr. Pietrov's killer, who was now wielding a high-powered rifle.

"As I said, I'm just a hired gun. I do what I'm told. I'm sorry if he was your friend."

Terry started unpacking the other rifle bag and opened the black backpack to reveal additional handguns. Sarah was quietly sitting in one of the metal chairs with Mark, processing the realization that her husband, the father of her children, was a hitman for a secret government agency.

Terry finished loading his guns and looked at David as if he just remembered something.

"By the way…there was *another man* who Pietrov was in contact with. A minister from South Carolina. He's here in D.C. now, I think. His name is Tommy Felton. They had me track him too, but I lost him in town a few days ago. He may have some more information for you."

At that moment, Terry, David, and Sarah heard a loud bang at the now-locked backdoor.

"They're here…" Terry said ominously as he grabbed an assault rifle and put a handgun in his leg holster.

He walked over to Mark, who was still watching the baseball game. This was a moment he had hoped would come – unfortunately, it was only to say goodbye.

"Hey buddy, be good for your mom, okay?" Terry kissed the top of Mark's head, not knowing what else to do.

Mark was confused by the interaction but nodded and quickly turned his attention back to the television.

Terry pulled Sarah by the arm into the hallway, with David following.

"You see the third door on the right?" Terry pointed even further down the dark hallway.

Sarah nodded.

> Behind that door, there is a secret stairwell that will take you up to the street in front of this building. I'm sure they have people on all sides of the warehouse, but I'll draw their fire at the backdoor, which will bring all the

operatives to the backside of the building. Take Mark and wait at that front door. Count to ten after you hear the first gunshots, then exit the door and sprint toward the main street. When you get to the street, make a left. One block down is a major thoroughfare. Your getaway should not take more than *sixty* seconds. Did you drive here?

"Yes, my car is parked just down the street. Once we get to the car, I'll get us out," David stated confidently. Terry continued.

"Okay, head back to David's apartment and stay out of sight. Pack your things and get somewhere off the grid for the night. You understand?"

"Terry...I lost you once...we have a chance to start over...please come with us!" Sarah pleaded. Terry shook his head.

"Sarah...I can't. If I run with you, it will only put a bigger target on your back. Let me finish this for you and Mark. I owe you both that much." Sarah folded her arms, hung her head, and nodded as she sniffled and held back more tears.

David removed the gun from his waistband in case they ran into trouble at the front door. Sarah retrieved Mark and explained they had to leave right away. Mark was irritated by the urgency of the request but sensed his mother's stress and acquiesced.

As they began to leave, Terry grabbed Sarah and kissed her one last time. David hurried Mark down the hall to prevent him from seeing the exchange, which would inevitably draw difficult questions.

"I love you, Sarah. I always have; raise him well!"

With that, Terry started down the dark hallway toward the backdoor. Sarah watched as the love of her life left her for the second time. She wiped her tears and ran to join the others. Sarah met up with Mark and David at the secret stairwell, and they began their ascent to the street level.

As Terry approached the backdoor, the bangs grew louder. The FARCO operatives were using a battering ram, trying to break down the door. He knew they would be in soon. Terry glanced back down the hall to make sure his wife and son were gone and positioned himself behind a wall adjacent to the door.

Another bang, and the door flew open. Two operatives came through the doorway, and Terry took both of them out with shots from his assault rifle. He waited a couple more seconds, knowing other operatives would be close behind. Another one came through the door firing, which peppered the corner of the wall in front of Terry. He took cover. The shadows on the wall indicated three more men had entered the building. Terry kneeled to get a lower vantage point and fired in the direction of the door.

By that time, the FARCO operatives had strategically taken cover inside the building's entryway. Terry traded gunfire with them, hitting one of them in the hip. Then, as he fell to the floor, Terry finished him with a clean headshot.

He saw a flash of light to his left, out of his peripheral vision. Terry felt a warm burn on his left arm and inhaled the smell of burnt flesh. He was hit. The weight of the assault rifle was now unbearable with just one good arm, so he drew his pistol from his leg holster. If he was going down, he was going down in a firefight. Terry turned the corner and fired four shots at the other operatives covered in body armor before absorbing multiple shots to his chest. He fell to his knees and uttered the word "sixty" before falling over dead.

----

Meanwhile, on the other side of the building, David and Sarah followed Terry's instructions to a tee. They climbed the secret stairwell to the warehouse's hidden front door. After ten seconds of gunfire, they opened the door and ran through the patchy grass in front of the building. They made a left and arrived safely at David's parked car. By then, nearby pedestrians were curiously looking in the warehouse's direction, concerned by the sound of gunshots. David knew they had to flee the scene immediately. He could still hear the pops of the gunfight, which sounded like firecrackers.

Mark was upset at that point, not understanding what was happening but recognizing the seriousness of the situation. Sarah was doing her best to console him as she buckled him into the backseat. David put his car into drive and looked down at his watch. It had been sixty seconds, and the sound of gunfire stopped. As they sped away, David realized Terry Gutierrez had saved their lives by surrendering his own.

# Chapter 41

Rita was pacing back and forth in David's living room. She was worried. She was worried about her brother's safety in prison, she was worried about David and Sarah, and she was worried about Mark. David had instructed her to stay in his apartment and not to speak with anyone until they returned.

She sat on the couch and opened her laptop. Upon checking her email, she saw multiple messages from Charles Morison to David to which she had been copied. Charles was not happy with David and Sarah for racing out of the mediation without much explanation.

In his last email, Charles said if he didn't hear from David by the end of the business day, he would consider the mediation failed and send the case back to Judge Callaway with a suggestion David be sanctioned for his unprofessional actions. Rita knew she would have to respond on David's behalf.

She drafted a short, fabricated email saying Sarah's son had an emergency and Sarah was unable to return to the mediation that day. Consequently, David was unwilling to attend the proceedings without his client. It was mostly true and explained David and Sarah's quick departure and non-responsiveness.

Rita also assured Charles that both David and Sarah would be present the following day, as scheduled. That may have been wishful thinking. However, she hoped her email would dissuade

Charles from prematurely involving Judge Callaway.

Rita set her laptop on an empty couch cushion and let her thoughts wander back to the dire situation at hand. She got choked up at the thought her coerced confession at Martin's Tavern may have severe consequences. She ran her hand through her graying hair and walked over to the living room window. She needed to feel the sunshine on her face, even if it was just through the glass.

Her momentary respite was interrupted by a sharp dinging sound from her computer, indicating she had a new email. She walked back to her laptop and saw an immediate response email from Charles. His response was concise and direct: *This conduct is highly irregular, and I expect a full explanation first thing tomorrow morning.*

Based on his response, Rita was confident Charles would take no further action that day. She was glad she had bought David and Sarah a bit more time. Feeling a slight sense of relief, Rita realized she misplaced her cell phone and glanced around the room to find it.

After a few moments of searching, she finally located her phone under the couch. It must have fallen out of her pocket. Rita noticed her ringer was turned to silent, and she had missed a call and voicemail from an unknown number.

She suspected it was Charles trying to reach David. However, as she listened to the voicemail, she didn't recognize the Southern accent of the caller but knew it wasn't Charles Morison.

> Hello, this message is for David Stoneman. I understand you may work with him. My name is Tommy Felton, and I got your number from one of your former colleagues at Johnson, Allen, Peters, and Branson. I have some

information that may help the case of Sarah Mercer. I really need to speak with Mr. Stoneman right away, but I would prefer to talk in person, so please have him contact me at 202-555-1986 as soon as possible. When he calls me back, please ask for *Bill Jones*. I can meet with him anytime today. Thank you.

Rita sensed this could be a promising lead and jotted down the message on a blank page of a yellow legal pad. She would inform David as soon as he walked in the door.

# Chapter 42

A call was made from a secure line in the FARCO headquarters to Senator Smythe's office on Capitol Hill. Senator Smythe was expecting the call and picked up after the first ring.

"Hello?" the Senator answered as he pounded his leg on the corner of his large desk.

"It's Henderson."

Senator Smythe was silent for a couple of seconds as he winced in pain until the throbbing ache in his right thigh began to subside.

"Well, Sergeant, I was told there was an issue...what is it?" Senator Smythe stretched out his leg to the side of his desk and untangled the chord of his dated landline phone.

"Sir, we had a snafu, but we fixed it."

"What do you mean a *snafu*? Greg Thomas told me Stoneman and the lady ran out of the mediation, and they haven't been seen since. This case should be thrown out by now!"

Sergeant Henderson took a deep breath and replied, "Sir, one of our operatives went rogue."

"What?! Went *rogue*?! How?!"

"Our guy took the boy to one of his secret locations. It's unclear *why* he took the boy, but we're looking into it. We had to take the operative out, and the boy is still in the wind, sir."

"You're looking into it?!" The Senator barked into the phone. The pain in his leg was nothing compared to the growing pain in his chest, which began shooting down his left arm.

"Well, sir, it hasn't been confirmed by our intel team, but we believe the operative may have been the boy's father and Ms. Mercer's husband. He was thought to be deceased."

Senator Smythe grew furious as the conversation continued.

"You mean to tell me, the primary FARCO operative assigned to deal with this situation was *married* to the plaintiff in this lawsuit?! How could you have missed that, Henderson?!" Senator Smythe screamed as his face turned blood red. His tone caused Tim to race into the office, thinking the screams were for him. However, he quickly retreated as Senator Smythe aggressively swatted him away.

Sergeant Henderson held his tongue. He was growing tired of the Senator's belittling accusations.

"Sir, this operative was one of our best. Unfortunately, the woman legally changed her name and the name of her sons. We didn't have much time to gather intel on the *secondary* targets, sir. There won't be any more mistakes."

"Do you know where Stoneman and the woman are now?"

"No sir, not yet, but we'll find them. The whole situation should be resolved shortly, sir."

"It had better be, Henderson. Or else..." Senator Smythe

threatened and then promptly slammed down the phone with such force that it nearly broke the receiver.

The Senator hobbled around his posh office. This state of affairs was becoming a pressure cooker, and Senator Smythe suspected it could blow up at any minute. He decided to call Greg Thomas and get his input. Things were getting out of hand, and this situation had to be contained *immediately*.

# Chapter 43

David, Sarah, and Mark entered David's apartment to find Rita still biting her fingernails and sitting at the kitchen table, looking uneasy. However, when Rita saw them, she sprung out of her chair and searched David's face for any sign of comfort.

"Is he okay?! Is Mark okay?!" Rita frantically asked.

Mark popped his head out from behind David and smiled. He then secured a spot on the couch and turned on the television.

"He's fine." David responded with a reassuring smile.

Rita let out a sigh of relief and collapsed back into her kitchen chair.

"I was so upset, Dave. I'm so glad you found him...where was he?"

David didn't have time to tell Rita the *whole* story, but he took a few minutes to give her the highlights. He also told her they were still in danger and asked if anyone came to the apartment while they were gone.

"Wait a minute...you're telling me a *secret government agency* is after us, and one of their operatives drugged me and took Mark?"

"Pretty much…"

"And they're coming *here, now?*"

"I don't know if they're coming here or not, Rita. We were told to get off the grid, but I just don't think we can do that at this point. I mean, where would we go?"

Rita's face froze as her eyes grew big, and she began to piece together the magnitude of the situation. She then snapped out of her momentary daze.

"Uh, to answer your question, no. No one came by, but someone called my cell looking for you."

"Was it Morison?"

"No, Morison *emailed* you. He wasn't thrilled about you running out of his mediation, that's for sure. So, I responded and told him you would be at the mediation first thing tomorrow – he seemed peeved but said he would talk with you in the morning."

"And the phone call?" David opened the refrigerator and retrieved a pre-made protein shake, which he chugged down in a matter of seconds.

"The call was from some guy who said he had information about the case and wanted you to call him back. He had a Southern accent, and I didn't recognize his name. I've got his number here if you want it."

David initially brushed off Rita's comment, assuming the caller was a low-level press contact at a second-rate publication wanting an update on the case's status. Unfortunately, due to the mediation's confidentiality requirements, David wouldn't be able to discuss much.

Sarah took the seat next to Mark on the couch. She was still in shock. Her eyes were puffy and swollen from crying – she was internally processing the day's events. David decided to retreat to his bedroom and change his shirt, which was soaked in sweat. As he was changing into a golf shirt in his bathroom, the thought suddenly hit him.

*What if the missed call on Rita's phone was from Terry's other target? The guy who knew Pietrov. Didn't Terry say he was from the South?*

David didn't bother to tuck in his shirt and jogged out to the kitchen.

"Rita, give me that guy's name and phone number. I'm going to call him right now."

Rita dutifully handed over the contact information on the yellow legal pad. He read the names *Tommy Felton* and *Bill Jones*. Tommy Felton was the name Terry mentioned.

"Why are there *two* names here? Which person called?"

"I thought it was odd too, but in the voicemail, he initially said his name was Tommy Felton but instructed you to ask for *Bill Jones* when you called him back."

David shook his head in confusion, dialed the number, and put the call on speakerphone.

"Hello, Good Samaritan Homeless Shelter."

"Yes, hi, this is David Stoneman returning a call from a Mr. Bill Jones. Is he available?"

"Let me check." The phone was silent for a minute. Then someone picked up. It was obvious they were out of breath.

248

"Mr. Stoneman?" the voice said in a breathless Southern accent.

"Yes, this is David Stoneman. Is this Bill or Tommy?"

"Both, I'll explain later. I have some information about your case with Ms. Mercer."

"Okay, *what is it*?" David asked as he took the phone off speaker and put it up to his right ear.

"I don't feel comfortable sharing it with you over the phone. Can you come to the Good Samaritan Shelter?"

"Sir, I'm not sure I can do that right now. But if you can send me an email or just tell me over the phone what the information is, I can determine if it's relevant to our case."

The phone was silent for a second. Then the voice on the other end of the line responded in a hushed whisper.

"I have documents I think you'll want to review…"

A spring of hope and curiosity welled up inside David. *Could I really be that lucky?* He wondered.

"Okay, give me the shelter's address; I'm coming now."

Tommy gave David the address and told him he would be waiting just inside the front doors and would jump in David's car when he arrived. Tommy didn't want to risk standing out in the open. David gave Tommy the make and model of his car and said he would be there in less than ten minutes.

David hung up the phone and told Rita and Sarah what Tommy had said and promised he would return shortly. David made sure his gun was in his waistband and hurried down to his black BMW. He had to move fast.

----

As David pulled up to the Good Samaritan Homeless Shelter, an older man with face scruff, a baseball cap, and wearing gym clothes hurried out of the front door with a garbage bag in his hand. He climbed into David's passenger seat. David thought he recognized the man but couldn't place him. Nevertheless, he had one hand on his gun, just in case this was a setup.

"Mr. Stoneman?" The man asked in a Southern accent as he put out his hand for an introductory shake. David recognized his distinctive voice from their call.

"It's nice to meet you. Let me pull into a safer spot." The men shook hands, and David pulled his car into an open street parking space. Once the car was safely parked, David turned to the man and asked his first question.

"First off, is it Bill or Tommy?"

"My name is Tommy Felton. I checked into the shelter with a fake name so *they* wouldn't find me."

"They?" David asked.

"Over the last few weeks, I believe I have been the target of a hitman who is trying to kill me. And, I think it's because I have information the government wants to keep quiet. Information I think is related to your case."

"Go on," David responded with growing optimism.

"You see, I received a call from a friend of mine, a scientist, who told me a secret—"

David interrupted, "Francis Pietrov?"

Tommy looked stunned and drew back in his seat. "Yes, how did you know that?"

"I'll tell you in a minute; please continue." David was eager to hear the rest of the story.

"Anyway, Francis told me a secret, and that night a man showed up at my house and killed my wife and tried to kill me. I've been on the run ever since. That's why I'm staying here under a fake name." Tommy pointed over his shoulder to the shelter.

"Okay, but on the phone, you said something about *documents*? Did Pietrov give you any documents?"

"Not exactly…I visited one of Francis's friends here in town, a guy named Jerry Hatfield, and *he* had copies of files the government tried to bury. They killed Jerry, but I was able to escape with these files."

Tommy held up the garbage bag. David looked at the bag as if it contained gold.

David snapped out of it when Tommy's words sunk in. "Wait, did you say *Jerry Hatfield*?"

"Yea, he was a counselor at the Fellowship Presbyterian Church in Foggy Bottom." After thinking for a moment, it clicked for David.

"I knew Jerry too." As he uttered the words, he felt sad the man who had been so kind to him in his hour of need was now dead. His momentary reflection was interrupted by another epiphany.

"Wait a second – I *have* met you before. You were at the church a few weeks ago talking to Jerry after the special service, weren't you?"

"Actually, yes!"

"I was there that night as well! You looked like you had been in an accident." David intentionally omitted that he had mistaken him for a homeless man begging for money on the sidewalk.

Tommy rolled up his sleeves to reveal healing burns and pointed to his neck and cheek.

"My beard grew out to cover the burns on my face, but, yea, I was in an accident. The hitman burned down my home with my wife and me still inside." He continued and held up the garbage bag a second time.

"But getting back to this…I read an article about Ms. Mercer's lawsuit, and I believe these documents can help her case. I'm giving them to you to ensure their safety. I was also hoping you could help get them into the hands of folks who can expose these people and protect us. Once the truth is out, I'll be able to go home!"

David was elated and terrified at the same time. He was now in possession of leaked documents the federal government assigned a crew of lethal assassins to keep hidden. David looked around cautiously. He saw a large gentleman in a tan jacket standing near the crosswalk on an adjacent street. It was unmistakable the man was looking at them. David glanced out his driver-side door and across the street where he saw a white van with no discernable company logo. The driver was meticulously dressed and was glaring at David.

"We have to go…you're coming with me." David put the car in drive and raced back to his apartment as the sun set over Washington.

# Chapter 44

As David and Tommy pulled into the parking garage, it was obvious they were being followed. The white van David saw near the homeless shelter was closely tailing them. Luckily, the garage's tenant keycard access forced the van to divert and park across the street from David's apartment complex.

David regretted not being more careful with the pick-up. Terry Gutierrez mentioned he had lost Tommy in D.C., and David had inadvertently led the operatives right back to him. Now, it was his job to keep Tommy safe.

As David parked his car, he pulled out his cell phone and called the apartment complex's front desk. The doorman answered.

"Hi, this is David Stoneman in Apartment 305. I just wanted to let you know there is a suspicious white van parked outside of the complex. Can you look into that for me?"

"We'll address that right away, Mr. Stoneman."

David knew the protocol for his apartment security was to call the police for any suspected illegal activity or suspicious characters on or near the premises. A police cruiser would arrive in minutes, and the operatives would be forced to leave the scene, at least for a while. David just bought some time, but not much.

He escorted Tommy into the elevator and up to his third-floor apartment. They walked in to find Rita and Mark playing a card game on the floor in the middle of the living room. Sarah was still sitting on the couch, wrapped up in the fetal position in a blanket.

"Welcome back!" Rita said as she continued playing go-fish with Mark. Sarah slowly and rigidly rose from her position on the couch.

"Hi, I'm Sarah," she said sheepishly without making eye contact as she shook Tommy's hand. It was evident to David she was simply being cordial to mask the emotional pain she was trying to process. However, her veiled attempts at hiding her distress were unconvincing to Tommy.

"Ah, yes! Ms. Mercer, of course. I'm so sorry to hear about the loss of your son, ma'am. As a minister, I have dealt with many folks who experienced the death of a child. I know it's tough!" Tommy said empathetically with a warm smile.

Sarah nodded in appreciation and retreated to the far end of the couch. Tommy moved to the center of the room and crouched down to converse with Rita and Mark, still immersed in their card game.

In the kitchen, David didn't waste any time pulling the files out of Tommy's garbage bag and sprawling them out on the table. He saw a file with Sarah's name on it and opened it. After realizing it contained personal information, David quickly hid it from view. He didn't want her to feel embarrassed by having her private information out in the open. David would ask her about it later.

"It's that one…that's Pietrov's report," Tommy pointed as he walked into the kitchen.

David sat down at the table and began poring over the document. It was getting dark outside, and he knew operatives could break down the door at any moment. David had to read everything he could before it was too late. Luckily, Johnson Allen trained him well, and he was able to review documents with lightning speed.

David smiled as he read each paragraph. *This was it! This was his golden ticket!* David's mind was racing. When he came to the Conclusion paragraph, his jaw dropped; he then quickly flipped the page to find the Author's Note. As he read the final sentence, he looked up at Tommy in disbelief.

"No way…" was all David could manage to say. Tommy was nodding, affirming the magnitude of the reveal.

David didn't take time to digest what the report meant for the country's future. Instead, he raced into his home office, scanned the document into his laptop, and printed another copy. He used the second copy to highlight key portions of text and write notes in the margins. David planned to take this evidence into the mediation the following day. Greg Thomas would be speechless, and the government's settlement number would skyrocket in an instant.

David paused for a moment – he had an idea. He printed a *third* copy of the report. He then carefully placed it into a letter-sized manila envelope that he sealed and inserted into a larger mailing envelope along with a handwritten note that he scribbled out on a half sheet of paper.

He jotted down a name and an address in the center of the envelope and affixed two stamps to the top right corner. David then ran down the hall to the mail deposit, dropping the envelope into the outgoing mailbox, and hurried back to his apartment to join the others. He hoped the envelope would make it to its secret intended recipient.

By that point, Rita was taking a break from playing with Mark and was casually standing in the living room listening to Tommy describe his treacherous journey from South Carolina. David felt better. All he had to do was show up at the mediation the next day with the Pietrov report, and the case should be finished. All of this would be behind him, and he and Sarah would emerge victorious.

Suddenly, the apartment lights went out, and three gunshots sailed through David's living room window. The sound of shattered glass echoed throughout the dark room. David hit the ground. He couldn't see anything but felt a warm body fall on his legs and heard Rita let out a blood-curdling scream.

He heard Mark yelling for his mother and recognized Sarah's frantic voice as they found each other behind the couch. David pulled his gun from his waistband and waited for more gunfire, but it never came. He turned on the flashlight feature on his cell phone and shined it across the room. He saw Sarah and Mark huddled behind the couch and Tommy hiding under the kitchen table.

David looked down and found Rita draped across his legs, gasping for air. It looked like one of the bullets hit her in the back and likely punctured a lung.

"No, no, no, no," David repeatedly shouted as he leaned over her.

"Please, Rita, no! We're going to get you to the hospital!"

Rita could only utter three words.

"Help me, Dave," she pleaded as her shirt began to redden with blood. She clenched David's shoulders as her eyes widened, and she continued to gasp for air.

Sarah covered Mark's eyes and looked on helplessly as Rita gulped a few times and then stopped breathing. She was gone.

"Rita?! Rita?!" David yelled as tears began to flow down his face.

David positioned Rita on her back on the floor and furiously crawled over to the window. He peeked over the windowsill, looking for any signs of the gunman. Instead, all he saw were dim lights from adjacent buildings and the red brake lights from cars on the street below. Performing a quick calculation of the bullet's trajectory, David concluded the shot must have come from one of the buildings across the street.

He collapsed in shock and leaned up against the living room wall. By then, the lights had come back on, and he saw the horrified faces of Mark, Sarah, and Tommy. David was speechless and heartbroken. Rita was like a second mother to him, and now she was dead.

Just then, the terrifying thought registered to David that the gunman may be making his way to the apartment to finish the job. He instructed everyone to stay down as he crawled across the living room floor to his front door.

"Guys…over here, we have to move!" David said in an urgent whisper.

He opened the door and ushered everyone out into the hall, still on their hands and knees. The hallway was empty and quiet.

"David, you're bleeding! Are you okay?" Sarah asked.

"I'm not hit…this is from Rita. Is anyone else hurt?" The group examined themselves.

"I led them to you…I'm so sorry!" Tommy said, distressed.

"No, they were onto us before I picked you up," David reassured as he attempted to deescalate emotions and devise an escape strategy.

"We have to take the back stairs down to my car in the garage. We're not safe here." David led the group down the stairwell with gun in hand. He vigilantly opened the metal door leading to the parking garage. His car was just a few feet from the stairwell door on purpose, just in case they had to make a quick getaway.

As David stepped into the garage, gunfire rang out from the street-side garage entrance. David could feel the bullets whizzing by his head.

"Get to the car!" David yelled as they ran toward his black BMW.

David fired four shots in the direction of his assailants. He didn't know if he hit anything, but gunfire stopped just long enough for the group to reach the vehicle. David remote-started the engine, opened the passenger-side door, and slid into the driver's seat.

As the passenger doors closed, he put the car in drive and sped toward the exit. The others were doubled over in the back seat, keeping their heads down. David saw a burly operative blocking the outlet by standing in the middle of the lane with an assault rifle. David stuck his pistol out the drivers' window and fired two more shots at the man. One of the shots hit him in the leg. The operative dropped his weapon and fell to the pavement, writhing in pain.

David blew past the fallen operative, nearly hitting him with his car's front-left bumper, then sailed through the exit gate and onto Wisconsin Avenue. He quickly veered down a side street and glanced in the rear-view mirror. No one was following him. David was sure he had taken the assailants by surprise when he began shooting back at them.

Still, he had to think. Mark was in the backseat crying, and Sarah was trying to calm him. Tommy was crouched down beside them, attempting to stay out of sight.

*What are we going to do?* David wondered as sweat dripped down his forehead. A comment came from the backseat.

"This has to be the same guy who is after me. The same guy who killed Pietrov," Tommy blurted out.

"Well, Tommy, I can promise it's not the guy who was tracking you," David said as he took an aggressive left turn down another street and glanced in his rear-view mirror.

Tommy popped his head into the front seat.

"How do you know that?" Tommy asked.

"I know because the man who was tracking you is Sarah's husband, and when he realized his family was in danger, he helped us get away from the people who were just shooting at us."

It took a minute for the difficult news to sink in. Trying to make sense of the situation, Tommy continued, "Well then, *who* are the people trying to kill us?"

"Not sure…a government agency of some kind. They are trying to bury Pietrov's research at all costs!"

"Why don't we just go to the cops?" Sarah pleaded, eavesdropping on the conversation.

"We don't know if we can trust the police. For all we know, the guys shooting at us *are* police. And, if we go to the wrong people, we're dead!" David responded.

David needed a plan. He attempted to tap into his thinking-while-driving talent, which had served him so well in the past. Then it hit him – there was only one surefire way the operatives would stand down. It was risky, but it was his only choice.

He pressed the voice activation button on his cell phone and said, "Call Greg Thomas."

# Chapter 45

Greg Thomas was surprised to see David calling him so late. He glanced down at his gold Rolex watch and answered.

"Hi, Dave, ready to drop the case?" Greg Thomas joked as he loosened his pink silk Tom Ford tie.

"Not a chance, Greg. I'm calling to let you know the game has changed a bit, and I want to lay down *new* ground rules." David was angry, and his stern tone sharply relayed that message.

"Piss off, Stoneman. You're not calling the shots; *we are*. You don't have a leg to stand on here, and you know it."

The line was silent for a couple of seconds, and Greg Thomas looked down at his phone to ensure it hadn't disconnected. Finally, David broke the awkward silence.

"You can't see it, Greg, but I'm smiling on the other end of this phone. You want to know why, you arrogant jackass?"

"Sure…" Greg Thomas condescendingly responded.

"Before I tell you, ask Senator Smythe to call off his goons. Second, meet me at the Johnson Allen offices in one hour."

Greg Thomas had his feet perched up on his desk and was pouring a three-finger portion of bourbon.

"Now, why would I do that, Davey?" Greg Thomas chuckled as he took a sip of his expensive drink.

"Because I have the missing Pietrov report...and if you don't do what I'm telling you to do, I'll release it to every major news network *tonight*. You think I'm bluffing? Try me; I dare you. See you in an hour at the office." David said as he abruptly hung up.

Greg Thomas immediately pulled his feet down from the desk and leaned forward in his chair. He was speechless, in disbelief by what he had just heard.

*He's bluffing; that report was destroyed – wasn't it?*

He set his drink down on a white stone coaster and decided to call Senator Smythe on his private line – the phone rang once.

"Hello?"

"Senator, it's Greg. We may have a problem. Stoneman claims to have the missing Pietrov report and wants to meet me at the firm in an hour. He wouldn't want to meet unless he had *something*."

"Do we know if he's telling the truth?" Senator Smythe nervously asked as he ran his hands through his thinning hair.

"I don't know, but we have to find out. You need to call off the FARCO team *now*! He said if they didn't back off, he would release the report to the press, and we can't afford to take that risk. I'll call Alex Mitchell and get him over here too."

Senator Smythe became anxious.

"If he has the report, we cannot let him release it – even if that means taking him out. I will go to those lengths to protect this information. And Greg?"

"Yes, Senator?"

"Make sure to turn off the security cameras in your building for our meeting. See you in a bit."

"You're coming here? I'm not sure that's a good idea. If Stoneman—"

Senator Smythe interjected.

"Greg…I'll be there. Stoneman needs to sense the gravity of this situation."

The Senator hung up, called Sergeant Henderson, and instructed him to rally his crew – he wanted FARCO at the meeting too.

# Chapter 46

David pulled up to Johnson Allen's offices at half-past ten with Rita's blood still spattered across his shirt. He didn't change clothes because he wanted Greg Thomas to see, first hand, what he was caught up in.

David carried a dated, brown leather briefcase, which contained all the documents he needed to ensure Sarah walked away from this case with millions of the government's dollars. David was no longer nervous or intimidated – he was angry and now had the upper hand.

The Johnson Allen offices were completely dark, which was unheard of on a weeknight. David suspected Greg Thomas required lingering associates to leave the office before this meeting got underway. The light in the large conference room was on, but the exterior shades were drawn.

David entered through the front doors, which were uncharacteristically ajar. Then, out of the shadows, stepped two hulking operatives donning military fatigues and assault rifles. He recognized one of the men by his limp – it was the man David shot earlier that evening in the parking garage.

The two men approached David and began roughly patting him down, searching for weapons. One of the men saw David looking at the security camera on the ceiling in the lobby.

"They're not on," the man smugly commented as he gave David a sharp jab to the ribs. David doubled over in pain but tried to regain his composure. He anticipated a heightened degree of intimidation, but it wouldn't work. And, David had left his gun in the car, expecting he would possibly be searched. If things took a turn for the worst, at least he had a weapon *close by*. However, with the bombshell he was about to drop, he was confident he wouldn't need his gun.

The men escorted David into the large conference room, where he was met by close to a dozen people.

David was thrown into one of the chairs with Greg Thomas, Alex Mitchell, and Senator Smythe sitting across from him. The other men in the room were armed operatives. Sergeant Henderson was nowhere in sight.

"Why are *they* here?" David asked as he pointed to the men.

Senator Smythe spoke first.

"They're here in case we decide to kill you tonight, David." The Senator's once charismatic and engaging demeanor had changed. He looked like a coiled snake ready to strike.

"Comforting, thanks, Senator," David sarcastically replied.

Greg Thomas chimed in, suspecting he would need to facilitate the meeting to prevent emotions from running too high.

"David, we're here tonight because *you* called this meeting. You claim to have documents that—" Greg Thomas could not finish his sentence before David interrupted.

"Greg, let *me* tell *you* how this is going to work." David leaned in and put his elbows on the conference table.

"First, the blood I have on my shirt is from my assistant, Rita Valore, who was viciously gunned down tonight in my apartment." David's gaze turned to Senator Smythe.

"Before she died, she told me *your* people blackmailed her into giving you inside information about our case. So, I can only assume one of these Neanderthals was responsible for her death. As a result, my settlement number just *doubled*."

Senator Smythe laughed. "And what makes you think that we're—"

David cut the Senator off.

"Second, you won't touch a hair on my head."

The FARCO operatives moved in closer to David. Senator Smythe nodded at one of them, who drew a revolver and pressed the cold metal against David's right temple.

Alex Mitchell, obviously uncomfortable with the situation, tried to excuse himself.

"Gentlemen, I did not sign up for this; I'm leaving."

"Sit down, Alex; you're not going anywhere," Senator Smythe barked.

"You'll stay in that chair until you're dismissed unless you want me to print copies of the photos I have of you and the prostitutes at The Senator's Club!"

Alex had no choice but to sink back into his chair and put his hands on his head. Senator Smythe put Alex in his place, then turned his toxic attention back to David.

"And why, might I ask, won't we hurt you?"

David smiled and confidently responded.

"Because if Sarah Mercer does not hear my voice in twenty minutes, she will release the documents to the press and on the internet for the whole world to see."

Senator Smythe shot a concerned look at Greg Thomas.

David continued, "And, before you go thinking you can just take out Sarah, I also have Tommy Felton in a *different* location. If he doesn't receive a call from Sarah *in twenty-one minutes*, he will release the information. You simply won't have time to eliminate both of them before the documents are all over the internet."

"That's no problem – we can just disable their email accounts. Then they won't be able to send anyone anything. It would take my operatives less than five minutes to do that," Senator Smythe smugly replied as he leaned back in his chair and folded his arms.

"That may be true, Senator, but it'll be hard to track the *secret third party* to whom I also sent these documents."

Senator Smythe smirked, unamused by David's attempt to outsmart him.

"We'll just hack your emails too and learn the identity of your mystery person in a matter of minutes! I bring the full power of the United States Intelligence Community to this table, Stoneman! You don't have a snowball's chance in—" David interrupted again.

"I thought you'd say that…it's a funny thing, Senator, with all the tracking power of the federal government, I bet your boys forgot to check the outgoing mail at my apartment complex, which was scheduled for a late pick-up this evening. So, the documents went out to my third party without a call, text, or email – no digital footprint whatsoever! They went out the old-fashioned way – snail mail. Good luck finding that needle in the haystack."

Greg Thomas began to wiggle anxiously in his chair, and the sweat started to run under his crisp, white shirt collar.

"So, I'll repeat myself, even with a gun to my head. You *can't* hurt me because if anything happens to me, Sarah Mercer, or Tommy Felton, your secret will become national news with juicy murder charges to go with it."

Senator Smythe was boiling inside. He had multiple guns pointed at David, all the power of the FARCO team, and the best litigator in the city, but he knew he was powerless.

David unbuckled his brown leather briefcase and tossed a copy of Dr. Pietrov's research report on the table.

"Oh, and just in case you thought I was bluffing…"

David continued, "You know, guys, it all makes sense now. This research absolutely would have killed the Division Act. This research *will* cost hundreds of millions of dollars, maybe even billions, in new wrongful death lawsuits against the government. Not to mention the multiple murders you directed to cover this whole thing up, and the fact that Senator Smythe is involved in an unprecedented conspiracy to dismantle America as we know it." David smiled.

Everyone in the room was silent. David knew he had them but decided to highlight their silver lining.

"Fortunately for you, my client's case is bound by confidentiality under the mediation rules. This means *if* we settle our case in mediation, I won't be able to share Pietrov's report or the information I have with anyone without risking the settlement amount."

By this point, Greg Thomas was hanging his head and staring at his expensive shoes, floored by the realization he had been bested by one of his former associates. David continued.

"If we don't settle the case, we'll just go back to court, and this report will be available in a public forum for all to see." David leaned back in his chair as the FARCO operatives holstered their sidearms and took a step back.

"Of course, Senator, even if you kill me, Sarah, and Tommy, and the report is released to the press by my third party, I won't care if I violated the mediation's confidentiality requirement because…I'll be dead. So, from where I'm sitting, it looks like your only option is to settle with me for my *new price* of twenty million dollars."

Greg Thomas lifted his head and locked eyes with Senator Smythe. He nodded, affirming that settlement was the only viable choice. Upon seeing the gesture, David reopened his briefcase and extracted another document.

"I drafted a settlement agreement which clearly states that, from this point on, neither my client nor I will share any information learned or discovered during this mediation."

"What about the pastor and the third party?" Senator Smythe angrily questioned.

David turned to Greg Thomas and Alex Mitchell, "Gents, please educate the Senator on the details of the Clergy-Penitent privilege. As far as the third-party individual – if I'm alive, they won't release the documents. Consider it my insurance policy to ensure my safety, the safety of my client and her son, and Mr. Felton." He turned back to Senator Smythe.

"Simply stated, Senator, we just want you to pay us and stop trying to kill us."

David stood up and fastened his leather briefcase, "Take the night to sleep on it, and I'll see you tomorrow morning. If you don't show up to the mediation with *that* signed settlement agreement, I'm withdrawing from this mediation, and we're headed back to federal court for some real fun."

David shouldered his way past the FARCO operatives who had positioned themselves near the conference room door. He left the conference room with a grin on his face, and turned around one last time and winked at Greg Thomas before the conference room door closed behind him. Greg Thomas, Senator Smythe, and Alex Mitchell sat in silence, realizing David had completely outsmarted them, and all of the muscle and power in the world couldn't help them dodge this bullet.

# Chapter 47

David started his car, again, half-expecting it to explode, and headed for the Four Seasons in Georgetown, where he instructed Tommy, Sarah, and Mark to wait for him. As he merged onto the highway, he called Sarah and glanced at the clock illuminated on the dashboard. It was a couple of minutes under the twenty-minute deadline.

"Hello, David?" Sarah sounded relieved as she answered.

"Yea, it's me, Sarah. I'm safe."

"Oh, thank God!"

David checked his rear-view mirror to see if a car was trailing him, but he didn't see anything.

"I think my plan may have worked," David chuckled in surprise.

"Is Tommy still with you?" David asked as he flipped on his left turn signal and switched lanes.

"Yes, should I tell him to come out of the bathroom now?" Sarah asked.

"Sure."

David's threats were sincere, but he lied about Tommy's actual location. Tommy was in the same hotel room with Sarah and

Mark but was told to stay in the bathroom and out of sight until David called, just in case FARCO operatives had eyes on Sarah. For his bluff to be compelling, David wanted to convince Senator Smythe that Tommy and Sarah were in different locations in order to complicate FARCO's attempt to eliminate them.

"Sarah, we need to report Rita's murder to the police. Can you call 911 and give them my address?" David decided it was best to report Rita's death immediately, rather than waiting until the following day.

"What do I say?" Sarah inquired.

"Just tell them someone has been shot in the apartment and give them the address. Then, jump in a cab with Tommy and Mark, and meet me there in fifteen minutes. They'll want statements from all of us."

"Are you sure it's safe to leave the hotel?" Sarah asked, worried they were still in danger.

"Oh yea, trust me; I gave the Senator plenty to think about. They won't bother us anymore tonight."

As the phone hung up, David breathed a deep sigh of relief because he knew they were finally safe, at least until the following morning. He suspected Senator Smythe, Greg Thomas, and Alex Mitchell were still huddled in the Johnson Allen conference room, trying to figure out if there was a way to avoid settling this case for twenty million dollars. David was confident they would ultimately conclude that settling was their only logical choice. They were simply not going to risk the information getting out, and they were in too deep to deny their part in the cover-up.

When David arrived at his apartment, the police were already waiting outside his door. They individually questioned David,

Sarah, Mark, and Tommy. The group gave their eyewitness accounts of random gunshots coming through the window but did not detail why they were together in the first place. The police didn't ask and seemed satisfied with their versions of the event.

Due to an outstanding warrant in South Carolina, Tommy was arrested and taken downtown. David was confident the charges against Tommy would be dropped but offered to represent him anyway and instructed him not to answer any questions until David could be with him.

After just an hour at the station, David got a call from Tommy saying the police received an anonymous tip that a man named Terry Gutierrez killed Rita, Jerry Hatfield, Francis Pietrov, and his wife, Marie. Still, the police chief wanted to keep Tommy in custody while he conferred with South Carolina officials.

David knew Terry didn't kill Rita. Terry was dead long before Rita was shot. David surmised Senator Smythe made Terry the fall guy to cover FARCO's tracks and to prevent Tommy from sharing too much information with the local police. Unfortunately, that was not a battle David could fight. He was exhausted, and because his apartment was now an active crime scene, he and Sarah packed some overnight clothes and headed back to the Four Seasons to turn in for the night. They needed to rest.

David would usually be up late preparing for the second day of mediation. However, this time was different. He didn't have to prepare a thing. All he had to do was show up the next morning, countersign the settlement agreement, and this fiasco would be over.

So, instead, David grabbed a quick shower and was asleep before his head hit the soft, cool pillow.

# Chapter 48

David and Sarah were the first to arrive at the mediation the following morning. David didn't even bother putting on a tie. He would only be there for a short while. The government had either signed the settlement agreement or not. If they chose not to sign it, David was going to insist the case be put back on the Court's docket that afternoon, and the Pietrov report would soon be breaking news on every major news station. David suspected that because he was still alive, the government decided to settle the case.

Greg Thomas, Alex Mitchell, and Charles Morison entered the conference room together. It was apparent they had been talking and concluded their conversation before sitting around the large conference table. Senator Smythe and the FARCO operatives were long gone.

Greg Thomas and Alex Mitchell looked exhausted with dark circles under their eyes. They stared daggers at David as they took their seats. David noticed they were wearing the same clothes as the night before, which indicated they had been up all night trying to evaluate possible alternatives to David's offer and ultimatum.

"Good morning, everyone." Charles enthusiastically began.

"I've conducted over thirty mediations, and, I must say, this has been the most non-traditional one, by far. First, the plaintiff and her counsel left abruptly and without explanation on the first day of the mediation. Then, I get a call from the defense's counsel at the crack of dawn on the second day telling me the case has settled."

David smiled. They had signed his settlement agreement. Charles continued.

Now, it is perfectly acceptable for the parties to meet outside of this mediation to discuss a settlement. I understand you met last night, and Plaintiff's counsel drafted and tendered a settlement agreement to the government's counsel. I also noticed the settlement amount doubled overnight. Again, not a problem, just highly unusual. Finally, I want to let both parties know *I'm not stupid*. Something happened yesterday that moved this case from a dog fight where the parties couldn't be more disagreeable into an amicable resolution, and all within twenty-four hours. I know the attorneys on both sides of this case, and I know neither of you settles cases quickly or easily. Regardless, my job is not to piece the puzzle together. My job is to offer support, guidance, and insight to increase the likelihood the case settles, and it has. So, Mr. Stoneman and Ms. Mercer, the government's counsel has signed your settlement agreement. Please countersign the document, and I'll ask Mr. Thomas's assistant to make three copies of the fully executed agreement for everyone's records. I'll also inform the Court this case has been resolved. Ms. Mercer, according to the agreement, you will receive the settlement amount of twenty million dollars within the next seventy-two hours into the bank account provided by your attorney. As a reminder, the information and evidence discussed in this mediation are considered confidential. From this point on, if either party breaches confidentiality, this settlement may be voided. Consider this matter closed.

Charles slid David and Sarah a copy of the settlement agreement, which they quickly signed and returned. Sarah began to cry, realizing this ordeal was finally over – she had won. Greg Thomas and Alex Mitchell swiftly retreated from the conference room in shame and disgust.

"It's okay, Sarah…Samuel can finally rest in peace knowing his mother and brother are financially secure for life." David put his hand on Sarah's shoulder.

"Thank you *so* much, David!" Sarah broke down again and gave David a big hug of appreciation.

"I couldn't have done this without you!"

David smiled and hugged her back.

David didn't get the far-reaching fanfare and publicity he had hoped for, but he realized he did something good for someone in need. In the end, he fought for those who could not fight for themselves. David stood up to a broken system, and in the face of giants, demanded justice for his client. Still, he was frustrated he could not share this news with the world – Senator Smythe had gotten away with murder, and countless other families would suffer because of the Division Act's restrictions.

Unfortunately, the mediation's confidentiality rules were airtight, and if David leaked the story to the press, it would jeopardize Sarah's settlement award. He wouldn't do that to her.

David collected his copy of the settlement agreement and escorted Sarah out of the building and to his car. He told her to wait for him in the parking lot; he needed to do one more thing.

David walked back into the Johnson Allen office building and took the elevator up to the eleventh floor.

As David exited the elevator, he was no longer mesmerized by the ornate fixtures and inspirational framed pictures. He was on a mission.

Greg Thomas's assistant, Stacy, saw David coming and tried to stop him.

"Mr. Stoneman, Mr. Thomas is in a meeting and can't see you right now." She tried to stand in his way, but David sidestepped and slid past her.

He walked behind her desk and opened the large wooden door.

As he stormed into Greg Thomas's office, Stacy frantically followed him, pleading for him to stop. David found Greg Thomas sitting with Alex Mitchell, obviously talking about the case.

"I'm sorry, Mr. Thomas, he just barged in," Stacy apologized.

"It's okay, Stacy, thank you," Greg Thomas responded as he raised his hand to dismiss her.

"Please, David, would you like to sit?" Greg Thomas extended his arm, inviting David to sit next to Alex.

"No, thanks…what I have to say will only take a minute." David curtly responded.

"I just want to let you know how lucky you are that Pietrov's report has to stay buried. I always knew you were an arrogant bastard, Greg, but I never dreamed you would be involved in one of the biggest government cover-ups in American history.

You have innocent blood on your hands – how will you live with yourself?" David asked as he sternly looked Greg Thomas up and down.

Greg Thomas just sat and frowned at David with his arms crossed. David then turned his attention to Alex.

"And, *you*! You're in way over your head, Alex. If I were you, I would get out why you still can. These guys will kill you if you don't go along with their charade. Do you think they're going to trust you to stay quiet? No way!"

Alex anxiously looked at Greg Thomas, whose eyes were still fixed on David. There was an awkward pregnant pause.

"Anything else?" Greg Thomas sneeringly asked as his eyebrows raised.

"Yea...*tell me you'll keep it up*, Greg. Because if you do, it's only a matter of time before you go down with the rest of them – and I can't wait to see your face on television as they haul you off to prison."

With those words, David turned and exited the large wooden door and strode back to the elevators and down to his car. Sarah was on the phone with Mark, telling him the good news. As they left the parking lot, David and Sarah knew they had achieved a historical victory – one that nobody would know about.

# Chapter 49

Senator Smythe was irate and pacing back and forth in the FARCO conference room. Sergeant Henderson sat with his feet propped up on the metal table, casually sipping his steaming hot coffee.

"Can you believe it, Henderson? We paid twenty million dollars to those bloodsuckers!" The Senator shouted with his hands in his pockets and the veins popping out of his neck.

"At least they have to keep it quiet…it seems, to me, like you got off easy." Sergeant Henderson replied, secretly satisfied that Senator Smythe had been bested.

Senator Smythe looked over at the trained killer, offended by his unsympathetic comment.

"Why aren't you more concerned about this, Henderson? Why do I even pay you? You're worthless!" The Senator threw his hands up in the air and kept pacing.

With that, Sergeant Henderson rose from his chair, and his relaxed demeanor quickly turned hostile. He had finally had enough, and the Senator just pushed him over the edge. He advanced toward the crooked politician. Senator Smythe began slowly backing toward the wall. When his backside hit the cold plaster, he dropped his head, not wanting to make eye contact.

The towering figure of Sergeant Henderson loomed over him, and the Senator could smell the stench of strong coffee on his breath. Senator Smythe realized he might be in trouble.

"Senator...don't ever talk to me like that again. I've taken your garbage for too long. You know who I *really* work for. You also know we can get to anyone, anytime, anywhere – even *you*, Senator." Sergeant Henderson was just inches from Senator Smythe's face. It was an overt threat, and Senator Smythe knew Sergeant Henderson was serious. The Senator nodded and slinked out of his vulnerable position, sitting down in one of the empty chairs around the metal conference table.

"We have to figure this out, Henderson. What if the report leaks?"

"Senator, I've led countless missions, and sometimes one or two witnesses are left standing. And, you know what I've learned?"

"No, what?"

"Those folks are so scared we'll come back for them; they *never* say a word. Sometimes trying to silence the loose ends is the very thing that gets you caught. My suggestion is to let it go. The pastor won't say anything, and we pinned everything else on Terry Gutierrez. We're in the clear." Sergeant Henderson resumed his seat and took another sip of coffee. He calmly continued.

"Plus, as you know, we have bigger fish to fry...this is just a minor setback...the plan is still on track."

Senator Smythe remained concerned.

"Do *they* know about the setback?" The Senator asked.

"Yes, they know."

"And…?" Senator Smythe was searching Sergeant Henderson's face for any sign of comfort or reassurance. But Sergeant Henderson enjoyed watching the Senator writhe in his seat.

"I don't know, Senator, you'll have to ask them yourself."

"Can we call them now? I want to call them right now! Where's a secure line?" Senator Smythe scanned the immediate area for a secure phone line.

Sergeant Henderson relocated a spider phone from the other end of the table and placed it in front of Senator Smythe. He then scrolled through his cell phone for a private number and dialed the numbers on the spider phone's keypad. It rang twice, and a voice answered. Sergeant Henderson began the conversation.

"It's Henderson, I have *Eagle* here, and he wants to know about next steps."

The phone was silent, and then a simple statement sent chills down Senator Smythe's spine.

"We'll see…" the mysterious voice said, and then the line went dead.

Sergeant Henderson kicked back in his chair and smirked, knowing that was not the reassurance the Senator desired.

"It looks like they're still deciding. Don't worry; I'm sure they'll let you live – however, you may lose your Senate seat."

The cheap shot did not amuse Senator Smythe, but he knew Sergeant Henderson's words rang true. The group behind the master plan would seal his fate – the real architects of the

Division Act. Senator Smythe knew this was only the beginning, and nothing could deter them from their *ultimate objective*.

# Chapter 50

Three weeks had passed since Sarah won her case. The settlement amount of twenty million dollars was successfully deposited into her bank account. David then put her in touch with a wills and estates attorney in Tysons Corner, Virginia, to help her manage the money.

Sarah gave three million dollars to a cancer research foundation in Samuel's name and gave another two million to the hospital where Samuel and Mark received their cancer treatments. Sarah personally presented the substantial check to the newly-promoted Hospital Director, Dr. Pam Winters. She knew the money was in good hands.

David, Sarah, and Mark were still staying at the Four Seasons in Georgetown. This time, however, Sarah was paying the bill. David didn't think he could move back into his apartment. There were too many bad memories and he needed a fresh start. So, he decided to move to McLean, Virginia, a community he liked just outside of town, and began to look actively at homes in the area.

In the weeks after the case settled, David helped to completely clear Tommy's name after overwhelming evidence emerged connecting Terry Gutierrez to the murders of Rita Valore, Jerry Hatfield, Francis Pietrov, and Marie Felton.

David even took police to Terry's secret warehouse hideout in Ivy City, but to their surprise, Terry's body was nowhere to be found. The entire building had been wiped clean, and there was no evidence Terry had ever been there. Nevertheless, the police seemed satisfied pinning all of the murders on Terry and closing the cases. Again, and not surprisingly, the news coverage on the murders was sparse. Terry's name was never even mentioned.

After being cleared of all wrongdoing in Washington, Tommy decided to go back to South Carolina. David paid for his flight home and told Tommy he would have his car shipped to him in Charleston so he wouldn't have to endure the long drive home by himself – he could simply jump on a direct flight and be home in a couple of hours.

Tommy had been through a lot, and David owed his case win to the eleventh-hour emergence of the missing Pietrov report. So, expediting Tommy's trip home was the least David could do to say 'thank you.' Tommy appreciated David's kindness and was eager to get back to the Lowcountry to clear up any confusion surrounding his uncharacteristic and immediate departure.

Later that afternoon, Tommy's daughter, Jenny, was waiting for him at the Charleston International Airport as his plane landed. Tommy stared out of the plane's small oval window as it slowly taxied toward the gate.

He had endured an ordeal. However, Tommy felt a peace that passed all understanding. Despite the tragic loss of his beloved wife, Marie, he felt good about his role in exacting justice for the Mercer family and his old friend, Francis Pietrov.

Still, he had a lot of explaining to do to his congregation and, most importantly, to Jenny. Staying true to the Clergy-Penitent confidentiality code, however, he would *never* utter a word about what Dr. Pietrov had told him or the information contained in the Pietrov report. He had a well-crafted cover story, which was *mostly* true, to answer any outstanding questions.

Tommy would simply say Marie was killed by a deranged, anti-religious zealot who chased him to Washington before being killed in D.C. by authorities. But, in reality, Tommy was just eager to put the horrific experience behind him and hoped his story would not invite further inquiry.

As he exited the plane, he put his hands in his pockets and took a few minutes to enjoy the sunshine cascading through the airport's tall windows. As he walked through the glass security doors, Jenny came running from the baggage claim area. They both cried as they embraced for several minutes. Finally, Tommy was home.

----

About the same time Tommy was touching down in Charleston, Sarah, David, and Mark were walking on the National Mall. They had attended Rita's funeral service earlier that morning, and their mood was somber. It was Sarah's idea to spend the afternoon downtown and to take a couple of hours to reflect on the recent events. David acquiesced.

They spread out a blanket on the soft, green grass near the base of the Washington Monument. Mark watched cartoons on his tablet, and David and Sarah were reminiscing about Rita and enjoying each other's company.

"Hey, Dave…?"

"Yea?" David answered as he reclined on the blanket to let the warm sunshine soak into his skin.

"We haven't talked about your fee for helping me with the case," Sarah commented as she sat down on the blanket next to David.

David knew this issue would be discussed at some point and had already generated a canned response.

"Sarah, it was my pleasure to help you, Mark, and Samuel. I've got plenty of irons in the fire for new jobs, so I'm good."

"What kind of jobs?" Sarah inquired.

David sat up and rested his elbows on his knees.

> Your case truly changed me, Sarah. To be candid, I didn't think it would, but it did. I used to only care about climbing the corporate ladder, but this whole experience showed me how fragile life can be and how fulfilling it is to help others. So, I think I'm going to change directions and try my hand at First Amendment law. Get out of Big Law and help those who are less fortunate find their voice. I may even start my own firm!

David said as he smiled.

Sarah nodded in affirmation and weighed her next words carefully.

"I did some research on the attorney's fee for a case like mine. The lawyer usually takes at least twenty-five percent of the settlement amount. David, I want to pay you that *same* percentage."

David couldn't believe his ears and quickly objected.

"Sarah…*absolutely not*! That money is for you and Mark so you can create the type of life you deserve and—" Sarah interrupted David mid-sentence.

"I know, I know, but I wouldn't have the money if it weren't for you. *I insist*, please. I've already spoken with my estate lawyer, and he set aside five million dollars for you. It's not up for discussion, I insist."

David was speechless. He couldn't believe it.

"I'll do good with it, Sarah. I promise, I'll do good with it!" David responded with sincerity.

"I know you will, Dave. That's what I like about you." She put her hand gently on his forearm. David sensed it was the appropriate time to ask a question he had wanted to ask for a month.

"Sarah, on another note, and this is in *no way* related to the fact that you just offered me millions of dollars, but…would you like to go to dinner with me sometime?"

That question caused Mark to look up from his tablet and chuckle before shaking his head and returning his attention to his show.

"I would love to, Dave," Sarah responded with a warm smile.

David, Sarah, and Mark spent the remaining hours of daylight relaxing on the lawn, in the shadow of the Washington Monument, without a care in the world.

# Chapter 51

Tommy and his daughter, Jenny, strolled past the famed Rainbow Row houses on East Bay Street and on down to the Charleston Battery. They enjoyed the warm breeze that sailed across the water as they wandered along the Battery wall. The sound of squawking seagulls served as their soundtrack. Tommy and Jenny had not said much to each other since they left the airport – neither knew where to start. After a silent moment, Tommy spoke first.

"Okay, what is it?" he inquired, sensing his daughter's uneasiness.

"Dad, we're moving back to Charleston. After all this, we want to be closer to you." Jenny looked out across Charleston Harbor as the wind disheveled her long, brown hair.

Tommy stopped walking and turned to his daughter.

"Honey, you don't need to do that; I'll be fine." He reassured her as he wrapped his arm around her shoulder.

"I know, but losing mom and not knowing where you were, or if you were even okay, made me realize we need to be here." Jenny hugged her father back.

Tommy's heart was full. He didn't tell Jenny, but he needed this. He put on a stoic face when times were tough, but he was dreading life without his darling Marie.

Tommy's eyes welled with tears as he held his daughter close. He took Jenny's hand as they walked down the wall's steps and across the street to White Point Garden and sat on one of the open park benches. A family of squirrels playfully chased each other up a nearby tree, and the constant stream of park walkers and joggers offered exceptional people-watching entertainment as Tommy's stress from the last month began to wane.

"Any news from the church since I left?" Tommy asked as he leaned back on the wooden bench and pulled one leg over the other. He had been avoiding that issue.

"Oh yea, big time!" Jenny answered with a laugh.

"When they couldn't reach you, the church board contacted me. They never assumed you were responsible for mom's death, but they still had *many* questions about why you raced out of town. I told them you needed an uninterrupted sabbatical, and I was not at liberty to share your location. Of course, I didn't know where you were or that a lunatic was trying to kill you, but I knew you were innocent and just needed some time." Jenny smiled at her father.

"Thanks, babe. You always cover for me, even when I got in trouble with your mother."

They both laughed.

"We need to have a proper funeral for her, don't you think?" Tommy asked.

"Yea…I already started looking into arrangements. Tons of folks have been calling and sending their condolences."

"Your mom and I talked about our funerals many years ago. She told me she didn't want a big funeral. Just something small with close friends and family. And, as you know, she loved the

Lowcountry marsh. So, let's do something near the water. She would like that."

Jenny nodded in approval as she took her father's hand and leaned her head on his shoulder.

Tommy gazed out toward Fort Sumter in the distance and reflected on the significance of the location where the first shots of the Civil War were fired. Sadly, the country was still divided. However, it was no longer divided by the Union and Confederacy but divided along religious, socio-economic, and racial lines.

The very name of "the Division Act" represented the country's ongoing societal schism and served as evidence that the deep scars from our nation's past had not completely healed. Tommy knew he had been involved in a historic event the public would never know about. Unfortunately, the headwinds against exposing the truth were still too strong, and, once again, the opposition had succeeded in keeping the truth hidden from the American people.

All Tommy could do was showcase his deeply held convictions by how he lived and lead his congregation to that greater truth – the truth about God, the truth about themselves, and the truth about each other. Dr. Pietrov's research simply affirmed what he had been preaching for decades, and he now could confidently share those core principles with his congregation each Sunday.

Tommy took solace in having scientific proof that prayer worked miracles. That fact alone was enough to motivate him to continue his ministry and even expand it. Tommy planned to return to the New Beginnings Baptist Church, assuming they would have him back. That's all he could do, but that was good enough for him.

As Tommy and Jenny sat on the park bench, enjoying the warm twilight hours, he missed Marie. Still, he knew she would be proud of him. And, she would encourage him to move forward and enjoy the rest of his life. He planned to do just that.

# Chapter 52

A couple of months had passed. It was still summertime, and David had purchased and moved into a new home in McLean, Virginia. With the generous gift Sarah gave him from the settlement, he was able to pay cash for a large, Colonial-style home with a pool and three acres. Sarah and Mark often came over to swim and enjoy the grounds.

Despite the windfall settlement award, Sarah decided to stay in their small condominium in Fairfax. Sarah told David she wanted to maintain a simple lifestyle, and her estate attorney encouraged her to invest most of the money in the stock market. David admired Sarah's fiscal prudence, even though he chose not to replicate it.

By then, David and Sarah had started dating and were smitten in their budding relationship. They were finishing a fun-filled Saturday by the pool when David logged in to his computer. He noticed a new email from a former colleague informing him that Judge Michael Callaway had abruptly resigned from the federal bench and retired completely from law practice. David found that odd and decided to research further.

"Hey, Sarah!" David hollered.

"Judge Callaway, the judge in your case, resigned unexpectedly!"

Sarah walked into the room, drying her blonde, chlorine-soaked hair with a yellow towel.

"Why?" Sarah asked.

"I don't know, but it's very odd for a federal judge to resign like that." David suspected something was not right and knew he wouldn't be able to enjoy his evening until he found a good explanation.

Sarah shrugged and walked back outside to join Mark by the pool.

David turned on the television to see if there was any coverage about Judge Callaway's resignation. He flipped the channels to one of the local networks. The text at the bottom of the screen caused his jaw to drop.

The headline read: *Newly Unveiled Secret Report Jeopardizes Division Act.*

"Sarah!! Get in here!" David yelled at the top of his lungs.

Sarah ran back into the living room and looked at the TV.

"Oh, my goodness…David, did *you* do this?!"

"No…I don't know how it got out." David turned the volume up.

David and Sarah were glued to the television as the reporter spoke live from the steps of the U.S. Capitol.

We have breaking news that a key member of Congress buried a government report during the passage of the controversial Division Act. This report allegedly states that certain portions of the Act, which limit religious gatherings and activities, may, in reality, be harmful to the public. Additionally, the Act's sponsoring member, Senator Stephen Smythe, may have been involved in a conspiracy to cover up that information. This secret report was just leaked online by an anonymous source. We will provide more information as it becomes available.

David and Sarah looked at each other, confounded and confused, as David scrolled through the other news channels. Each station was running the same story.

David immediately called Tommy Felton.

"Hello?" Tommy answered in his Southern accent.

"Tommy, it's David Stoneman."

"Hi, Dave, good to hear your voice! How have you been?"

"Tommy, did you leak the Pietrov report to the press? I need to know *now*! Did you leak it?!" David asked with urgency.

"No, Dave, I didn't. Why? What happened?"

"Someone leaked it. Turn on the news and call me back." David hung up and nervously ran his fingers through his damp hair, debating what to do next. At that moment, his cell phone rang. It was Greg Thomas. David didn't answer. In seconds his phone lit up, signifying he had a voicemail. David pressed the button to listen on speakerphone.

"Stoneman, you stupid jackass! Congratulations! You just invalidated your settlement agreement. I promise we're going to claw back every penny of Sarah Mercer's money. I'm also going to have you disbarred for this. Who do you think you are? You're an idiot to think you could get away with this. I'm taking you down, Stoneman!" The message ended abruptly.

David wasn't surprised by the tone of the message. He knew losing the case had been eating at Greg Thomas for months. David was, however, mulling over multiple scenarios in his head about who could have done this. Then, his cell phone rang again. It was an unknown number this time. David was curious, so he answered.

"Hello?"

"David, this is Michael Callaway."

David was shocked. Why was the now-retired judge calling him? No doubt it was to reprimand him for the leaked information.

"Yes, sir, Judge Callaway, what can I do for you, sir?"

David was surprised by his response.

"Well, you can start by calling me *Michael*. I'm sure someone told you I retired from the bench this week."

"Yes, sir, I heard that. Congratulations on your retirement." David didn't know what else to say.

"David, I'm calling to let you know that *I* was the one who leaked Francis Pietrov's Division Act report to the press."

David was stunned but responded quickly.

"Judge...I mean, Michael...when I sent you those documents in the mail, I gave you explicit instructions in my letter not to read the documents *unless my client and I were killed*. I put the report in its own sealed envelope for that very reason—" Judge Callaway interrupted David.

"I know, and I didn't open the envelope with the report until after your case settled. But I *had* to know what was in that envelope, David. And when I knew, I felt obligated to share the information with the world. The information is too important not to share." Judge Callaway was silent for a second, then continued.

> You see, I was very concerned when I read your cover letter. You were wise to acknowledge the importance of maintaining the mediation's confidentiality requirement because, *technically*, you did not divulge any confidential information to anyone. You simply put an insurance policy in place, which was very clever. Now I know why you did that. So, I waited until your case was closed, and then I opened the sealed envelope against your instructions. When I read that report, I knew why the government was eager to settle the case. I also knew I couldn't do anything with the information as a sitting judge. However, because I disobeyed your explicit instructions not to open the document, I could then release the information to the public without invalidating the settlement *if* I resigned from the bench. There's solid case law on this issue and, I promise you, the validity of the settlement will be upheld. You and Ms. Mercer are in the clear. It's *all on me* at this point.

"Michael, I'm not sure what to say..." David was dumbfounded.

"I plan to tell the press it was me who leaked the information right after I get off this call. I just wanted you to hear it from me *first*." Judge Callaway seemed resolute in his decision. Nevertheless, David felt compelled to warn him of the potential consequences.

"But, Michael, you'll likely be disbarred for this. Maybe even worse."

"I know, but I always wanted my legacy to be based on transparency and justice. This information staying buried is *wrong*, and the American people deserve to know the truth about the Division Act and the conduct of their elected officials. If they disbar me for it, or worse, then so be it. It's worth it to me. Take care of yourself, David."

The call ended, and David explained the situation to Sarah.

"When did you send the report to the judge?" Sarah asked as she tried to recall the events of that fateful evening.

"Remember when I brought Tommy back to my apartment and began making copies of the report? The night Rita died?"

"Yea…"

"And, recall, I told you I sent a third copy in the mail to a secret third party who would release the document if we were killed?"

"Yes…but that was just a bluff, wasn't it?" Sarah asked.

Yes and no. I didn't want to scare you, Sarah. I also wanted to give you plausible deniability. If the plan backfired with Judge Callaway, it would have been entirely on me. So, I sent a sealed copy of the Pietrov report to Judge Callaway and scribbled a short cover letter telling him there was additional evidence in the envelope and to open it only if we were killed. After the case settled, he opened it anyway and released it to the press on his own. So, we didn't violate any terms of the settlement agreement, and the information came out! It's a win-win!

Sarah smiled.

"You're brilliant; you know that?"

David smirked and leaned in for a small kiss.

"I just can't wait to see the look on Greg Thomas's face when he realizes he can't do anything about the leak." David suspected it would only be a matter of time before the press contacted him for a statement.

----

David and Sarah kept the news on for the rest of the evening and watched as additional information began to trickle out regarding the secret source of the broadcast bombshell. Judge Callaway was wise not to divulge *how* he received the Pietrov report and didn't even mention Sarah's case in his comments to the press. Consequently, neither David nor Sarah's name was mentioned at all. David suspected Judge Callaway destroyed the cover letter and mailing envelope, which were the only pieces of evidence connecting David to the report.

How the report was leaked quickly became less important than the information it contained. It didn't take long for the press to connect the Pietrov report to Senator Smythe and the sudden, violent death of Francis Pietrov began to raise a lot of questions.

In the days following, allegations of murder and a government cover-up resulted in the U.S. Senate announcing they would be launching a full investigation with the FBI. David knew other attorneys would soon begin to file similar wrongful death lawsuits, and the government would be forced to spend billions to fight them in federal court. The Division Act was now under intense scrutiny and would inevitably be amended. The teeth had been extracted from the tiger, and the government fallout in the coming days would be immense.

# Chapter 53

Senator Smythe sat in his spacious office on Capitol Hill with his aide, Tim. He was fuming. The phone had been ringing off the hook most of the day. Tim fielded more than a dozen calls from news outlets worldwide, inquiring whether or not the Senator knew about Dr. Pietrov's report. Tim was instructed to say "no comment" to all such inquiries.

Senator Smythe had just gotten off the phone with Greg Thomas, who indicated he couldn't legally do anything to retract the Pietrov report – it was out. Even if he filed an injunction, the information would forever live on the internet, and there was no way to prevent its continued circulation online. Greg Thomas also shared the bad news that they could likely not prove David Stoneman leaked the information, which would make it impossible to invalidate Sarah Mercer's settlement agreement – a fact that Charles Morison had reiterated to Greg Thomas earlier that morning. So, Greg Thomas's hands were tied, yet again, and all he could do was suggest Senator Smythe remain quiet and not speak to the press.

"What would you like me to do, sir?" Tim sheepishly inquired as he sat rigidly in the Senator's office with notepad and pen in hand.

"I want you to shut up until I can figure out what needs to be done!" The Senator barked as he circled his desk.

Senator Smythe picked up the phone for his private line and attempted to call Sergeant Henderson at the FARCO headquarters. No answer.

He hung up and realized he didn't have many more options.

As he sat in silence, Tim's conscience was getting the better of him, and he couldn't stay quiet any longer.

"Senator? I heard the woman you told me to threaten was killed. Is that true?" Tim turned to face his boss and continued.

"Sir, I didn't sign up for this. I didn't know anyone was actually going to get hurt."

"Get out, Tim. You're fired! And, remember, you signed a non-disclosure agreement with this office. So, if you say anything to anyone, I will personally guarantee your career will be over."

The young aide sat frozen in his chair, shocked by the Senator's intensely hostile reaction.

"I said GET OUT!" Senator Smythe screamed as he pointed at the door.

Tim fearfully got up from his chair and left the room with his shoulders hunched.

Senator Smythe heard the alert of a new email in his inbox. It was from the Senate Minority Leader. Senator Smythe knew from the first line it was not good news.

> It has come to our attention that you, or someone in your office, may have engaged in unethical and possibly criminal behavior related to the passage of the Division Act. As such, according to Article 1, section 5 of the U.S. Constitution,

*the Senate has decided to evaluate whether expulsion proceedings are appropriate…*

Senator Smythe didn't need to read any further. He suspected the email had already been leaked to the press, and the public blowback from this news would be severe.

Tim suddenly re-entered his office. He looked terrified.

"Didn't I just fire you, moron?!"

"Yes, sir, you did. I just wanted to let you know the FBI is outside, and they want to speak with you right away."

"Stall them for two minutes…tell them I'm on the phone."

The terminated aide complied in an attempt to redeem himself and hurried out of the office to stall the federal agents.

Senator Smythe hurriedly picked up his phone to dial Greg Thomas's number. He needed his legal advice *immediately*. Greg Thomas's assistant answered, which was unusual for his private line.

"Greg Thomas's office, Stacy speaking."

"This is Senator Stephen Smythe; I need to speak with Greg Thomas right now."

"I'm sorry, sir, Mr. Thomas is unavailable."

Senator Smythe could hear loud voices in the background. The last thing he heard before the line went dead was, "ma'am, I need you to hang up the phone. We have a warrant…"

No sooner had the Senator hung up the phone, the FBI stormed into his office, with Tim objecting behind them.

"Senator Stephen Smythe?" A tall FBI agent sternly asked.

"Yes?" The Senator responded, acting surprised to see the federal agents.

"We received an anonymous tip you may have been involved in a string of homicides and other illegal activity, and we're going to need you to come with us for questioning." The tall FBI agent grabbed Senator Smythe's arm and led him to the door.

Senator Smythe was escorted out of his office with many of his congressional colleagues looking on. He instructed Tim to keep trying to reach Greg Thomas but suspected that would be an act in futility. He was right. Across town, Greg Thomas was also being escorted out of the Johnson Allen offices by the FBI.

----

Once in custody, Senator Smythe and Greg Thomas quickly turned on each other, blaming the other for being the mastermind behind burying the Pietrov report. Both men told the FBI about FARCO and blamed FARCO operatives for the murders of Francis Pietrov, Marie Felton, Jerry Hatfield, and Rita Valore and gave them the address of the FARCO headquarters in Northern Virginia.

When the FBI arrived at the FARCO building, all of the operatives were gone, and the documents and computers had been destroyed. The only remaining items were a handful of manila folders on one of the empty desks, which contained emails, pictures, and transcripts of phone conversations between Senator Smythe and Greg Thomas. All of the identifying information for the FARCO team was removed or redacted. These documents proved that while Senator Smythe and Greg Thomas did not pull the trigger, they were definitely complicit in the murderous attempt to keep the Pietrov report hidden.

The FARCO operatives also included evidence of Senator Smythe and Greg Thomas laundering money and witness tampering long before the Division Act was passed. Clearly, the FARCO team knew this day would come, and they knew the FBI would salivate at the opportunity to take down a United States Senator and D.C.'s top litigator.

After that, it only took one day for Johnson Allen to release a statement disclaiming any knowledge of Greg Thomas's wrongdoing and indicating he had been fired. The firm quickly distanced themselves from their fallen star attorney. He would be lucky to see the inside of a law office again.

# Chapter 54

As summer turned to autumn, the press heavily covered Senator Smythe's fall from glory. He and Greg Thomas were charged with various crimes and accepted plea deals, which included jail time for both men.

As suspected, by October, the government was flooded with hundreds of new wrongful death lawsuits, based on the same research included in Sarah Mercer's case. As the number of lawsuits increased, the U.S. Supreme Court called a special shadow docket session to address the potentially unconstitutional portions of the Division Act to try to stop the bleeding and avoid an international embarrassment. However, after very little deliberation and strong dissents from two of the Justices, several sections of the Division Act were rendered unconstitutional. The legislation was then remanded to Congress for immediate re-drafting.

The revised legislation that emerged was nothing more than a skeleton of the former Act and was devoid of any restrictions on religious activities. After the new legislation passed, the government quickly settled all related lawsuits. The final settlement amount for the collective suits was in the billions of dollars.

David and Sarah had been closely following the news for weeks. It looked like this ordeal was finally behind them. The public outcry and the government's rapid, knee-jerk response was, no doubt, a pivotal moment in America's history. Yet, sentiments were calming, and life began to return to normal.

What encouraged David and Sarah the most was the positive impact Dr. Pietrov's report was having on the world. There were, of course, strong objections to some of his conclusions by the scientific community, but at least the report was getting the attention it deserved. Many religious institutions increased their corporate prayer sessions to help sick members of their congregation, and many ill people improved. The stories of healing and hope flooded the internet. Dr. Pietrov's research sparked a global obsession with seeking the truth and preserving the basic religious tenets guaranteed to Americans under the First Amendment to the Constitution. Dr. Pietrov's research and legacy would continue to make a positive impact for many generations to come.

# Chapter 55 – Epilogue

The fall breeze was cool that October in Charleston, South Carolina. It was Sunday night, and Pastor Tommy Felton had just concluded his evening service at the New Beginnings Baptist Church. As the large crowd filtered out of the sanctuary, Tommy recognized two faces sitting in the back pew. He grinned, shook his head, and walked up the aisle to greet them.

David and Sarah met him halfway down the aisle with smiles and hugs.

"It's great to see you two again! What are you doing here?"

"Thought we would take some time away from the craziness in Washington. We're just visiting Charleston for a long weekend and wanted to stop by and surprise you," David replied as he slapped Tommy's back.

"Well, I'm sure glad you did! Where's Mark?" Tommy glanced around the sanctuary.

"He's in the foyer playing a game on his tablet," Sarah smiled and rolled her eyes.

"Well, it's great to see y'all again! Hey, can we grab supper while you're in town?" Tommy's eyebrows raised in optimistic anticipation.

"Actually, yes, we were hoping you'd say that. Are you free tonight by any chance?" David asked.

"I'm free, and I'm famished," Tommy replied as he rubbed his stomach.

The three of them began to walk up the aisle toward the foyer. David slowed and looked around to ensure they were alone. Sensing David was about to say something privately, Tommy stopped and waited for his friend to speak.

"You know, Tommy. It looks like we started a worldwide awakening here. That's got to excite you!"

"Dave, everything happens for a reason, and I'm just glad I was able to help."

David nodded and looked at Sarah.

"Well, Tommy, we wanted to show our appreciation for everything you did for us," Sarah said with a bashful smile. She continued.

"David says that without Dr. Pietrov's report, we would have been dead in the water. None of this would have happened without you. That's why David and I insist you take this." She handed Tommy a check.

Tommy's face lit up when he read the dollar amount.

"Two million dollars?!" Tommy blurted out.

"I'm sorry, y'all, but I simply cannot accept this." Tommy tried to hand the check back to Sarah, but she took a step back and put her hands in the air.

"Please, take it. Consider it a reflection of your contribution to our case victory!" Tommy was overwhelmed, and tears rolled down his face. He sniffled a few times and composed himself.

"I'm giving half of it to the church," he said resolutely.

"Are you sure, Tommy? This money is *yours*," David exclaimed.

"No, Dave, it's perfect, don't you see? The Division Act was meant to limit my church's ministry. So, it's only fitting I use their money to grow the ministry."

David and Sarah sensed the irony and nodded in approval.

"Plus, I think I can buy a pretty nice boat with a million bucks!"

The group roared with laughter as they left the sanctuary, collected Mark from the foyer, and headed to Market Street for a relaxing, Southern-style dinner.

They had won. Even if nobody but God himself knew the extent of their tribulation, they had emerged from their battle victorious. Or so they thought...

----

Sergeant Henderson watched as Tommy, David, Mark, and Sarah filed down the steps of the New Beginnings Baptist Church. Then, he turned to one of his fellow FARCO operatives.

"Keep a safe distance, but don't let them out of your sight. We'll reconvene at location Alpha at 2200 hours."

"Roger that." The operative said as he crossed the street to trail his targets.

Sergeant Henderson pulled his secure cell phone out of his pocket and dialed the most private number in his contacts list.

"This is Henderson; we're following them like you asked."

The ominous voice on the other end only uttered a few sentences.

"The plan is still moving forward. *Eagle* is out of the picture. Stand by for further instructions. We're still on schedule."

The call went dead. Even with the recent challenges, Sergeant Henderson knew everything was going according to the *master plan*. Senator Smythe was just a pawn in a larger shell game, and he had failed. However, his failure would not deter the group that set the plan in motion decades earlier. They would get what they wanted; they always did. And when they did, America would never be the same again.

## THE END